The Secrets of Mudge Bay

Ron McCormack

Text © 2018 Ron McCormack

Editor: Allister Thompson
Proofreader: Britanie Wilson

ISBN (print):
ISBN-13: 978-1729648612
ISBN-10: 1729648614

In memory of Daniel George Dodge,
may he rest in peace

Two great people,
Don + Darlah,

Enjoy the read,

Don

Chapter 1

The crack from the dynamite blast rolled over the choppy waters of the North Channel like thunder. Minutes later, a second blast was much louder. The screams of terror from the few that witnessed the ensuing horror never made it to the water, lost in the towering pines of Spirit Island.

The Canadian north offers many things: incomparable beauty, a euphoric level of solitude, and uncompromised freedom are but a few. Its isolation frees the mind, allowing the imagination to roam. It invites trial, challenging you to act on things you had only dreamed of. Risks don't seem as great in its vastness; you seem inconsequential when you live in its grandeur. It allows you to run from something or chase the something you think might be there. There are pros and cons to reclusion. For those that can handle it there is no better world, while for others it can be life-changing, since it reveals all of your honesty — or lack of it.

But this particular place adds more to the equation, complicating the decision to stay or move on. Aptly named, Spirit Island not only presents all the seclusion and splendor the north has to offer, but it also combines it with a power or an energy that cannot be explained.

It's as if the island chooses its own and provides, almost

protects its selections. It seems to control what is to be known about its history and its inhabitants. Should the island embrace you as its own, you will never leave, at least in spirit. Many have visited, even called it home for a period of time, and then left, never to return, unaffected by its power. There is no explanation why some people are influenced and others are not, but it is apparent the decision is not anyone's to make.

Spirit Island offers one thing that stands alone, rising above all its other attributes: *it keeps the secrets of its people* — forever.

*

In 1931, the world found itself treading water in the depths of the Great Depression. The unemployment rate was over 25%, and the average wage for those lucky enough to be working was about thirty bucks a week. The recession had impacted the classes of society with different degrees of severity. The unfortunate by-product of the depression was it had widened the gap between the haves and the have-nots. Society's elite, the super-wealthy, were enduring — sure, with a little heartburn here and there, but they were getting by. The middle class was barely hanging on, and the lower classes were on the street.

George Rausch was blessed to be born into the mega-rich.

George was the son of an American industrialist who had made a fortune manufacturing parts for the automotive business. His father and his uncle had built a multimillion-dollar business that was growing at an alarming rate, and with the war clouds looming in Europe, demand for their automotive products was about to quadruple.

George's father passed when George was three years old. He was raised by his mother, Mattie, until he was eight. Mattie was a loving, nurturing mother, perhaps overprotective, compensating for the loss of George's father. She would let no harm come to her son and allowed his social development to occur only in the class he was born into. If she wasn't on guard ensuring George's safety, she made sure others were. He was under the constant watch of tutors and Mattie's staff, twenty-four hours a day, seven days a week. George had little freedom in those early years, seldom given time on his own to venture, discover, and learn. He would not really know what he was missing until his mother remarried in 1925.

Fred Gaston would be a gift to young George.

Fred gave George space, allowing George to open doors, make mistakes, and more than anything, grow as a person. He would be given the opportunity to regain what was taken away by his fatherless years. Free from the smothering affection of his mother's environment, he would be shown the path to a full life, with all of its choices, including all classes of people, from every walk of life. A world George new nothing about.

Fred and Mattie had been introduced by mutual friends two years before. They found themselves attending similar fundraisers and charitable events and started dating a year before they married. Fred was from an affluent background, nowhere near the staggering wealth that Mattie had inherited from George's father, but he was upper class, something that was very important to Mattie.

George had a wonderful relationship with his stepfather from the beginning. Fred was kind and understanding and unselfish with his time. Fred never had children, and George was too young to remember his father. It was the perfect relationship for both. Fred did everything with George; from homework to baseball, he was there. Fred knew what it was like to be a boy growing up. He also knew what Mattie thought she wanted: a safe, insulated child. Insulated from the influences an association with other classes of society could bring. Fred respected Mattie for that and loved her and the life she was providing both himself and

George. But Fred was a bright man and identified what George needed in his life to be better equipped to deal with what the world would bring.

To that end, he would keep parts of the relationship he had with George to himself, for better or worse.

Fred loved cars and boats, and when he married Mattie, he married into an impressive collection of both. He never had to ask George twice to go for a ride in one of the sports cars or speedboats. It would be their common passion that would be the cornerstone of their relationship for the rest of their lives.

Fred was also a fisherman. By the time George was nine years old, he was a seasoned angler. The two spent countless hours on Lake St. Clair and in the bays of Lake Michigan chasing trophy fish. When George was twelve, Fred took him on his first "fly-in" fishing excursion to upstate Michigan, most specifically Mackinac Island.

It would be a watershed moment in the boy's young life. He fell in love with the rugged beauty of the area and could not get enough of the incomparable fishing. He also had his first interaction with the state's Indigenous people. He was fascinated with their culture and way of life and wanted to learn more about their knowledge and talents.

George knew nothing but private schools, tutors, and servants. They tended to his every whim. To the credit of Mattie and later Fred, it was a very loving environment filled with teachings of respect and responsibility. When George was ten years old, he left his cherished bicycle at a nearby playground and walked to his friend's house for a glass of lemonade. An hour later, he returned to find an empty bike stand; his prized possession was gone. Devastated, George ran home in tears to his mother, claiming his bicycle had been stolen. With minimal cross-examination, Mattie concluded that her son had left it unattended in a public place for over an hour.

"You are responsible for the safekeeping of your property, George. Unless it turns up, you will be doing without a bike for the rest of the summer."

Strict? By all means, but a life lesson that George never forgot. The family could have provided George a different bicycle, in a different color, every hour of every day for the rest of his life. But they chose not to. That was the way Mattie and Fred taught George to look after his property.

The value of those possessions would increase exponentially in the coming years, and George would exhibit a level of responsibility second to none.

The Rausch home was set on twelve acres of land in a northern suburb of Detroit. From the eighteen-foot iron gates, you would travel on the tree-lined stone driveway, a quarter of a mile until you reached the magnificent mansion.

It had thirty rooms with a full-time staff of six, including a butler, cook, two maids, and two housekeepers.

The home had an additional four full-time staff responsible *only* for the grounds, which were impeccably manicured, including tennis courts, an indoor and outdoor swimming pool, and an equestrian center, where George learned to ride and jump. In the winter, parts of the grounds were flooded to produce a magnificent skating trail that meandered through the property. On weekends, they made skating available to charitable organizations. The grounds were a destination for locals during the Christmas holiday season. The Rausch family decorated the property with over 100,000 lights to celebrate the festive time.

Linda, the property manager, was Mattie's closest friend. They had met in primary school and were inseparable from that day forward. Not only was Linda immensely competent at her job, but she also had been with George since his birth.

Linda watched over George as if he was her own. As if poor

George needed another mother, Linda was there — always. She was Mattie's second set of eyes, and George called her Auntie Linda, even though there was no blood relationship.

Linda managed everything from staff to parties. She was a business manager given a budget and a full-time staff of ten. But above all, she made sure Mattie and Fred's little boy was behaving well and respectful of others. Linda did make it more difficult for Fred. If he tried to loosen the reins for George, Linda was watching to see if Mattie's wants were being followed to the letter.

With wealth, incredible wealth, came incredible toys. To compound the issue, the family's business was automation. They were machinists, engineers, the people who were to lead the United States into a dominant position in the global transportation market.

George grew up privy to the leading edge of automotive power; more importantly, his family *had* what was next before the rest of the world owned a car. With the Rausch collection he had access to cars and boats that the locals, even the very rich locals, viewed with amazement and jealousy.

At the age of fourteen, George was driving cars with his stepfather in the passenger seat.

When it came to cars and boats, Fred gave George a long leash at a very young age. Adding length to the leash were very undefined driving laws. The law was vague as to what age a person had to be to drive a car. It was nonexistent when it came to boats.

As a young teenager George was happiest at the marina, where he would arrive driving a high-powered sports car and then park it in front of his twenty-two-foot mahogany speedboat. Either the car or the boat always drew a crowd.

A crowd that included one or two wide-eyed teenage girls.

George was growing up fast, and Fred was giving him as

much freedom as he dared, knowing this would not be looked upon favorably by his wife.

One day, Fred was talking to another boat owner who had a daughter that had caught George's eye. The young lady was standing by herself, admiring the Rausch's pristinely polished boat. George found the courage to walk over and introduce himself, a first for the young man. Sure, he had spoken to female classmates before, but never an unknown girl in a public place; uncharted waters for George indeed.

"Hi, my name is George. You like my boat?"

"Wow, I have never seen a boat so shiny. It's beautiful. Oh, I'm sorry, my name is Mary. That's my father over there talking to your dad."

It was the first time George had heard anyone refer to Fred as his "dad." It caught him off guard, but as he digested it, he really enjoyed how it made him feel.

"Do you come here often, Mary? I've never seen you here before."

"No, my mother says this is a place for men and not a place for young ladies."

Another sentence that really hit home with George, knowing the restrictions his mother had placed on him growing up.

"But my father said I could come today to see the boats."

George reached down further in the confidence pool. "Maybe you and your father would like to go for a ride in our boat. I will go ask permission."

Not waiting for an answer, George left Mary like a shot and sprinted over to Fred.

Minutes later, the four were cruising Lake St. Clair, and of course George was driving. Mary was sitting up front with the two dads in the back, and life could not get any better for young George.

When they were driving home, Fred put his arm around

George. "Let's keep today between you and me, no sense bothering your mother with the details."

A huge grin appeared on George's face. "Yes, sir, whatever you say!"

Fred had never invited Mattie to these outings at the marina, which was just fine with her; Mattie could not swim and had feared the water her whole life.

This was an amazing situation given that the Rausch family owned the largest steam yacht in the state of Michigan. Before George's paternal father passed, he and his brother had built the state-of-the-art boat, *The Rose*, which measured over 200 feet in length. Used primarily by the company for corporate outings and fundraising events, the yacht was harbored on the Detroit River. The Rausch family did use it for family vacations, which were usually spent on Lake Erie cruising to the Niagara region.

Mary's father and Fred were forming a nice friendship, which was perfectly fine with George. They had one thing very much in common: neither spouse would approve of what was going on with their children.

After one Sunday's boat ride, George asked Mary's father if he could walk her home, unchaperoned, for the first time. After looking at Mary's puppy dog eyes, her father reluctantly agreed.

He walked hand in hand with Mary through the lakeside park, working hard not to look as nervous as he felt. As they walked around a large fountain, they found themselves alone in a densely wooded area.

He put his arms around her waist and enjoyed the first real kiss of his life.

Actually, the first fifteen kisses of his life, but who's counting.

That night, when it seemed impossible the day could get any better, Fred and Mattie announced that the family was taking the yacht on a seven-day cruise.

George was thrilled since it would be the first time he and his family would head north to Lake Huron.

George was going to miss his first love terribly but had always wanted to see the northern reaches of Lake Huron. He remembered every minute of his fishing trip from a couple of years back and could only imagine the experience awaiting him in the next few days.

That night, as he lay in bed thinking about the upcoming cruise, an intense thunderstorm with high winds passed over the Rausch estate. Suddenly, the strong wind knocked out the power and forced open the large window in his room. George stumbled through the dark to locate the candle on the night table and close the window. The dim light from the candle revealed a book that had fallen from his shelf. He bent over to pick up the book. It had opened to a page displaying a map.

A map of Spirit Island.

Chapter 2

George woke to the sounds of sawing and chopping.

Mattie and Fred were surveying the damage from the August storm. A couple of trees had fallen, and the groundskeepers were busy restoring order.

"Quite the storm last night. The wind blew my window open at 2:00 a.m."

"Yes, good thing you had walked your friend home long before that. You would not want to be caught out in such dangerous weather."

George looked over at Fred, who was staring straight ahead with eyes opened wider than they were before Mattie's comment. Mattie gave George a penetrating look with raised eyebrows and walked away.

"Did you tell?"

Fred looked at George with disappointment. "I didn't say a thing, I would hope you knew that."

"Then how does she know?" Fred put his arm around George and pointed to the grounds staff being berated by Linda.

"I don't know, George, but I have a hunch."

*

The Rausch yacht was grand. The largest yacht of its time, *The Rose* was the ultimate symbol of the super-rich.

A large crowd watched as she pulled away from her Detroit home. A crew of twelve, including Captain Joseph Bolan, were to look after George, Mattie, Fred, and Fred's brother and his wife.

They planned to travel from Lake St. Clair to Lake Huron, then north on the west shore to Saginaw Bay. They would anchor there for a day or two of fishing and swimming. The yacht carried two boats, one twenty-two feet long and a second sixteen-footer.

From there they would proceed north, passing through the Mississagi Strait that separated Cockburn Island and Spirit Island. Providing all were enjoying the trip, the plan was to turn east and cruise the North Channel to the town of Little Current.

George had flirted with the idea of asking Fred to invite Mary and her parents along for the trip. But that was dismissed quickly after George thought it through. Fred had not known Mary's father very long, and his mother had never met the family.

Not a great idea. Best to keep that part of his life away from mother. Although Mary for a week on his yacht had visions of sugar plums dancing in his head.

George was spending time with the captain in the wheelhouse, going over the proposed route. Charts by the dozens were laid out, detailing every "fathom" of the trip. It was here that George received his first history lesson about the northern tip of Lake Huron. Captain Boland had the young man's full attention as he detailed the treachery of the waters they would be navigating.

"Over two hundred years ago, 1679 to be exact, the first sailing vessel on the Great Lakes, called the *Griffon*, met its demise in the Mississagi Strait. The very same strait we will be passing through."

Suddenly the monster steam yacht George was so comfortable

on didn't seem so big. He loved the water and felt as at home on it as he was on land; he urged the captain to continue.

"There is some mystery about the *Griffon*; she was apparently headed for Montreal, loaded with furs. The most accepted explanation of the disaster was that the "magnetic reefs" that mess with compass readings made the ship head toward the rocks they were trying to avoid. That is the explanation that I subscribe to, as do most nautical sorts. We will be sailing right by them. I will point them out to you when we get there."

"And Captain Boland, what is the other school of thought?"

"Mr. Gaston, Fred, tells me you have been become a student of the Indigenous people of this area, so you are probably more knowledgeable about this than I am."

George had moved up on his leather chair, sitting a little more upright. "Do tell, Captain."

"Many believe that Spirit Island is a place of 'mystery.' Manitoulin Island, as it is now called, means 'The Island of the Great Spirit.' The *Griffon* met its demise off the coast of this island, just adding to the mystique."

George was reminded of the book that had fallen from his shelf a few nights before. A part of his young mind was not ready to concede to the magnetic reef explanation.

"You know, Captain, there are a few interpretations of the name. 'Mysterious being,' tied more to the legend of Manitou, is another. The Odawa called it 'Mnidoo Mnis,' your 'Island of Great Spirit.' Regardless, it is indeed mysterious. It's a magical place."

"You see, George, you know more than I will ever know. I am very impressed. We should all take the time to learn more."

George thanked the captain and promised he would seek him out when they were passing through the strait.

*

The first day traveling through Lake St. Clair and up the St. Clair River was old hat for the fourteen-year-old young man, having driven his speedboat with Fred in these waters many times.

George was alone standing on the port deck watching the many boats come closer for a better look at the magnificent vessel. One particular boat had several young ladies aboard, dressed in swimwear that by any measure was borderline acceptable.

To George it was very acceptable, as it would have been to any teenage American boy. It was becoming abundantly apparent that George liked the young ladies and was liking them more as each day passed. He was a bright, personable young man, fond of fast boats and faster cars.

Could fast women be far behind?

His position in society and his enormous wealth made him the number-one catch for any and all eligible young ladies. Given the economic conditions of the early 1930s, it was very obvious that many would be after a taste of his lavish lifestyle.

It was this that his mother worried about every day. The femme fatale that would devour her innocent boy. If it wasn't the main reason for her overprotection of young George, it was certainly in the top two. But Mother was not privy to the total relationship Fred and George now shared. Her son was not as naïve as she thought. In fact, over the last year George had matured a great deal. Driving cars and boats and getting away from the house allowed the young man to grow and see so much more of life. He was beginning to understand how fortunate he was, how different his life was than the vast majority of the population.

He understood it and he liked it — a lot.

They were approaching the mouth of the river where it opened to Lake Huron, boats still circling, waving at George and George waving back. Fred was approaching with a broad smile.

"A first for you, George. You are about to enter Lake Huron.

It is better than an ocean voyage; the water is as vast but with incredible vistas the whole way. I hope the weather remains like this for the entire trip. This water can get nasty, very nasty."

The day was spectacular. It was later August, warm and not a breath of wind. George was excited about the next several days. "Have you ever been through the Mississagi Strait?" he asked.

"Never have. I have never been in the North Channel."

George gazed out at the endless blue. "Captain Boland was telling me about the *Griffon*."

Fred smiled. "Ah yes, I know the story. Don't let it bother you. *The Rose* is equipped with the most sophisticated navigation system in the world, and besides, that was in the 1600s!"

It was not the reefs that were on George's mind. Over the last couple of years, he had studied the history of the Anishinabek. He had convinced his mother and Fred to allow him to make a monthly financial contribution out of his massive trust fund to three hospitals that provided medical assistance to the Indigenous people of Michigan. George wanted to talk to Fred about expanding his support to Manitoulin Island. An amazing display of generosity and maturity from such a young man. But he chose to continue the conversation with Fred about that another time.

George remained on deck. *The Rose* increased its speed to ten knots and was proceeding north to Saginaw Bay. Basking in the sun under crystal blue skies, the group enjoyed an afternoon lunch on the aft deck in the most tranquil water the lake could offer.

That evening, with *The Rose* anchored, George and Fred boarded the smaller runabout and headed to a shoal for some bass fishing. Lines were not in the water one minute before each had a fish on.

"I have read that the bass fishing on the north shore of Manitoulin Island is the best in the world. We will have to make time for that. That's providing, however, we survive the Mississagi Strait."

Fred looked through the corner of his eye, waiting for a response from George.

"I'm not worried at all, but there is something I need to tell you."

George explained what the captain had told him and about the book falling open to the map of Spirit Island.

"The two things happened so closely together, it has me thinking."

"I'm not a believer in ghosts and goblins, George, and you shouldn't be either. There is a scientific explanation for 99% of everything that happens, and the *Griffon* was one of them. As far as your book is concerned, strictly coincidence."

"You and I will never agree on that, I'm afraid."

At that point George got a strike that almost ripped the rod out of his hand. He played the fish for over five minutes before landing a six-pound smallmouth bass.

"Yahoo, that's the way to end the night!"

Fred and George sat back, immensely proud of themselves. The ship's hand who had done everything except reel the fish in shuttled them back to *The Rose*.

George lay awake, thinking about the day's events. The discussion with Fred had almost closed the book for him on the "spirit" of Spirit Island.

Almost.

He knew the name was Manitoulin Island, but he would always call it Spirit Island. If for no other reason than just to bug Fred.

The other thought occupying his head was the young ladies waving at him earlier that day. They were exciting to him, very exciting. Was that normal? He had been enjoying the feeling of his first real crush, his first kisses with a girl. Mary was his first and had been on his mind constantly.

But those girls in the boat!

Mary was on his mind, just not as much as she was before. Was that wrong? Should he be only thinking of Mary? He wrestled with that one for a while until the fresh air of the trip's first day pushed him to sleep.

*

The morning brought weather vastly different from the serenity of the day before. The sun was still shining brightly, but the prevailing west wind had stiffened, producing swells of five to six feet. Lake Huron was baring some of her teeth; a high-pressure front had moved in, with cooler air replacing yesterday's humidity. *The Rose* was over two hundred feet long, so the ship's rolling, while noticeable, was hardly worthy of panic. However, the movement was enough to add a greenish tinge to Mattie's complexion. She would spend the remainder of the day in luxury in the confines of her master bedroom.

It was late in the afternoon. George was on deck with Fred and the other guests, taking in the fresh air and spectacular view of Cockburn Island. It would not be long now until *The Rose* would enter the Mississagi Strait.

George left the starboard deck and made his way to the wheelhouse.

Captain Boland was looking very nautical with binoculars pointed at the southern point of Spirit Island. The first officer was behind the wheel. The captain turned to see George looking at the outline of Cockburn Island off the port bow.

"George, at this exact point we are straddling the US–Canada border. The port side of *The Rose* is in US water and the starboard side is in Canadian water."

Having grown up in Lake St. Clair and the St. Clair River, he was used to seeing Canada and then turning around and seeing the U.S.A. It was not top of mind right now.

"Where is this infamous magnetic reef, Captain?"

"Let's you and I go up with some binoculars and have a look."

George looked off the starboard bow. The shore of Spirit Island was crystal clear. He felt the fresh breeze, and for some reason, he started smiling.

He didn't know why.

He could see the Mississagi lighthouse and its flashing white light. He felt exhilarated, like the light was telling him he had arrived at a special place.

"There are magnetic shoals here, south of the point of land where that light house sits. We are in plenty of depth here and on a course to take us around the northwest corner of the island, to Meldrum Bay. As I told you before, in years gone by these shoals would affect compass readings. Many boats have run aground in these waters. Take the binoculars and enjoy the scenery before it gets too dark. I am going back to work."

George was alone, staring at the light from the lighthouse, as dusk surrounded *The Rose*. He could see no life, no movement, just the noise of the wind and the diminishing waves. The strait had calmed the water considerably. His previous concerns about the reefs were long gone.

In the distance he could see another steam ship, not a yacht but a working cargo ship. He had seen many at home, traveling to Detroit. This one was also heading in the direction of Meldrum Bay. He continued to patrol the shoreline with the binoculars, but there was nothing. Trees and untouched wilderness, so natural. He was still smiling. It reminded him of Mackinaw Island; it was love at first sight.

They were anchored a short time later in the middle of Meldrum Bay. Much to George's surprise, the dock was full with other steamships.

It was dusk, very limited light, and dinner was about to be served in the grand dining room of the yacht.

George and others heard several loud explosions coming from the town.

All were caught off guard except for the captain, who was hosting this evening's dinner.

"No cause for alarm. It's dynamite. They are blasting rock. Get used to it, you will hear it as we travel along the north shore of the island."

George had heard dynamite before as a small boy. He did not remember it ever sounding so loud. That crack was miles away, but it sounded like it came from the bow of the boat!

"Captain, does the blasting always sound so loud?"

"The water, George. The sound is unimpeded, and it rolls across the water."

Dinner conversation was boring. George was also mildly depressed about today's cruise through the strait. He wasn't sure what he expected with the reefs, but they didn't measure up.

The island, on the other hand, was a different story.

He was off to bed.

After reading a book about Detroit's newest sports cars, he was not as sleepy as expected. Cars always got his heart pounding; he put on his robe and went up to the aft deck.

The stars took his breath away.

They were different than any he had ever seen before. There were thousands and thousands, so bright they painted the sky white. The constellations were so defined, it was easy to identify them.

The lights of the town at the end of the bay seemed dim in comparison. *The Rose*'s reflection in the water was like midday. George was only sorry he couldn't paint; this would have been a canvas for the ages.

He stood alone in amazement for what seemed like an eternity before deciding to return to his cabin. He walked down the stairs past his mother's room, where he heard Fred's voice at a level that would only be required should he be speaking publicly.

"I am getting tired of this conversation. I think you need to understand that George is a young man capable of mature decisions, including decisions about the opposite sex! He is almost fifteen, and his hormones are raging. You need to understand that. We have brought him up well, sheltered, but well, let him make mistakes, Mattie."

"So many girls, young women will try to seduce him. They will offer sex to win him and his money! That cannot happen. We have to intervene. He has to stay with young ladies of similar upbringing. Not with those harlots we saw today!"

"Please, Mattie, don't let me remind you about *your* background. You were George's father's secretary, remember? You turned out very well, prospering in the elite class, a class you were not from. The same could hold true for your son."

With that, there was silence on both sides of the door.

Chapter 3

The Rose had been steaming along the north coast of Spirit Island for thirty minutes. George arrived late for breakfast.

"Good morning, sleepyhead! I trust you slept well?"

Fred was sitting back in a leather chair, reading telegraphs that were piled on the table beside him.

George looked him straight in the eye. "Yes, a little trouble falling asleep, but after a while I slept like the dead."

Mattie, looking much better having regained her sea legs, said, "I don't care for that expression, George. A different analogy, if you don't mind!"

Fishing was the agenda for the morning, a good thing as far as George was concerned. Mother didn't look like a lot of yuks today.

This morning's route took them around Cape Robert into Bayfield Sound, where they would anchor and the fishing party would head into Cook's Bay. The day was pleasant and still, a mix of sun and cloud, as the runabout motored Fred and George toward a sawmill on the lee side of the bay. Fred's brother and his wife were aboard the larger lapstrake on a sightseeing tour of the sound.

This area was known for its bass and perch, so well known that commercial fishing boats were regular visitors.

"Supposedly the best small-mouth bass fishing in all the Great Lakes is right here."

George was not interested in Fred's fishing commentary. "I couldn't fall asleep last night because I was consumed with the knowledge that I know nothing about my real father, my mother, and most importantly myself!"

Fred realized last night's heated conversation with his wife had been overheard. "George, I'm sorry, you need to know my discussion with your mother was in your best interest, please believe that."

George had never been able to express the true feelings he had for his stepfather. Fred was not good at it either. He did his best by trying to show his love through actions rather than words. George had struggled with it from the time he was ten. Fred had given him everything he wanted. But more than anything, he had freed him from his mother's smothering. He couldn't hold back any longer.

"From what I overheard, I absolutely believe you, and even if I didn't hear you, I would still believe you. You are my best friend in the world."

Fred could not hold back the emotion, eyes welling as he hugged George like the boat they were in was going down.

For the first time, their feelings for each other were out in the open. They had both felt the mutual love and respect for years, but it had never been put on display.

The hired hand piloting the boat was trying not to notice; he was not fooling anyone. He said, "Please forgive me, I am trying to allow you the privacy this moment deserves."

George, still in a bear hug with Fred, was trying to regroup.

"Could you please drive back to the yacht? Fred and I will fish alone today and thank you for your confidence."

They said little to each other for the next hour. They did what they loved to do: they fished, and the action was crazy. Fish were being landed with bare hooks and no bait. They smiled and laughed until Fred broke the silence.

"You need to know your mother loves you more than anything in the world. You need to know where she's coming from."

George shrugged. "My mother and I have a guardian-child relationship, nothing more. We haven't shared anything meaningful. She was never my friend. I never felt at ease; I always felt like I was being scrutinized."

"I know, George, and you are not wrong. Your mother first and foremost wanted you to be safe, as she does today. She had to raise you, until I came along, by herself. You are asking a woman to raise a son without a male influence around, no easy task, as I'm sure you can understand. Was she overprotective? Of course, and she would be the first to admit that."

"So why couldn't she tell me that? I am almost fifteen; we could have 'grown-up' dialogue, but she chooses not to. She continues to be the 'keeper,' allowing me little freedom. I would be totally devoid of normal development if it wasn't for you! She finds out I walk a girlfriend home and makes me feel like I've committed a crime."

Fred looked out at the sawmill in the distance, loading a steamship with the island's lumber. "How much do you know about your father?"

"Not much other than the obvious. He and my uncle made a fortune in the automotive business. My mom inherited the business when he died. I was three. Mom and my aunt sold the business when she met you. I was eight. I remember that very well; I read pages and pages about the sale in all the newspapers. My name even appeared in some of the press. Mom said he was a brilliant engineer and a wonderful man and father. That's it. I do not remember him at all other than from photographs. And yes, I am very much aware we are one the wealthiest families in the United States because of him."

"George, what I'm about to tell you is to help you understand where you and your mother are. My hope is you will absorb this information and be able to make better sense of the relationship, or lack thereof. Mattie is the most charitable, giving person I have ever *heard* of, let alone known. She shares her fortune in so many ways, trying help the needy and make the world a better place. You should know, by the way, that she had tears of joy running down her cheeks when she found out you wanted to give some of *your* money to those hospitals.

"You are one of the richest people in the world, George, you are heir to wealth that is difficult for most to understand. Your mother and aunt sold the business for over 140 million dollars. You see that sawmill over there? Those hard-working people work fifty hours a week, every week, every month, all year. Not one of them will make two thousand dollars for the whole year. My point is you are a person that enjoys a life that everyone wants, a life that people only read and dream about. Your mother's fear is that some will do anything to get into your life — anything! But therein lies her conflict. Do you know how your mother met your father?"

"I do not."

"Mattie was your father's secretary."

George looked at his rod over the side of the boat, seemingly oblivious to the fact that it was bent double from the pull of a fish. Seconds later he realized and started reeling in. "I had no idea. I'm shocked. Mom was a secretary?"

"George, I can stop if you want. I have much more to tell, but if you are uncomfortable please tell me."

"No, no, keep going I want to know everything."

For the first time in George's life he viewed his mother in a different light. Initially he felt anger, thinking she had held this from him, lied to him. But he softened as he started thinking what he would have done if he were in her shoes.

"Your mother is a kind, loving person, very intelligent. She graduated business school, but given the economic conditions, jobs she wanted just weren't there. She took any job she could get. As fate would have it, your father, recognizing her business ability, hired her as an executive secretary. So during that time she saw a lot of things that have stayed with her until this day. She saw countless people trying to get a piece of your father's wealth, business people, social people with their hand out, and, of course, women.

"George, I know you are very attracted to the opposite sex, as you should be; it's only healthy for a teenage lad. Your father was very attracted to the ladies as well. Why not? Hundreds threw themselves at him on a regular basis. He dated many while your mother was his secretary. Some were sincere, socially acceptable, and would have been worthy of your father's continued attention. Others were not and were dismissed by your father in a short period of time. Your mother was privy to many of these relationships because of her position as his personal secretary.

"What I am trying to say, I guess as the expression goes, is 'fruit doesn't fall far from the tree.' Your father loved automobiles, and the fastest ones he loved the most. He loved boats, the faster the better. Your father was a risk-taker, not only in business but in boats and cars and in other things. Mattie is seeing all of this in you, and while she is pleased that you are the image of the man she loved, the rest of it is scaring her crazy."

George sat his rod down and looked across the sound, saying nothing, trying to make sense of all he had heard. His mind was numb with information overload. He looked back at Fred, who looked drained, spent from the emotion.

"I never thought my mother was a bad person. I never knew."

George's eyes were moist, and he dropped his face into his hands.

"George, the first thing I said to you was she loves you unconditionally and only wants you to be safe. Unfortunately, just because you and I have had this talk, that doesn't mean she is going to change. I did this for you, to help you understand."

George moved across the boat and hugged Fred again. "You are a wonderful man, you are a friend, a father, better than a father. Thank you."

*

The Rose pulled out of the sound, continuing toward Little Current. It was midafternoon, and all passengers were on deck playing shuffleboard under the bluest skies you could order. George had selected his mother as his partner, the first time he had ever taken *that* initiative in any circumstance in his life.

Mattie did not like the water. "It's so hard to concentrate on your shot with the boat heaving like this!"

The water was like a pool table, the most placid condition.

"Mother, I think you are looking for any excuse to explain your total inability to play this game."

Mattie laughed and retired with her lemonade to a lounge chair to catch a few rays.

A couple of hours had passed, and George was the only person still on deck. He was focused on the outline of Clapperton Island, which lay straight ahead. It had been the most traumatic but satisfying day of his young life, a day he would never forget.

The Rose had noticeably slowed down in the last few minutes. George made his way to the wheelhouse to see what was up.

"George, you need to be alert passing between Maple Point and Clapperton Island. Nothing to worry about, you just need to watch your depth."

Curiosity satisfied, he returned topside.

He was looking at a peninsula of Spirit Island that Captain Boland had identified as Maple Point when a calm came over his body. He had felt this once before, years ago in the hospital. He had broken his wrist falling off his bicycle and was given a needle for the pain. The feeling he was experiencing was identical to the feeling he experienced on that drug. Total relaxation, almost floating in air, no stress or pressure; he could feel nothing.

What was going on? It was like he was in some euphoric trance, unable to move or think, and to make things more bizarre, not really caring if he moved or not. He continued to stare at Maple Point, and while they were over a mile off shore he could make out the trees and rocky shoreline as if it were only a few yards away.

He could see wigwams past the point, farther into the bay. The faint outline of a small town with a few boats along its dock were visible to him. There was no way he should be able to see that far.

His legs were able to move, but their movement seemed predetermined. He seemed to follow himself, not out of body but like someone was driving his body. He found himself in the wheelhouse, and all came back to normal.

"Yes, George, can I help you with something?"

"I'm not sure, Captain, I'm really not sure?" George took a few steps towards the door then turned to face the captain. "Can we anchor in this bay for the night?"

"It was not the plan. We were going to dock in Little Current, but I can ask your mother if you would like?"

"No, I will look after that, thank you."

A short time and a brief conversation later, they were anchored in the bay under the incredible night sky.

Fred was on deck with George after dinner, the stars illuminating the bay like flood lights.

"What is the attraction to this place, my boy?"

"I don't know, I can't explain it."

"Try."

"No, you said before you don't believe in ghosts and goblins.

You will roll your eyes and take another sip from your brandy flask you think no one knows exists."

Fred burst out laughing, hysterical belly laughter. "I will give you credit, George, I'm positive your mother doesn't even know! Besides, it will all be socially accepted in the near future. Prohibition is all but over."

"I felt something weird today, and as I said before, I can't explain it. I need to stay here tonight, let's leave it at that."

"You and I continue to add to our chest of secrets. My flask and I are off to bed. It's been an emotional day."

George remained on deck, looking, waiting, thinking something was going to happen. There were stars, flickering lights from shore, and a faint smell of smoke, and while all his senses were on full alert, there was nothing more.

The day had taken its toll. His bed felt better than ever, and there would be no problem drifting off tonight.

Nature called in the wee hours of the morning. George opened the bathroom door and found himself standing on the shore of Maple Point.

The Rose was nowhere to be seen, just a starlit bay that was smooth as glass. It was comfortably warm, and the smell in the air was sweet, the trees tall and motionless. The feeling from this afternoon had returned: euphoria.

George was not frightened — exactly the opposite. There was a cabin by the water with a light on inside. His body moved slowly in that direction. He wasn't sure how he was moving, but he felt his hand on the knob of the cabin door.

Inside there was something in front of the window overlooking the bay. It was motionless, continuing to face the water. He heard words, but they didn't seem to come from the shape in front of the window.

"Hello, George. This is your home. You will always be at peace here. Welcome to Maple Point."

Chapter 4

George opened his eyes, not sure where he was.

The ceiling looked familiar; he turned his head and saw a painting of *The Rose*. Yes, he was in his bed, and the sheets were soaked in sweat. His pajamas were stuck to him like he had showered with them on.

What had happened?

He showered, without pajamas, dressed, and went on deck. It was early morning. The air was cool and the sun hadn't been in the sky long. Maple Point appeared as tranquil as it had the previous afternoon.

There was no cabin.

Why not? He was sure it would be visible from the water.

The whistle from a steamship behind him was heading west towards Meldrum Bay; nothing out of the ordinary was going on. What did he expect? Something happened last night, he was sure of that. A dream? A vision? Whatever it was, it was vividly etched in his mind.

Twice yesterday he had the same feeling take over his body. He was conscious for one, not sure what he was for the other. He continued his surveillance of the shore. Maybe he was mistaken about the location of the cabin. He looked up and down the entire shoreline, trees, rocks, and seagulls, nothing else. He stood motionless, wondering, hoping the feeling would return; nothing was going on.

Mattie approached from the aft deck. "Good morning, son. You are up early. I have to say, George, I am not sure why you wanted to stay here last night. It doesn't seem any different from any other bay we have been in on this island."

Mattie waited for a response, but there was none forthcoming. "We are heading to Little Current shortly. Everyone wants to go shop and do some touristy stuff."

Despite his new respect for his mother, there was no way he was going to confide in her *his* last twelve hours.

"To be honest, Mom, I'm not sure why this place either; it just seemed different for some reason."

Mattie walked briskly inside when she felt *The Rose* turning out of the bay.

George had one last look, hoping for something, but there was the Canadian north and nothing else. They rounded Trudeau Point and headed to Little Current.

There was no doubt in his mind that what had transpired was real. He was convinced he would be back; for him the only question was whether his return would be under his own control, conscious or otherwise.

*

As always, *The Rose* attracted a large crowd, moored at the Little Current dock.

Little Current was the largest town on Spirit Island, located where the island and the mainland almost touched. A strip of water, not two hundred yards wide, separated the two. The dock was only feet from the main drag.

The shore party was short one person: George had decided to stay on board. He watched from above as the four hustled into Turner's Department Store, a short distance from the boardwalk.

George was watching a coal freighter being loaded on the other side of the narrow harbor. A picture of black on black, the dark of the freighter was darkened further by the black cloud of the coal.

George was totally preoccupied. The freighter could have burned and sank and it would have gone unnoticed by him. He moved to the port side of the boat and waved at people parading past the grand yacht. Naturally, he noticed two girls standing, staring directly at him. He waved, they waved back, he waved again. They were not moving, so George, being George, held up his index finger, motioning he was coming down.

He ran down the stairs and onto the boardwalk. The girls had not moved an inch.

"Hi, my name is George Rausch, pleased to meet you."

Upon closer inspection, he noticed one girl was several years older than the other, maybe nineteen, even twenty. More importantly, the elder was looking directly into his eyes and smiling, while the younger was giggling, looking at her feet.

"Hello, George, my name is Lilly, and this is my younger sister, Olivia. That is a wonderful ship. Is it yours?"

"Well, sort of, yes, it is my family's. Do you girls live here?"

"No, we are from Toronto. That's our sailboat over there."

They pointed at a beautiful white schooner with *Toronto Bound* written across the hull. It was easily the second most impressive vessel at the dock.

"What a beauty. Your father must be an excellent sailor. How long is that?"

Olivia, who was no more than twelve, had no interest in any of this rhetoric. Lilly responded. "Fifty-seven feet, yes, we have sailed all over the Great Lakes. We leave in May every year and don't go back home until the end of August. We are on our way home now. I am taking Olivia back to our boat. Do you want to walk the boardwalk with me? There is plenty to see."

Another first for George: an older girl wanted to go for a walk with him.

"Sure, let's go."

Olivia had been dropped off.

"George, do you live in Detroit, like your boat says?"

"Close, just north of there."

They took a few steps farther, and Lilly grabbed George's hand.

George almost pissed his pants. He didn't even know this *older* girl's last name, and they were already holding hands. Fighting embarrassment, George collected himself and figured *why not?*

"Do you have a boyfriend, Lilly?"

Lilly didn't answer as she led George from the boardwalk behind an ice cream shop.

"I have one right now!"

The words weren't completely out of her mouth when she pushed George up against the shop's wall and gave him a long, wet kiss.

For the first time in George's life he could feel a girl's tongue inside his mouth!

There was no one more surprised than George when after a few seconds, he realized this wasn't all bad and placed his tongue on top of hers! This continued for almost a minute until they heard someone coming and jumped back on the boardwalk, still holding hands.

George, unable to look at Lilly, was staring at his feet when they walked head-on into Fred and Mattie.

In his lifetime, George couldn't ever remember soiling himself and was hoping this wasn't going to be the first time.

"Mom! Hi! Ah, this is Lilly, she is sailing back to Toronto today!"

Lilly had dropped George's hand, but it was too late. The guilt was splashed all over his face, and if that wasn't enough, his last sentence had been delivered like his pants were too tight. His voice was operating at a pitch an octave higher than normal.

"Pleased to meet you, Lilly. I'm Fred and this is my wife, Mattie. We are George's parents."

"Hi, a pleasure, Lilly Edwards."

"Well, we will let you two carry on. See you back at the boat, George."

George could feel Fred holding back the smile. His choice of words, "carry on," was for George's benefit as well.

"Sorry, George, I hope I didn't get you in trouble."

George grabbed Lilly's hand and said, "No trouble at all, everything is fine."

They walked back over to the side of the ice cream shop and picked up where they left off. George was closer to twenty than he thought. He escorted Lilly to her schooner and said goodbye. Walking to *The Rose*, he was smiling, thinking about all that had happened in the last twenty-four hours.

This Spirit Island was amazing and fast becoming his favorite place in the world.

Fred was at the top of the stairs, looking like the welcoming committee for an arriving dignitary.

"You better get that lipstick off your face before your mother sees you!"

George started frantically rubbing his mouth, but Fred burst out laughing,

"There's no lipstick, Mr. Gullible, but there might as well be! The first thing your mother said walking away from you two was 'how old is that *harlot*?'"

"Oh great, she said 'harlot'? Is Mom mad?"

"I smoothed things over, George. She won't say anything, especially after our conversation you overheard the other night."

George and the four grown-ups were dining at the Anchor Inn, the main hotel in Little Current. This hotel had been hosting Great Lake's mariners since the late 1800s. The walls of the dining room were covered in paintings and photographs of the era.

The dinner conversation centered around an upcoming state election in Michigan. George was *so* not interested, so he asked to be excused and wandered around the hotel looking at the old works of art. Sailing ships, steamers, and wrecks made up most of the subject matter.

George was in the men's room, staring at a painting of a tugboat while he was taking care of business. The painting was old and nothing special, but there was something that kept his attention.

A tugboat in choppy water, two men in rain gear pointing at something off in the distance, the lake's spray soaking the bow of the boat. The backdrop was a nondescript rocky shoreline with nothing visible except trees and a few gray clouds.

He noticed a small brass plate embedded in the wood frame. It was covered in years of grime and was not legible. He wasn't about to touch it; he grabbed tissue and began wiping away the grunge.

The engraving read, *Maple Point*.

George didn't move, fixated on the words.

There were so many questions he wanted answered. What were the two men on the tug pointing at? Was that the same shoreline where he had his cabin visit last night? And finally, what was going on? Was this another message from Maple Point saying, 'You can't get away from me'?

A weathered old salt in his eighties had been taking his time washing his hands, watching George.

"You like that painting, boy?"

George was caught off guard, thinking he had been alone all this time.

"Just curious, I was at Maple Point yesterday, that's all."

The old man moved over to the painting and looked at it closely, not saying a word.

George had one foot out the door when the man, still looking at the painting, said, "Are you wondering what they are pointing at?"

George let the door close. "Yes, as a matter of fact, that's exactly what I want to know."

The man moved toward the door that George was blocking. He looked into the boy's face and stopped dead. He rubbed his bloodshot eyes; they widened, creepy wide.

"They are pointing at something they see on the shore, but only *they* can see it, and when they look for it again, it won't be there."

The man continued to look at George for an uncomfortable period of time then left.

George, rejoined his dinner party, looking vacant. His appearance prompted Mattie to say, "You okay, George? You feeling alright?"

George sat down, nearly missing his chair. "Yes, I'm fine, Mom, just tired, I guess, long day."

Fred, with his napkin over his mouth, noticed George's scattered appearance. "Well, I for one am ready for bed. I agree with George, are we all ready?"

Fred walked back to *The Rose*, arm around George's shoulders. "You don't look good. Can I help? Something you want to talk about?"

"I do, maybe tomorrow. We start back in the morning, right?"

"We are. Get some sleep. I will see you topside in the morning, and we will talk."

*

George didn't know where to begin with his analysis of the day's events. He was exhausted, his head spinning. Light from the stars cascaded around his room. Did the old man know about his experience from the night before? How, in Little Current, in a men's room no less, did he uncover a painting of Maple Point?

He met a twenty-year-old lady and five minutes later was wildly kissing her seconds before his mother came by?

No wonder exhaustion was taking over.

Spirit Island offered him everything he wanted.

His mind was made up, even at the tender age of almost fifteen. He was coming back; he felt at home here. He felt like the island was his, where he was meant to be.

He felt free and alive.

He was going to talk to Fred in the morning.

He was fighting sleep now, a fight he was glad to lose.

Chapter 5

Little Current's swing bridge that connected the island to the mainland completed its turn, allowing *The Rose* to cruise past Strawberry Island. They had begun their trip home to Detroit.

Fred, coffee in hand, was marveling at the engineering of the massive structure. "You look so much better. I was worried about you last night."

George wasn't sure how much he was going to tell Fred. The lighter side involving Lilly Edwards was a given; that would be funny and only confirm what Fred already assumed. He wanted to sell Spirit Island to Fred. He wanted his dad to want it as much as he did. Or at a minimum understand why George wanted to be there.

The whole Maple Point thing with the cabin visit and then the old man at the Anchor Inn was a heavier decision. He was closer to Fred than anyone in the world, but how could he explain something that he didn't understand himself? Fred had already made his position on "ghosts and goblins" clear. Even if he could make sense of the "spiritual" experience, it would be an uphill fight to make Fred believe.

Fred was a businessman. This area of the world was untamed, almost virgin real estate — perhaps a discussion about a property investment should be his approach?

He wanted Fred to know this was not a visit or a stop on a Great Lakes vacation. This island, Spirit Island or Manitoulin Island for Fred, held something special, something he wanted to be a part of for years to follow.

"Mom didn't say a thing to me about Lilly last night. You were right."

Fred was grinning, "You know, Miss Edwards is exactly the type of female that scares her to death. A little more 'experienced' and blessed with the 'attributes' most men desire. By the way, she was a beautiful young lady, big-city girl from Toronto. Well done, my boy."

George was fashioning a grin of satisfaction, "I wonder, was she kissing me or *The Rose*?"

Fred turned to George with an equally large smile. "I wish your mother heard you ask that. As long as you keep that thought in mind, Mattie and I can rest easy for the rest of our lives."

"You know, the whole thing came out of nowhere. I was thinking about how much older she looked, the makeup she was wearing, then she grabbed my hand! Two minutes later, lip-lock!"

George was so proud of himself, almost exhibiting a swagger in his voice.

"George, you are a handsome young man with immense wealth. That combination will attract an endless line of Lilly Edwards. You seem to understand that, and you will need to keep your guard up at all times. Some will lie — no, check that, many will lie to you. Only you will be able to determine their sincerity. I am thrilled we are talking about this; you are confirming all the points about your maturity I made to your mother. So here is my wish for you, that we will never discuss this again, agreed?"

"Of course!"

"You are a wonderful young man, grounded, and I'm

confident you will not abuse your good fortune, so I am comfortable with what I am about to say. Don't be shy about enjoying life, especially with the ladies. You are blessed, so enjoy the fruits of being a Rausch!"

Fred winked at George and raised his coffee, like he was toasting the young man. George figured there was no better time to discuss Spirit Island than right now, so he dove right in.

"These last few days have been the best time of my life. I have never felt so alive. Do you want to know why?"

"Well, I think I have a good idea, I met her!"

Fred raised his eyebrows, giving another frat-house expression of approval.

George grinned and said, "That was a small part of it, for sure, but not what I want to talk about. I realize I am different than most, not just the family fortune and social status, but because my best friend is my stepfather."

Fred smiled. "It may be different from the norm, but certainly not in a bad way."

"I agree totally. I think it is different in a *good* way, especially for me! You have raised my opinion of my mother and my affection for her. You have remedied the 'dark' years spent under Mother's control with your time and attention. If I had good buddies, or a best friend for the last couple of years taking up all my time, I would not be where I am today in my development and maturity."

Fred continued to look at George in amazement. "Are you sure you are not turning twenty next month instead of fifteen?"

"So, my point is with you as my best friend *and* my stepfather, I can feel relaxed and open with about what I want to discuss."

"George, this sounds like it could get deep. I feel the need to freshen my coffee, wink, wink!"

Fred did a little jig, patted the breast pocket of his smoking jacket, and disappeared inside the boat. *The Rose* chugged toward "The Hole in the Wall," a passage of water on the northeast corner of Spirit Island. Once navigated, the family would head south through the northwest portion of Georgian Bay into Lake Huron and home.

Fred returned with a larger cup of coffee, positioned two deck chairs, and tapped the seat on one gently, "Sit, my boy, what's on your mind?"

"I cannot accurately tell you the feelings I have experienced on and around this island these past few days."

"To my recollection, George, you have never stepped foot on this island?"

"Sit back and keep an open mind."

Over the next half hour George detailed his nocturnal trip to the cabin and his visit with the "thing" inside. He was on to the conversation about the old timer in the men's room when Fred finally made it a two-sided conversation.

"I would suggest the visit to the cabin was a dream, nightmare, or whatever. A stomach disorder causing abnormal rapid eye movements during an uneasy sleep; and the old guy, merely a coincidence."

George looked at Fred with disdain. "You are not entering into the spirit of this thing, excuse the pun."

"You are aware of my position on ghosts, and that is what you have been talking about, so I can't look interested in something that I do not believe in."

"I had my body taken over by something — twice! I was awake, totally awake the first time! The old guy said, unsolicited, '*They* are the only ones that can see what they are looking at and when they try to see it again, it *won't* be there!'"

"Granted, George, an untimely coincidence for you, but a coincidence all the same."

George jumped up and paced around, kicking at the deck like there was a ball in front of him.

"George, I believe there are two separate issues here. Please don't confuse them. I don't believe in the supernatural, but I do believe *you* when you say this place makes you feel alive and excited. We both know the freedom Manitoulin Island represents for you; that alone makes this place better than anywhere else you have been in your life. The unknown always raises blood pressure. That combined with the energy and enthusiasm of a fifteen-year-old young man makes this place a desired destination."

George slowly returned to his chair and in a subdued voice said, "I know what I saw. It wasn't a dream. This place holds something special for George Rausch, and I believe it always will."

It was Fred's turn to pace. "So, what do we want to do about it?"

George raised his head like he had been given new life. "Like what? You tell me!"

Fred continued to walk, enjoying the fresh air and gazing at the open water ahead. "*We* can make a point of coming back here every year for as long as you want. We can take *The Rose* or we can fly back, whatever you'd like."

It was a step in the right direction for George, but not totally what he had in mind. He was focused on Maple Point. Sure, returning to visit there was a start, but he wanted more; he wanted to belong, he wanted Maple Point.

"I am thinking about something a little more permanent. We both like to fish, and there is no better fishing in the world than here. While we are not huge hunters, from what I have read, the island offers world-class deer hunting."

"I think I know where you are going. George, you are turning fifteen in a matter of days. Still a little young for a summer home, wouldn't you say?"

"For me maybe, but not for you! We could buy land for a

fishing and hunting lodge on Maple Point!"

George's enthusiasm was boiling over; he was bouncing around Fred like a little puppy. Fred looked at George with a grin, then turned, taking a long look at the shore of Manitoulin Island waning in the distance.

"Do you have any idea the selling job required on your mother to pull this off?"

George reached inside Fred's jacket, removed the infamous flask, and handed it to Fred.

"Take a drink, a toast to the future 'Rausch Lodge'!"

Fred followed George's direction and took a more than ample swig.

"This will take time. Let me do my homework. We may be talking a year from now, maybe two."

Naturally, George wanted them to turn *The Rose* around and bolt to the real estate office, but nonetheless, he was ecstatic!

*

The Rose returned to Detroit, and soon after, life was back to normal for George. The summer of 1932 was drawing to a close, but he felt a new excitement for his life ahead. A day did not go by that thoughts of Spirit Island and Maple Point didn't cross his mind.

Over the next year and half, George would pass on "land notices" to Fred on a regular basis. George never asked Fred how the discussion about a fishing lodge purchase was progressing with Mother; he trusted his stepfather that talks were happening, and it would only be a matter of time — he hoped.

George spent much of his time driving his boat, and when possible, one of the many family cars. He was becoming quite the lady's man and was dating many of Detroit's better known younger ladies. Most were screened and approved by Mother, the rest were under the cover of Fred.

On his sixteenth birthday, in the late summer of 1933, Fred and his mother presented George with a red sports car. George found out later that Mattie agreed to the gift while kicking and screaming. This convertible was Detroit's latest and greatest and a conversation piece wherever George would take it.

On one early fall evening, George was followed by the local police while driving a young lady home after a college party. It seemed he had been driving at a very high speed and had actually lost the trailing officer. When leaving the home of the young lady, two police cars converged on George, pulling him from the car.

"That is some fast car, son. You left me in the dust a few miles back."

George, figuring "no comment" was the best thing to do, shrugged and said, "Am I being arrested?"

"Do you own a driving permit, boy?"

George handed him the permit, and the officer walked back to his partner. A few minutes later, he returned to where George was standing.

"Mr. Rausch, I suggest you drive more responsibly in the future."

The officer walked back to his car and drove away. On more than one occasion the Rausch name paid George dividends when caught for driving fast — very, very fast.

It was Christmas Day, and the Rausch family were opening gifts. Mattie and Fred had just said goodbye to newspaper photographers from the *Detroit News*. George's parents had donated five million dollars to Michigan University and had agreed to a Christmas shot of their property to accompany the announcement.

George was opening a large gift, one of many for the day. However, this one was different. Fred was looking at him like the box was going to ignite.

The gift was light for its size; all it held was an envelope, addressed to George. He opened it and began to shake uncontrollably.

It was the deed to six hundred acres of land in the District of Gore Bay, known as Maple Point.

Fred had tears running down his face seeing the absolute joy in George's eyes,

"We take possession in the spring. Soon as the snow lifts, we can start building."

He hugged his mother first. "It was your father's idea. I know how much you two wanted it."

George moved to his stepfather. Both of them crying, they hugged like never before.

No words were spoken; no words were needed.

Chapter 6

The Rausch family owned a couple of planes.

George's fascination with speed wasn't limited to ground and water, and with the ink barely dry on the Rausch land transfer, he wanted to get to "his" Maple Point as quickly as possible.

So, the sea plane holding George, Fred, and an architect headed north from Lake St. Clair.

A team of tradesmen and laborers had gone ahead to set up camp. George did not know what to expect as he viewed Spirit Island from above. It looked as he had left it two years before. But was it? Would his "cabin" reappear when he approached the location? He was reminded of the old guy's narrative of the painting showing two men in the tugboat: "*When they look for it again, it won't be there.*"

Or would only he see it, prompting Fred and others to have George seek psychiatric care?

It was spring, and the snow was gone — barely. The plane banked left over the west shore as they made their final approach into Mudge Bay. Fred was a bit of a "white knuckler" at the best of times, and landing on water, albeit a calm day, was pushing his comfort zone to the limit. George was laughing to himself watching the flask make numerous appearances on the plane's final descent. When it came safely to an abrupt stop and the engine's roar subsided, Fred looked at George and said, "That wasn't so bad!"

George, pointing at the flask, burst out laughing. "Think you could have made it alone?"

George had been instrumental in the planning process over the winter. Given a sketchy survey of the land, he worked long hours with surveyors and the architect planning the lodge. They wanted to hit the ground running in early May. The timeline had a fall completion. Initial drawings planned a ten-bedroom, five-bathroom, four thousand-square-foot residence.

There were two sites under consideration, and a decision had to be made quickly.

The team was to dine and stay at the Havelock Hotel, in the tiny town of Kagawong at the foot of Mudge Bay, a short boat ride from Maple Point. It was also accessible by car, but on a single-lane gravel road with potholes you could take a bath in. If you could achieve ten miles per hour you were lucky. The only vehicle was a pick-up truck, so few would have to ride in the back; hence, a water ride was chosen. The boat was a cross between a tug and a mini-barge that had been purchased in Little Current the week before.

The staple for the evening feed was fresh whitefish. The local joke was, with the hotel so close to the water and the bay's reputation for great fishing, just keep the widow open and the fish will jump right onto your plate!

Fred looked across the table at George. "Exciting! We will have a site chosen by this time tomorrow and be ready to break ground on Rausch Lodge!"

The group applauded, and George was all smiles.

"I want to thank you all for the time and effort you put in planning this project. I can't wait to get started."

Fred had arranged a shot of bourbon for everyone. "To a successful project!"

The property, six hundred acres worth, had over four thousand feet of frontage. It was wild, virgin land, untouched by construction equipment of any kind. A part of Maple Point was believed to be a native campground, but all the wigwams were gone, at least to the naked eye. There were some remnants, but none that needed to be removed. George's education on Indigenous matters had him taking steps to ensure all was completed without compromising any aboriginal law. George had great respect and admiration for the island's native people.

"The water front here is shelf rock, perfect for docking large boats, even our plane."

The water dropped off sharply only feet from the shore, and the grade of the land was level, where the lodge and two other buildings would be built.

The view of Clapperton Island looked like a backdrop some artist had flown in from Hollywood. There had been a couple of possible sites on paper, but once viewed live, the decision was easy.

George was walking around the site, enjoying the water view when he tripped and fell toward the massive trunk of a birch tree. Bracing for the impact, he held his arms straight out in front as he tumbled forward.

His arms went right through the tree. Like the tree was invisible, a hologram, there was no contact.

George, brushing himself off, looked around to see if anyone else had witnessed the incident. No one was watching, of course.

"Hey! Come over here quick!"

Fred and the others ran to George's side, thinking he had injured himself.

"Are you okay?"

"Yes, fine, feel the trunk of that tree?"

The architect, looking at George a little differently, kicked the trunk gently then slapped it with his palm a couple of times.

"It's a tree alright, been there a long time I'd imagine. Did you hit your head, George, by chance?"

George was looking at the trunk like it was going to speak to him. "It felt like rock, that's all, no, I'm fine."

The men moved back to what they were doing. Fred squinted at George with a puzzled look. "You sure you're okay?"

"I'm great. That view of Clapperton Island is amazing. I was so enthralled, I did a face-plant. Let's get to work!"

There was no way he was sharing this episode with anyone, not even Fred. Maybe he missed the trunk; in the excitement of the day, anything was possible.

He *didn't* miss the trunk, but he was convincing himself he did, no matter what.

A few hours had passed, and George returned after a healthy, eventless hike through the property. The architect and two other workers were carrying blueprints, driving stakes into the ground and marking the footing locations of the two buildings and the main lodge. The architect spotted George and yelled, "Your infamous 'cement' birch tree is coming down. It is in the exact location of the corner footing of the lodge."

Like George needed to be spooked one more time.

This was not helping him believe he missed the trunk during his fall. Maybe this was confirmation from the island that this was to be "his" place? Perhaps Maple Point had preselected the site and used the birch tree to confirm the exact location? Too much to consider right now; the stakes were in the ground, time to move on.

The first two major tasks were the dock construction and their driveway into the lodge from the gravel road that went to Kagawong. George intended to be hands-on with both projects. He started with the road crew on a job that was to take three weeks; George lasted forty-five minutes.

George had gained more knowledge about the island: they

grew big bugs, big in number and big in size. Black flies by the trillions, deer flies, and horse flies you could ride on.

George moved out of the bush and on to the dock project, where he lasted a full two weeks, until the dock was completed. He learned from this experience that the waters of the North Channel were crystal clear; you could read the date on a fifty-cent piece, ten feet down in the water. This was a good thing, because you spent a lot of time in hip waders, so the clarity made it easy to identify your body parts that had dropped off from the frigid temperature of the channel.

The summer was one of work and little play. Fred and George fished a few times here and there, but their focus was on the lodge.

The locals from Kagawong, Gore Bay, and Little Current were aghast at the dollars being spent on the Rausch Lodge.

It was the talk of the island; money was no object. For three months, a barge arrived every other day, loaded with different types of wood, glass, slate, and hand-crafted furniture to fill four thousand square feet, including ten bedrooms. The dining table alone sat eighteen people and was one single piece of wood, weighing over a thousand pounds.

One of the richest families in the world had opened the purse strings. Shipping expenses alone were staggering; they were employing all the tradesmen and laborers available in the area and flying in and out three or four times a day.

The fireplace in the grand room of the lodge was magnificent, by far the most expensive and time-consuming project of the entire construction. It was twelve feet across at the mantle and was the height of the lodge, continuing above the roofline as a massive chimney. The stone was brought in from upstate Michigan, a stone the family chose years ago for their country home.

George was becoming a celebrity and a household name in

Gore Bay and Little Current. During the construction period, he would arrive by boat or pickup truck, arranging supplies, buying whatever was required, and, of course, spending money like it was growing on the trees of Maple Point.

On a hot day late in August, with the lodge near completion, George was needed in Little Current to sign some papers. Leaving the bank, the ice cream shop caught his eye. Wonderful memories from a few summers past surfaced. With cone in hand, looking like an unshaven movie star, he strolled along the boardwalk, talking to everyone and anyone that said hello.

Floating Alone, on the transom of a forty-eight-foot beauty, made George laugh. He heard music coming from inside the craft, but no one was around.

"What is so amusing, Mr. Rausch?"

The voice seemed to come from the boat, but he still couldn't see anyone.

"I found the name of your vessel quite clever. How do you know my name?"

A head finally popped up from beneath the deck. "Sorry, hi, I'm Johnny Griggs. I don't think there is a person in Little Current who doesn't know who you are!"

Johnny reached over the side of the boat and shook George's hand. "Would you like to join me for some lemonade? Please, come aboard!"

George quickly found out that Johnny was the owner of the Anchor Inn.

He was watching the swing bridge, enjoying his drink, listening to Johnny talk about the history of the inn and the town itself.

"So, who named the boat?"

"I did. My dad, who actually owns the hotel, took ill a year ago, just after he purchased the repossessed boat from the bank. I told him we couldn't really afford it, but he remortgaged the inn and thus the name."

George smiled. "Very clever, and a beautiful boat, I might add."

"Thanks, we got it very cheap. Someone else's misfortune was a great opportunity for us."

Johnny topped up George's glass. "We are kind of humbled your family chose Manitoulin Island. You are the biggest thing *ever* to happen here!"

George modestly replied, "I love it here. I have never felt so comfortable."

George told Johnny about the dinner his family had two years ago at the Anchor and the infamous meeting with the old art critic.

After digesting George's story, Johnny shook his head. "I've known you less than an hour, but this island isn't that big. I know we will be seeing a lot more of each other, so take this for what it's worth. My family has been here for over seventy-five years, in Little Current and Gore Bay. My grandmother and grandfather grew up in Gore Bay in the 1870s. My father told me a long time ago that Maple Point was always a topic of discussion with the sailors and crews that stayed at the inn. The stories were focused on 'sightings' at night when they passed the point."

George felt a small shiver go down his back. "What kind of sightings?"

"Always lights from a cabin, fires nearby that burned a different color."

George's eyes widened.

"Would you have a bit more lemonade?" Johnny went on, "Very strange, they *all* talk about a 'cabin.'"

"Well, that's not *that* strange, is it Johnny?"

Johnny looked out over the harbor. "There has never been a cabin there, ever, in over a hundred years."

Chapter 7

It answered the question for George.

He had visited that "cabin" that others had only seen. He did not see it from a distance — he found himself there. The cabin could have presented itself to George as it did others, from the deck of *The Rose*; but it chose not to. In fact, it may have *chosen* George. But to the best of his knowledge, the cabin was exactly where the lodge was now sitting.

Did that mean the cabin or its inhabitant would never appear again?

The lodge was finished, and it was more than he or any of the Rausch family could have hoped for. Unfortunately, the humane weather was also done for the year.

George would finish school this winter and head back to Maple Point in the later spring. He couldn't wait to enjoy his new digs and live the experience of Spirit Island. He had worked hard this summer. It was time to bring some toys from home; it was time to start having fun.

Mattie and George were spending more time together back in Michigan. Mattie's charitable work with local colleges had gained national recognition. She had helped George with his studies, and the two were closer than at any other point in their lives.

She appreciated the independence Manitoulin Island provided her son and acknowledged the personal growth he realized from his time there. George would be eighteen in a matter of weeks, and he was indeed a mature young man. He still lived for excitement and speed and the thrill of the unknown, but he carried himself like the gentleman Mattie had hoped for.

Mattie and Fred were proud of how George turned out, an intelligent, loving individual. A man from great wealth, humble enough to realize it and gracious enough to share it. George, on his own, decided to avoid the red tape of an American making charitable donations to the two hospitals on the island and made them anonymously, although the doctors and administrators knew exactly where the funds were coming from.

It was April of 1935, and George was itching to head north. The ice had not totally cleared from the inland lakes of Spirit Island, and the snow drifts at his Maple Point estate had not completely melted. Fred and George were planning a shipment from their Michigan home to arrive at the lodge by the first week of May. A barge arrived from Gore Bay, two days after they arrived.

The cargo was the red convertible he received on his sixteenth birthday and his twenty-two-foot speed boat. They were the "must haves" for Mr. Rausch to maximize the island experience.

The boat was polished mahogany, wrapped around a 220-horsepower inboard. Only a handful of these existed — anywhere. George had driven it for three summers on Lake St. Clair, and Fred had total confidence in his ability. As far as the convertible, he had been cruising the college campus and suburban Detroit for a couple of years now and was as competent as anyone behind the wheel. But George only knew one speed.

This candy-apple-red sports car with the bright white rag top was one of one, manufactured for the Rausch family.

George stood out in Detroit whenever he drove this car; on

the island he may as well have had fireworks spewing from the exhaust as he drove down the road. This vehicle with the young millionaire behind the wheel would attract crowds everywhere he went. And those crowds would be largely made up of young eligible ladies, hoping to catch the eye of Manitoulin Island's famous new bachelor.

Fred and George were at the dock tinkering with the boat.

"You know, my boy, now that we are settled, we should think about a full-time hand around here. Jack of all trades sort of guy."

With a smirk George replied, "Gee, what about the girl that did the paperwork at the barge yesterday?"

Fred winked at George and said, "Your mother isn't here, but I still have to look her in the eye sooner or later!"

George had been giving thought to this before Fred brought it up. He had been impressed with Johnny Griggs; he liked his personality and the fact that he ran a business. While Johnny was not the person, he was as good as anywhere to start his search.

George traveled the horrible bumpy road from the lodge up to the "highway." Once there, he increased his speed dramatically and cruised on over to Little Current to have a word with Johnny.

"No shortage of men looking for work, especially when they find out they are working at the lodge!"

"Well, Johnny, I am hoping I can lean on your knowledge of the locals to find the best person available?"

"You know, Mr. Smith at Smith's Grocery in Kagawong knows everyone, and everyone knows him. A finer gentleman you couldn't meet. Pay him a visit; you will certainly need no introduction. Leave it with me as well for a day or two. I will put the word out."

George jumped in his car and drove slowly down the main street of the town. Several onlookers waved.

"Good day, Mr. Rausch, very nice wheels!!"

George waved and took off to Gore Bay. He had not driven the rag top in that village; time to check it out. In 1935 the Depression was still very much alive, but Gore Bay was somewhat insulated, serving as home to the island's government buildings and the island's telephone office, as well as its busiest port.

It was the first warm day of the year, over seventy degrees. George parked the car and strolled along the boardwalk, taking in the sights. He was not out of the car five minutes and already a crowd was circling and pointing at the sports car.

George smiled at the crowd, which included a couple of young ladies.

A tall gentlemen walking toward him called his name. "Mr. Rausch, George if I may, I am Carmen, Carmen Piercy. I own the marina over there. I've been looking so forward to meeting you!"

"Hello Carmen, my pleasure."

George held out his hand.

"I wanted to say whenever you're here, please feel free to park your car at the marina, or your boat, for that matter. I will look after them. And besides, the crowds you attract are good for business!"

George took him up on his offer and moved his car to the dock beside the marina, which was getting crowded. He was starting to believe he was the attraction after all. When George returned to his car, he was shocked to see someone sitting in the passenger seat!

Someone he didn't know.

"Excuse me, who are you and what are you doing in my car?"

The young lady took off her sunglasses, showing her blue eyes and said, "I was admiring your car, and I just had to sit in it. I hope you don't mind?"

George got in behind the wheel, noticing his passenger's

skirt was cut well up her leg and she was making no attempt to cover herself up.

"And you are?"

"Susie. I work at the bank."

"Would you like to go for a ride, Susie?"

Susie reached over and rested her hand on George's *upper* thigh. "A long ride, Mr. Rausch. I'd like to go wherever you want to take me."

George took a gulp like he was swallowing a watermelon and headed out of town, west, along the highway.

"You must have so many girlfriends, Mr. Rausch, I'll bet you can't keep track of them."

George was reminded of the talk he had with his stepfather. *There will be many girls, George. You will have to decide. Keep your guard up.*

"Actually, Susie, I'm very new here. You are the first girl I've met!"

With that little trinket, Susie moved over, almost on top of George. "Well, why don't we go down here to the water. We can walk a bit."

George took directions well, turning the convertible down a skinny gravel road. A few moments later the car came to a stop, only a few feet from the water. It was an isolated part of the shore, highlighted by tufts of high grass and hard-packed sand.

Susie hopped out of the car, now in bare feet with the skirt blowing in the breeze. George was beside himself. How could this place get any better!

He was about to find out.

He grabbed Susie's hand and took off along the shore.

"When do you have to be back at work, Susie?"

"Well, I guess one thirty, but I can be a little late."

George was trying to contain his excitement. This girl was coming on like a train. The little man in his head was saying,

'No, no, no, Mom would not approve.' But it had been a while since Detroit and the college life, so the little man in his head was mugged and silenced.

She turned to George, put her arms around his neck and said, "So we don't have much time!"

She licked George's upper lip then proceeded to bite his bottom one. She let out a tiny squeal when George placed both hands on her firm ass.

Susie pushed George down on the sand and unzipped his pants. The split skirt covered a pair of pink panties that soon went missing. She straddled George, moving slowly up and down on him, George's hands still guiding her tight backside.

She bent over and licked his lips again. Her eyes had a wild look, a look that freaked George out. She moved faster and faster. "Welcome to Gore Bay, Mr. Rausch. You know you are never going to get rid of me!"

George quickly pulled Susie off him and exploded all over her pretty split skirt.

Susie was not what George was expecting. Fast women were one thing, but this girl had an air of Lizzie Borden about her. He had let himself get caught up in the moment. He was a celebrity now, and an eighteen-year-old millionaire in the middle of the Depression. Fred's image blazed in his mind. He pulled his pants up quickly,

"I better get you back to work."

He dropped Susie off, thanked her for a *lovely* day, and tore off back to Maple Point.

He was still in a fog, a satisfied one mind you, when Fred called out from behind the boathouse, "You've been gone a while. I hope it was time well spent. George, we really need someone to look after this place."

In George's opinion, the time *was* well spent, but he wasn't sure Fred would share his opinion after he heard the details. He sat Fred down and told the lusty story.

"It wasn't your first, and it won't be your last. I hope it was as good for you as your story was for me!"

Fred laughed and went back to the boathouse.

*

It was time to pay a visit to Mr. Smith at the grocery store in Kagawong.

The store was small. A gray-haired, slightly built man was filling an elderly lady's bag with a few things.

"Thank you, Ruth, I will add that to your bill."

George was surprised that anyone would give credit in these economic times.

"Mr. Smith, I presume?"

"Well, well, Mr. Rausch your reputation precedes you. We finally meet! I have filled a few grocery orders for your people. I have been looking forward to this day!"

"I can say the same about you. You are a different kind of business man that doesn't ask for payment at the time of purchase. That is very nice of you."

"These are tough times for many around here, I do what I can; it is a small community."

"Kind of the reason for my visit. I am trying to hire a full-time property manager, caretaker for our place on the point, and Johnny Griggs from Little Current suggested I talk to you."

Mr. Smith smiled and said, "There would be a line a mile long if you advertised for that position! Is this a live-in position?"

"Yes, if required, the person would have his own room, or he could come and go. My family and I need to feel comfortable with the person. A high level of trust would be required, I'm sure you understand."

Mr. Smith walked to the back of the store and opened a

drawer of the dustiest old credenza on the island. He slowly pulled out a piece of birch bark. He motioned at George to come over. He methodically, unraveled the paper. "My father gave me this. God knows where he got it from. It is an aboriginal drawing of this area. You see the area in heavier shade? That is your point of land. It was native camp, going back over two hundred years. But I'm sure you knew that, right?"

"I knew it was a native campground, but this is so interesting. Thank you for sharing this with me."

"My father was very good friends with the Long family, an aboriginal family that only had one daughter, Angeni. She married, much against the wishes of her father, a white man from Espanola named Bob Short. Funny, eh, Long and Short?"

George stood straight-faced, still fixated on the map. Mr. Smith's body language showed his disappointment in the reaction to his attempt at some humor.

"The daughter's family did not think it was funny either. They produced a son named Glenn. He is an extremely talented guy. He worked for me as a child, sweeping up, stocking shelves, et cetera. He went to Toronto to school, graduated at the top of his class, and has just returned to the island. Glenn is very proud of his mother and his background. He is a fine young man. You would do very well to have him in your employ."

The two men were chatting for over an hour about the town and its history when a woman entered the store. "Angeni, your ears must be ringing. I was *just* talking about Glenn. Angeni, please meet George Rausch. George, may I present Glenn's mother, Angeni."

George explained how the previous discussion had included her son. Her beautiful smile lit up the store when George indicated he would like to discuss an employment opportunity with Glenn.

"Thank you, Mr. Rausch, he will be at your home this evening at seven. He is a good man, and he will work hard."

George and Angeni continued to talk while Mr. Smith tended to a customer.

"I am very pleased to have met you, Angeni. I have studied the history of the Anishinabek and this island for the last few years. I am so impressed with the history. We owe your culture so much. If this works out with Glenn, I hope you will join my father and I for dinner one night?"

"Mr. Rausch, I would be honored."

*

George answered the door to find a dark-haired, clean-shaven young man, not much older than himself.

"Mr. Rausch, my name is Glenn Long. You met my mother earlier today."

"Please come in, Glenn. Very nice of you to come here tonight."

Glenn entered the family room and sat down facing the massive fireplace. He was only seated a short time when he placed both hands over his ears, placing his chin in the middle of his chest. A minute later, he looked up at George, who was shocked watching Glenn's actions.

"Are you okay, Glenn?"

"Yes, I'm fine, Mr. Rausch." Glenn stood and looked around the room. He sat back down and looked at George. "Is anyone else here right now?"

"Unfortunately, we are alone. I was hoping my father would be here to meet you, but he took our sea plane to Detroit late this afternoon. Kind of a business emergency, so it's just you and I tonight, sorry."

"Please don't be sorry, Mr. Rausch. That's fine, but I can assure you, we are far from alone."

Chapter 8

George was thinking about several things, not really focused on any of them. This recommended, supposedly astute hired hand enters the lodge and in two minutes drops a bomb.

Glenn's eyes followed George pacing around the room.

There was an eerie stillness while George looked into the dusk that shrouded the waters of the North Channel. He turned to the corner of the family room, where a "chair" may have once been, where he listened to "something" talk to him, possibly from another dimension.

"This isn't exactly how I planned on starting your employment interview. You will have to forgive me. When I explain to you what I have experienced over the past couple of years since arriving here, I'm sure you will appreciate the state I am in right now."

Glenn was noticeably uncomfortable. "I don't know what to say, Mr. Rausch, I really don't know whether I should leave, apologize, or what?"

George put his hand on Glenn's shoulder. "I am the one who needs to apologize. Please, we have lots to discuss. Would you like something to drink?"

"Maybe just a glass of water, please."

While George was in the kitchen, Glenn made his way over

to the corner of the family room. He squinted and slowly moved his head, like he was battling a headache.

"Mr. Rausch, having met my mother, you are aware of my background. You must also be aware that Maple Point was an aboriginal campground?"

George had moved to the center of the room, holding two glasses of water. "Yes, Glenn, to both statements."

"Well, Mr. Rausch, at the risk of ending this interview before it starts, you must know I am a spiritual person. I have beliefs about the energy that exists on this island."

George took his time with his response, placing the two glasses on the oak table. "A few things, Glenn. Come sit down. First, I appreciate the respect you are showing me by calling me Mr. Rausch, but from now on, it's George. Second, I also believe in the spiritual energy of this area and will tell you why shortly. Finally, the person we are looking to hire must protect our family's privacy. We expect the person to keep all conversations confidential. We have become the 'talk of the island' with the purchase of Maple Point, and people love to gossip. The candidate for the job must understand that fully. Are you okay with that?"

Glenn nodded. "Yes, totally."

"Now that we have that out of the way, please tell me how you are feeling. What happened to you when you came into the lodge?"

"George, I am not a visionary, nor do I believe I can tell the future. But I have seen things, and I *feel* things, and they are not imaginary." Glenn paused, rubbing his forehead. "I get the feeling you have already decided I'm not the person for this job. I get the sense the more I talk, the closer I get to the door."

"Exactly the opposite, please continue."

"When I entered the lodge, I felt nothing, but as I moved to the center of the room I felt an energy. I saw you in parts of this lodge, but it was strange — I saw you as you are now, and I saw you in a different form."

George stood so fast, it was a wonder he didn't get light-headed. He remembered the voice in the cabin: "*You will always be at peace here.*"

George had a decision to make, and fast. If he opened up about all that he had experienced and then chose not to hire Glenn, he ran the risk of him telling everyone on the island about George Rausch the psychotic. Or, he could trust his first impressions and the glowing recommendation Glenn received from Mr. Smith and hire him.

"Glenn, can you keep the confidence of the Rausch family? Can we trust you with our property and money? Can we rely on you to be here, whenever we need you?"

"Yes, George, I will be the best hire your family ever made."

"You start right now, fifty dollars a week for the first month, going to sixty if all is satisfactory. You can live here if you want or travel back and forth to Gore Bay, or a combination of the two, whichever you please."

George held out his hand. Glenn stood and looked him right in the eye,

"Thank you, George, I accept. You will not be sorry."

George led Glenn outside to show him the property and talk. He spent the next hour telling Glenn about his love for the island and respect for the Indigenous people. He went on about his studies of the Anishinabek and how impressed he was with Glenn's mother. He spoke of his visit to the "cabin," the "being," and what they said. He continued with how his hand passed through a tree that stood where the lodge was built. He ended with the story about the art critic at the Anchor Inn, and of course he spoke respectfully about Fred.

The two returned to the lodge in total darkness. George was sure Glenn was sick of listening to him.

"Your family may have purchased this land, and the deed may have your name on it, but you cannot control its inhabitants. You met one at their cabin. They will never leave; this is their home. But from what you have told me, it would seem they have accepted *you*. They want you to stay. They pointed you where to build, with the *tree*. They made themselves *visible* to you."

George was pacing again, analyzing Glenn's words.

"George, you are the most famous person on Manitoulin Island. Your every move will be big news. I will do my best to keep you informed and alerted to all I know, but beware, you have more money than people can understand, and some will try anything to get at it."

George looked at Glenn with a sheepish grin. "Fred has lectured me numerous times on that very subject. You think I would have paid attention!"

"Really, something else you want to share?"

"Oh, I got caught up in myself the other day in Gore Bay thinking I was every women's fantasy. A girl came on to me at 100 mph, and I didn't see it; I was so stupid. She came out of the bank and got right in my car, and I wasn't even there. You know, in hindsight, it was rather scary."

Glenn put his hand over his eyes, kicking at nothing on the floor. "Blue eyes, showing lots of leg?"

"Yes, exactly!"

"Sorry to hurt your ego, George, but Sue is very well known in these parts, and she really likes money!"

George was now giggling, and it was his turn to put his hand over his eyes. "So, it wasn't my charm, and I wasn't her first?"

Glenn was now bent in belly laughter. "Not even in the first fifty, and I should know, I think I was number thirty-seven!"

The two laughed hard for several minutes.

"Glenn, I'm feeling so much better. I think we will get along famously!"

*

George woke to the sound of a seaplane landing in the bay. He ran to the dock.

"Welcome back, that was a quick trip."

Fred, standing beside his two suitcases, watched the plane turn into the gentle morning breeze and takeoff. "It was a quick trip. Anything exciting happen when I was gone? Any candidates yet?"

George wasn't sure how Fred would take the news or what would be the best way to deliver it, so he decided to blurt it straight out. "I hired a guy last night. He's actually already on the clock!"

Fred was in the process of picking up his bags and nearly did a header over the luggage into the brisk water of Mudge Bay.

"I see, and his title is caretaker of *George's* Lodge? I thought we had agreed to select a few candidates, and *we* would interview them?"

George wasn't sure whether he was kidding or genuinely upset. Fred was a very even-keeled man and had never even raised his voice around George for as long as he could remember.

"Johnny Griggs of Anchor Inn fame suggested I speak to Mr. Smith here in Kagawong. He gave him the highest endorsement possible, and I even met his mother, a charming aboriginal lady from Gore Bay."

Fred tilted his head to the side and raised his right eyebrow. "Now we get down to it — 'aboriginal' lady? Let me guess, the interview was conducted by an open fire under the stars, while you told stories of unexplained happenings on Maple Point?"

"As a matter of fact, with the exception of the open fire."

"Well, at least you didn't hire a bosomy girl who wouldn't know a hammer from an anchor!"

George had concluded that Fred was mildly pissed.

"When can I meet this man?"

"In about fifteen minutes. He is returning this morning to start cutting and stacking firewood."

"George, I trust your judgment, but that doesn't mean I approve of the process. This is the Rausch Lodge, and more than one Rausch needs to be involved in the decision. Let me talk to him alone for a while. I assume you conveyed that trust and confidence were one and two on the list of requirements?"

"Of course, and you need not worry. This guy has been brought up well and has also completed college in Toronto. It took him five years instead of three because money was an issue; he had to support his mother here in Gore Bay."

*

George decided it was best not to be there for the next few hours. It was supposed to be in the low seventies and sunny, so he hopped in the ragtop and took off for Gore Bay.

It was a Saturday, and the dock and park were packed. If George was trying to slink into town unnoticed, that wasn't happening. He pulled up to his friend's marina and parked the car as far from the action as possible.

It didn't matter; he hadn't closed the door when two guys in their early teens were standing five feet from his trunk.

"Mr. Rausch, that is the coolest car!"

"Thanks, boys, listen, you want to make two dollars each for the next hour or two?"

"Sure!"

"Keep an eye on the car, and don't let anyone get in it, okay? Here's two bucks, and I will give you the other two bucks when I get back."

George cruised the boardwalk, talking to everyone, checking out the boats.

There were a few girls sunning themselves on picnic tables at the end of the boardwalk. One of the more brazen ladies walked over to George and from a distance resembled Sue from the bank! George was preparing to bolt to the car, but as the girl neared, his fear subsided.

"Hi, please excuse me for being so forward. I wanted to introduce myself, I'm Margaret Mahon. I have heard all about you and your car and your huge home. I just had to say hello."

George cringed at the "I have heard all about you," wondering if Sue from the bank had spread the word.

"That's very nice of you, Margaret. I'm George, but you already know that. Do you live in Gore Bay?"

"My dad is Dr. Mahon, the dentist in town, and yes we live a mile west of here, on the water."

George and Margaret talked for quite a while. The girls she was sunning with had long gone.

"I'm sorry, Margaret, it seems I have caused your friends to leave you."

"Oh, that's okay, we are all meeting at a friend's house later for a BBQ. I'm sure I will get an earful from them then."

George shook her hand and said. "I should be getting back. My father is meeting with our new groundskeeper."

"It was so nice talking to you, George. I hope we can see each other again?"

He could see silhouettes of Glenn and Fred and anyone else that had told him to "keep his guard up."

"It's a small island, and you seem to be a very nice person. I don't see how we won't see each other again."

George walked back to his car, thinking about how things were going with Glenn and Fred. In the distance he could see the two guys still standing by his car, talking to a group of curious onlookers.

He stopped walking for reasons unknown and looked to his

left. There was a girl lying on top of a picnic table, all by herself. She was wearing a black bathing suit, resting on her elbows with her long athletic legs bent in front of her. She was looking into the sun with her eyes closed, oblivious to him or anyone else.

She was stunning.

He couldn't take his eyes off her. He stood staring at her, mesmerized. He didn't move, and she didn't open her eyes. From what he could see, she was a tallish, very fit girl and looked about his age.

He didn't want to move; she was incredible.

He finally began walking, leaving her as he found her, eyes closed, facing the bright, warm sun.

"Thanks, guys, here's your money. Any problems?"

"None at all, Mr. Rausch, and thanks!"

George pulled out and turned right instead of left; he wanted one more look at that girl.

To his disappointment, the picnic table was empty. She was gone.

He drove back to the lodge with the picture of her burning in his mind. He had to find out who she was — and soon.

Chapter 9

The road to the lodge was bumpy and narrow. The maximum speed was twenty, and that was only if your eyes were glued to the road, avoiding hundreds of potholes. If you added night driving to the equation, the top speed obtainable would be ten miles per hour, providing you didn't hit a deer, or, God forbid, a moose.

From the lodge, as long as the winds were not in a bad mood, Gore Bay and Little Current were more easily accessed by water. With the spring temperatures warming, George would be using his speedboat more. Not only was it faster and more enjoyable, but the road was killing the suspension of his roadster.

Glenn was chopping wood. Fred was sitting on the far side of the lodge with fishing line everywhere except in his reel.

"Well, I see Glenn is still here, so I can assume your talk went okay?"

"Sit down here a minute. We should talk."

George noticed Fred's flask lying on its side. The cap was off, and nothing was running out.

"You know, George, life is funny. You never stop learning. For instance, Glenn told me one of the best bass locations in the area is right in the middle of the channel! I figured the water had to be over 150 feet deep in the middle, so what bass would be there?"

George surmised Fred was feeling no pain, but with a little bourbon might come a lot of honesty, so he looked forward to the dialogue.

"Foster Banks!"

"Who is Foster Banks?"

"No, George, not who, but *what* is Foster Banks. It is a shoal in the middle of the channel that is located off Bedford Island. Many a steamship has run aground there, but it is also home to thousands of smallmouth bass. Glenn says not a lot of people fish there because the water can be very rough and it is very difficult to find!"

George was finding Fred's inebriated state rather amusing and was doing his best to keep a straight face.

"Glenn also told me about his mother and his childhood with no father. I got the impression it was difficult for him, not having a father and all. I felt for the young man."

George was feeling more secure about Glenn's future as groundskeeper for the Rausch lodge.

"I guess what I'm trying to say, George, is I am so proud of the choice you made with Glenn. He is a fine young man, very impressive. I too would have hired him last night if I had been in your shoes."

George could see the Jim Beam misting up Fred's eyes.

"I'm glad. I think he will work out great. Did you talk about anything else, say, like ghostly stuff?"

"I made my position clear that I do not subscribe to the 'island's energy' as you do. Not that I am against those who believe, but it is just not me."

George was smiling ear to ear, looking at the yards of fishing line lying at Fred's feet.

"A little problem with the line here?"

"I got a crow's nest when I tried to spool the line."

"That's some crow."

Fred laughed, rose to his feet like his legs weren't his, and said, "I'm going to take a nap. Good talk, George."

Glenn had stacked a cord of wood and was sitting on the sawhorse. George came around the corner of the lodge with a pitcher of water. "Wouldn't be thirsty, would you?"

"Thanks. I had a good talk with Fred today. I think I passed the test. He seems a very nice man. You are lucky, George."

"You made a great impression, as I knew you would."

"So funny, George, this is the oldest native campground in the area, and he couldn't care less, could he?"

"Nope, it's you and I around here as far as that's concerned. Glenn, I have to ask you about someone I saw in Gore Bay this afternoon."

"By the look on your face, I don't think this is about Wally the blacksmith with the wart on his nose?"

"Glenn, I saw a girl today that left me breathless. I mean like, had me in a trance! I stood there just leering at her legs. I can't get her out of my mind!"

"Wow, you may need this water more than I do, or maybe some of Fred's flask! By the way, I knew I had made the cut when Fred felt comfortable enough to pull out the hooch in front of me."

"You must have made him feel *quite* at ease, because that flask's contents are long gone!"

"So, can you give me a bit more to go on than great legs?"

"I didn't get closer than fifty yards. She was alone, lying on her back on a picnic table wearing a black bathing suit. She was facing the sun, with her eyes closed. She was tall and looked athletic, her legs muscular and perfect."

Glenn looked at the waves pounding the shoreline. "Yes, you've mentioned the legs. Sorry, I can't help you, I need more information. How old was she?"

"My age, I think, maybe a year older at most."

"I can only think of one person it could be, but I have never seen her alone. She is *always* with her friend and her baby."

"No, she was alone. After I got back to the car, I drove around to have another look, but she was gone."

"George, you were in Gore Bay, not Toronto or Detroit. You will see her again, guaranteed. It's a small island."

George walked toward the water, thinking of only one thing. The wind was beefing up; the water moved his prized boat up and down against the dock. The noise from the swaying pines was loud, so loud he didn't hear Glenn right behind him. "Annie Arnold."

"Geez! You scared the shit out of me! I thought you didn't have enough to go on?"

"I don't, but nineteen years old, tall, athletic legs, sunning herself sounds like Annie Arnold. But she is always with her friend Claudette, who has a new baby, maybe a year old. Annie works at the telephone office in town. She is an operator, I think. It will be easy for you to verify."

George wanted to jump in the boat and head to Gore Bay but quickly changed his mind while watching the water crash onto the shore. Annie Arnold; he wondered what she was like, how he would approach her, and if she knew about him. He had been with several ladies back home who were both charming and attractive, but none had stopped him dead in his tracks. None of them had rendered him speechless, unable to do anything but stare. Sure, Annie was wearing a black bathing suit showing all that she owned, but there were bathing suits in Michigan, and he had dated many of them.

Then paranoia set in. What if she was friends with "Sue from the bank"? Glenn had said more than once, "this a small island." Or the dentist's daughter he just met? Granted, Annie meeting Sue would be a lot worse than meeting Margaret, but it wouldn't take long for Annie to gather that George was a player. Or the biggest concern — what if Glenn was wrong and it wasn't Annie Arnold, it was a girl from a boat that was just passing through Gore Bay?

The last thought was one he didn't want to think ever again.

*

"I caught two bass off the dock this afternoon, George. I have some of Mom's spice in my bag. I carry it with me all the time. Mixed with a little flour, you will love it."

Fred never made it for a feed of bass. He slept right through the dinner hour.

Good bourbon.

The fish was amazing; as far as George was concerned, Mom's batter was a business opportunity for Glenn's family.

"I think that is marketable back home, Glenn. I am taking it with me. My family knows the right people."

Fred kept several bottles of Jim Beam and finer bourbons in the pantry. George had consumed moderately over the last year, heavily on occasion at college with his fraternity buddies, but was not by any means, a "drinker."

"Do you drink alcohol, Glenn?'

"I do from time to time, more when I was in Toronto. I never drink at home. According to my mother, my father had a real problem. It was supposedly the reason he left."

"How about you and I have a drink?"

"Why not? I was planning on staying here tonight. Lots of wood to cut tomorrow."

George didn't know which was more relaxing, the conversation or the bourbon. Regardless, the evening was fantastic. Glenn told stories about growing up on the island with no money, and George answered with tales of wealth and opulence that would have staggered the Shah of Iran.

If opposites did indeed attract, this evening was proof.

Glenn poured his third drink and made it clear he was done with Mr. Beam for the night. George, on the other hand, was celebrating his new lady interest in Gore Bay. Even though he wasn't sure her name was Annie or if he would ever see her again.

"Glenn, you have no idea how beautiful this girl was!"

George's appreciation of Annie, if that was her name, grew with each ounce of Jim Beam. By the end of the night she would make Aphrodite look like a warthog.

The wind had dropped and the stars were putting on a dazzling show. The water was calm and the air fresh and cool.

"George, let's have our nightcap with a fire on the shore, it's perfect outside."

George was feeling very laid back at this point in the bourbon-soaked evening and wasn't all that gung ho about making a fire. He peered out the window, hoping the star-studded water would ignite some energy.

He was not ready for what he saw.

"Glenn, come here, quick."

Glenn saw a fire burning on the shore with the outline of something seated beside it.

"Glenn, tell me you see what I see! Am I looking through whiskey goggles, or is that for real?"

"I see it."

The two of them, drinks in hand, made their way slowly toward the water's edge some fifty yards from the campfire. Whatever it was, it was still facing the other direction. They inched closer.

It was different for George this time. Inside the cabin he felt like he was floating, a mystical, out-of-body experience. This time it seemed very real. He was not dreaming. He was very alert, and all senses were in play.

As they moved within ten yards, the thing, wrapped in a blanket, started shaking and moving up and down. This was followed by a muffled, grunting sound.

The blanket dropped, and the thing stood up. It was Fred!

"You boys enjoy my whiskey tonight?"

Fred was laughing hysterically. He could be heard for miles across the waters of the North Channel.

"I'm sorry, guys, I woke up from my afternoon nap around ten and heard you guys enjoying yourselves. I couldn't resist the opportunity."

George and Glenn were not amused. They said very little as they finished their drinks under a midnight sky. A sky that unfortunately produced light bright enough to see the smirk on Fred's face.

*

It was late morning, and Glenn was chopping and stacking wood. Fred was spooling his line, only this time successfully, and he was drinking coffee not bourbon. Weatherwise, the day was a continuation of the previous night. The water was calm; it was a beautiful day.

The boat was gone. George was on his way to Gore Bay. When he pulled up to the dock there was only room for his boat. The town was hopping.

He walked to the picnic table where he had seen Annie the day before. The telephone office was in sight, and it was a few minutes before noon. It was a long shot; maybe she wasn't working today, or maybe her shift was at another time.

Or maybe it wasn't Annie at all; maybe whoever she was left on a boat yesterday, never to be seen again.

"Hi, George!"

Oh, God. George turned to see Margaret walking toward

him. He was thinking of an excuse even before he responded to her greeting.

"You were right, George, we would see each other again!"

"Hi, Margaret, how are you today?"

"I'm better now. What are you doing here?"

George was looking past her, watching people walking in and out of the telephone office. "Actually, I am just leaving, I have to call home to Detroit. I am heading into the telephone office."

He was sure she knew he was lying. Why was he sitting on a picnic table if he had to go to the telephone office?

"I will see you later, Margaret. I hate to be rude, but I need to get back. Lots of work to do today."

Margaret said nothing, but as George walked away, he could feel her disappointment. That wasn't him. He felt terrible. He couldn't bring himself to turn and see the expression on her face.

The telephone office was a reception area with two phones and the two operators seated at the back of a larger room. George really didn't know what to do. He stood there for minutes, looking lost, trying not to bring attention to himself. He looked quickly at the operators, neither of whom resembled Annie.

He left the office and walked back to his boat. As usual, it had attracted a few people. He smiled, said hello, and jumped in the back.

"Nice boat. You must be George, right?"

He looked up and tried not to wet his pants.

It was her.

Chapter 10

The winter months in suburban Detroit were no picnic. As a boy, he couldn't wait for the first warm day of spring to feel the sun hitting his neck. He told his mother *that* was the best feeling ever. Years later, as a junior in high school, he lost his virginity to "Mabel," who was a senior in the same private school. He told Fred *that* was the high point of his life, a moment for the ages.

The bar had now been raised.

Less than a day had passed since he first saw Annie sunning herself. He had not been able to think about anything else, and that vision had rendered him incapable of any intelligent thought.

And now she stood in front of him on the boardwalk, elevated some three or four feet, making him gaze up to her beautiful, smiling face framed by a crystal blue sky.

"I am, and you are?"

"Annie Arnold."

She crouched down and held out her hand. George took a step closer and stumbled, missing her hand altogether. He collected himself and tried again.

"Sorry, pleased to meet you, Annie."

An awkward few seconds went by as they stared into each other's eyes, smiling and saying nothing. George looked down, shaking his head nervously. "Beautiful day, isn't it?"

Annie straightened up, turning around as if she were looking for someone. "I love your boat. I have heard all about you, your car and plane, and even your steamship! I feel like I'm talking to a movie star!"

"Oh, not really, just fell in love with this island and built a home here, that's all."

George's nervousness was bothering him. He wanted to say the perfect things, but he felt he was failing. Annie continued looking around the boardwalk.

"Are you expecting someone, Annie?"

"Well, I was supposed to meet my friend here before I go to work at two o'clock, but I don't see him."

George felt the air leave his lungs. He tried to hide the sag in his shoulders, but it was difficult. *Him?* He could have handled any word but that one.

"Boyfriend?"

The instant the question left his mouth, he wanted it back. He knew that was a tad too personal, having known the girl a full two minutes.

Annie crouched down again, looking so directly into George's eyes that he felt his knees weakening. "Just a couple of dates, nothing serious."

In the next brief instant George felt the largest emotional swing possible. The euphoria of that information was immediately followed by the crushing low of watching a guy turn Annie around and kiss her on the cheek.

Annie pulled away from him, and looking embarrassed, she pushed her hair back. "George, this is my friend, Harold. Harold, meet George Rausch."

Harold looked at the boat, then at George, with a blank face. "Nice to meet you."

Harold didn't offer a handshake, standing motionless,

staring at George then back at the boat. He turned to Annie, reached for her hand, and said. "We should go if we want to have a coffee before you start work."

Annie looked over her shoulder, smiling as Harold led her away. "Nice to meet you, George, have a nice day!"

George watched the two of them head down the boardwalk. He sat in the back of his boat, trying to process what just happened. He decided quickly he was not going back to the lodge to stew about this all day. George waited until Annie was out of sight and jumped onto the dock.

An older gentleman had been admiring the boat. "Can I ask you something, Mr. Rausch?"

George, totally preoccupied, looked at him and said, "I'm sorry, have we met?"

"No, we haven't met. I'm Art. I work at the phone company, same place as Miss. Arnold."

The comment refocused George. "Hello, nice to meet you. I didn't know Annie worked there. What do you do there?"

"I'm a repair guy, lineman, more or less."

"And Annie?"

"Operator."

"So, what was your question?"

"How fast does your boat go?"

"Fast. The engine is over 200 horsepower."

"Wowie. You best be careful with that boat. This water can get real rough, and at that speed, boy oh boy!"

"Thanks, Art, I will be careful for sure."

George shook his hand and said goodbye.

"Oh, by the way, Annie is a nice girl. She is very popular here in Gore Bay, gets asked out on dates a lot, you know, operator and all. Annie's very personable, and as you can see, she's a real looker!"

Art winked at George and walked away.

Annie and Harold were standing in front of the hotel. To George's delight, not only were they not holding hands, but an animated discussion was taking place. Then, for the second time in a matter of minutes, George's emotions were tested. The discussion ended, and they walked to the front door of the phone company, where Harold planted another kiss on Annie's cheek.

George was beside himself. What was going on?

He entered the general store and purchased a pencil and piece of paper. He proceeded around the block and picked some spring flowers from an overgrown garden. On the paper he wrote, *Annie, you took my breath away a few minutes ago, I'd like it back. Please have dinner with me Saturday night. I think we will have a nice time. I will wait at my boat for your answer, take as long as you need.*

George

George wrapped the paper around the flowers and gave a young lad a dollar to deliver them. Then he went back to his boat and waited. He talked to everyone, as he always did, answering questions about his boat, the lodge, and anything else the people were curious about. He enjoyed the conversation; it helped calm his nerves while he waited for Annie to respond. Two hours went by, and no Annie, no messenger boy — no indication of any kind.

Maybe he had been too forward. After all, he had just watched another man kiss her twice! Who did he think he was anyway? But she had said it was "nothing serious." Wasn't that opening the door?

He was getting depressed; too much time had passed. George started the boat and was undoing the dock lines when he couldn't believe what he saw.

Harold was walking quickly toward the boat from the far end of the boardwalk.

Oh my God. George was not a fighter or ready for any type of altercation. He didn't know what to do. He retied the boat to the dock but kept the engine running. Harold was closing in. George tried not to make eye contact, but he could *feel* him staring at the boat. Harold, glaring at George, sped up and tore past the boat to engage two other men standing at the opposite end of the boardwalk. An argument began between the three.

Harold yelled, "My father asked me to have the roof completed by this weekend, and now I hear it will be another two weeks!? That is unacceptable for the money he is paying you!"

"Harold, the material never arrived from Sudbury!"

"Then get it from somewhere else. This roof better be completed on time, or you won't work again anywhere on this island! My father and I will make damn sure of that!"

Harold stormed by the boat, eyeing George like it was his fault the roof was not completed on time.

George concluded nothing was happening with Annie. He scanned the boardwalk one last time, hoping, but there was no Annie. However, a girl was walking quickly toward the boat. He wanted no part of any more girls and pulled away from the dock.

"Mr. Rausch, George?" The girl was yelling his name, with the boat well away from the dock.

"Yes?"

"Could you please come closer? I'm a friend of Annie's!"

George circled and docked the boat in seconds.

"My name is Claudette. I'm Annie's closest friend. Pleased to meet you, George."

Glenn popped into George's mind — Annie's girlfriend with the baby! He had failed to mention she was so young-looking!

"Annie is the only operator working. She couldn't leave to answer you, but she wanted me to give you this."

"Thank you, Claudette, thank you very much."

"I have to go. Nice meeting you. I hope we see each other again."

Claudette hurried off the boardwalk and down the street.

She had handed him a small piece of paper taped closed at the end. There were lips, like a kiss, in red lipstick on the outside. He opened it very carefully, as nervous as he had ever been in his life.

That is the sweetest thing anyone has ever said to me. I would be honored to have dinner with you. My heart is beating so fast, you have made me so happy. You know where to find me. If I'm not here, leave a message with someone. I can't wait to hear from you.

He was ecstatic.

George pulled away, heading to Mudge Bay. He had mentioned to Art, the guy from the phone company, that this boat was fast. Too bad Art wasn't around right now. George had it full throttle, and in seconds, he was out of sight. He ran into the lodge and threw his arms around Fred like he was never going to see him again.

"She said yes. I have a dinner date Saturday night with the most beautiful girl on this planet!"

George was jumping around like a five-year-old on Christmas morning.

"I take it we are talking about the girl on the picnic table?"

"We are! Oh geez, I can't believe it, she is incredible!"

Fred had something to say, but it could wait. A talk about keeping your guard up would fall on deaf ears right now anyway.

George ran out the back, where Glenn was chopping,

"Glenn, I am going out for dinner with Annie, yes, Annie Arnold, on Saturday night!"

Glenn slapped George on the back, smiling like *he* was going on the date. "I'm happy for you, George. Where are you going to take her?"

In all the excitement, George had not given that one thought. This was not Detroit; there were two or three choices if you included *both* Little Current and Gore Bay.

"Good question.

Years ago, Fred had mentioned, "Enjoy being a Rausch."

It was time to use a tiny portion of his thirty-thousand-dollar monthly trust fund. Prior to George's father's passing, he had established a trust fund for his son. When he was twenty-five he would inherit ten million dollars. Until that time, George would have to make ends meet on $360,000 a year.

The average salary on Spirit Island was about $1,900 per year.

The Anchor Inn had a small dining area, and on the other side was a bar with tables. He would ask Johnny Griggs to close the dining area after seven.

He would make it worth Johnny's while.

George had gone over what he was going to say a hundred times, and he was confident he would come across perfectly. He jumped back in the boat and headed to Gore Bay.

As nervous as a young man could be, he stood in the reception area of the telephone office. Annie was at her desk, headphones on, unaware of a suitor coming to call. The receptionist recognized George. "Can I help you, Mr. Rausch? Would you like to make a call?"

"Actually, I would like a brief word with Miss Arnold if that would be okay?"

The receptionist smiled and went over to Annie, who was still talking with someone. She looked up and saw George smiling, looking directly at her.

Her hand went over her mouth and her eyes sparkled like the night's brightest star.

His eyes were fixated on Annie as she moved slowly toward him. There was no one else in George's universe at that moment, oblivious to several other people in the office. Annie carried herself confidently. In total control of her feminine power, there was a seductive aura about her. George, sweaty palms, heart racing, was praying words came out of his powder-dry mouth.

"Thank you for taking the time to see me, Annie, and thank you so much for accepting my invitation to dinner this Saturday."

Annie inhaled and spoke so softly that George leaned over to hear her clearly. "I'm so nervous, George, I can barely talk. I still can't believe you want to go on a date with me. You could date the most beautiful women in the world. I think I am in shock."

George smiled and held her hand, and in even a softer voice said, "I'm about to date the most beautiful girl I've ever seen."

Annie's hand went over her eyes. "You are making me blush, George. I can't wait until Saturday!"

George looked around to make sure there wasn't anyone standing too close. "Tomorrow could be Saturday, if you are not busy?"

Annie's eyes opened wide. "I'm finished work at five."

"I will pick you up here if that's okay?"

"I can't wait."

George ran back to the boat and for the second time that day put the boat through its paces back to the lodge. Fred was fishing off the dock.

"I'm glad the water is lying down today. We are going back to Gore Bay."

"You have got to be kidding?"

"I need to call your mother; I haven't spoken to her in a week."

As much as George wanted to see Annie, he remained in the boat while Fred made the call home to Mattie.

George could not wipe the grin off his face. He was positive he would not sleep a wink tonight. Tomorrow was sure to be the longest day of his life.

Fred hopped back in the boat. "Your mother will be flying here day after tomorrow with a special surprise. Please look surprised when you see Trevor."

"Our cook?"

"The one and the same. He has agreed to look after you and I and Glenn for the balance of the summer. You remember Madeline, his assistant? Your mother is letting Madeline take over the duties at home. I'm wondering if Mattie has been sampling my bourbon? Arriving on a sea plane AND giving up Trevor? What has got into that woman?"

The news about the cook and his mother went in one ear and out the other. He was in another world. Fred, shaking his head, looked over at George with a smile of his own.

"Did I tell you I caught a fish earlier today that asked me to put him back in the water?"

George, looked straight ahead with glassy eyes and replied, "That's nice."

Chapter 11

It was late spring, and sunlight was hanging around until eight thirty. "Someone" was doing their best to ensure the weather was in George's favor; for the second straight day it was pleasantly warm, and there was no wind.

George had spent the day in Little Current, making sure Mr. Griggs had all in order. It was Monday evening, slow at the best of times in the dining room. So, when George gave Johnny a hundred dollars to make sure the evening went smoothly, you could imagine the owner's elation.

Johnny had servers ready to back up the servers. Nothing was left to chance. The hundred dollars would equal the dining room's revenue for a week.

Annie Arnold was in the lady's room at work, fifteen minutes before George was to pick her up. She was with Claudette, who she had asked to join her for moral support more than anything else.

"I still can't believe this is going to happen. I'm expecting one of his staff to show up and say 'Mr. Rausch sends his apologies.'"

Annie had scrubbed her face raw with the industrial strength soap and was starting her face from scratch.

Claudette was sitting in the corner, watching the makeover unfold. "Do you have any idea who you are tonight?"

"What?"

Claudette moved over, looking at Annie's reflection in the mirror. "There are thousands and thousands of women in the United States and Canada who would murder to be in your shoes this evening."

Annie was doing a nice job on the reinvention of Miss Arnold; she looked amazing.

"If I were in your shoes, Annie, I would make sure George felt special tonight. Keep in mind he did see you with that idiot Harold. What you see in him I have no idea. Sure, he's the doctor's son, but what a pompous ass."

"Claudette, I make fifteen dollars a week! I am almost twenty! He has taken me out twice, paying for dinners that I could never afford. He treats me like gold. Why wouldn't I go out with him?"

Annie turned to Claudette, arms stretched out from her sides, hoping for a positive appraisal. "Can you imagine the women he's been with? Their wealth, their class, their clothes? Oh, honey, I'm scared to death."

"Annie, you look like Myrna Loy. You will reduce him to jelly. He is not worthy, darling!"

*

George walked up the steps of the telephone office, taking a moment to look to the sky, praying for a perfect evening. Annie walked out the door, and George stood like he was in cement. He thought he was prepared for any vision, any eventuality.

He was wrong.

She was perfect.

Her eyes sparkled, the skirt was snug to below the knee and split, just far enough. The smile on her face was sincere; she genuinely looked as excited as he was. George was struggling to remain composed. "Hi Annie, you look beautiful. You have no idea how nervous I am."

Annie stood as close to him as you could get without touching. "You couldn't have said anything more appropriate. I am praying I don't pass out. I haven't been able to think straight since I left you last."

George took her hand, and they headed down the street to the water. "The weather is good. I thought we would take the boat to Little Current. I will have you back before dark."

"Sounds wonderful, I love the water; I grew up in boats."

The trip to Little Current in calm waters was thirty to forty minutes. The Rausch boat could make it in twenty. By car it would take hours. The boat was therapeutic for both of them, helping to relieve the anxiety.

"I like to go fast. Are you okay with that? It's a very solid boat!"

"I can't wait to see how fast this will go. This is so wonderful!"

As if George needed another reason to love this lady, he pressed the throttle forward and the evening began. They were going 40 mph across smooth waters, and it was a tossup who had the bigger smile on their face.

They were still holding hands.

"Are you okay?" The wind was swirling Annie's hair all over her head.

"This is great, the speed, so exciting, oh my goodness!"

George slowed and steered closer to shore as they passed Maple Point. Annie's eyes widened as she realized the size of the lodge.

"Oh, George, you could have a hundred people there!"

George wanted to say something but decided to keep driving. He did not want to sound presumptuous by saying, "You will see it soon enough."

Johnny Griggs was waiting, like he was expecting royalty. He seated the couple in the middle of the room; all the other tables were empty. George thought of the inn's painting showing two men in a boat pointing at Maple Point. He decided that would be a conversation piece for a date to follow. The first date was too early to discuss beliefs about the island's energy and mystery.

A huge vase of fresh cut flowers sat in the center of the table, and a small red box with a yellow bow was waiting in front of Annie.

"I hope you like it."

Annie looked at the box then back at George. "I don't know what to say. This whole experience is overwhelming."

Annie opened the box revealing a small bottle of perfume. "Blue Grass?"

"It was just launched in New York City by a lady named Elizabeth Arden. I can pretty much assure you it's the only bottle in Canada."

Annie leaned over and kissed George on the cheek. "I'm sorry, I had to do that. You are the sweetest person. This is already a day I will remember for the rest of my life."

"I wasn't sure you would accept my invitation to dinner. Having met Harold only hours before, I mean, I still can't believe I did it. It's a real compliment to you, totally out of character for me. I'm so attracted to you."

Annie took a sip of water and reached out to hold George's hands. "I have been on lots of dates, and I have had a couple of longer relationships, but at this time in my life there is no one special. Harold is the son of one of the two doctors in Little Current. His father is a friend of my dad's, and my dad did some work for him."

"What does your father do?"

"He is a captain. He pilots a few tugs around the island. He hauled material in for Harold's father's new house."

"*Not* all the material, I hear."

Annie looked at George with a curled eyebrow. "How do you

know about that?"

George sat back and told her about the argument he'd overheard on the dock. They both laughed and Annie added. "You see, Harold was trying to play the big shot. He's done that more than once. He didn't know *what* to do when he met you!"

"Have you always lived in Gore Bay?"

"A little time here in Little Current, but yes, my whole life on the island."

"And Claudette, the same?"

"Yes, she married her high-school sweetheart and had a baby. She has never been anywhere other than Gore Bay."

"Can I ask how old she is?"

"Nineteen, same as me. Do you think she is pretty?"

What kind of question was that? Here he was, gaga over the lady across the table, and she was asking if she thought her best friend was pretty? What do you say to that?

"Yes, she is quite attractive."

"So, George Rausch, you like fast cars, fast boats, and pretty girls. My dad would want me to run out of here right now!"

Annie had a huge smile on her face and broke out laughing.

George did not know how to react, and even worse, had no comeback. He was thankful she kept talking.

"How about fast girls?"

Annie had the water glass covering her mouth to hide her giggling, but her eyes gave her playful mood away. George knew immediately that she knew about Sue from the bank! He picked up his napkin to wipe his mouth, even though no food or drink had passed his lips.

"Oh boy, my first test of the evening. If you are referring to what I think you are referring to, the answer would be, "No, I don't like fast girls, per se.' That incident caught me totally off guard."

Annie was laughing even harder. She reached over, grabbed

both of his hands again, and said, "I'm so sorry, I'm awful! George, I am so nervous about tonight, I thought by being outgoing it might help my nerves, you know, break the ice. Please forgive me. Sue and her actions are well known here. Please believe me, I am not passing judgment at all! You are the most eligible bachelor in the world. You are young, handsome, and wildly rich. It's all totally natural to me, her actions and yours."

George smiled, holding Annie's hands firmly. This girl was fun, beautiful, and had no pretenses. She had just validated his promiscuity, making him feel almost *good* about it! He hadn't picked up the menu yet and was already enjoying himself more with this lady than the many others he had shared a dinner with.

"Annie, you are a treat. My nerves are starting to behave. I want yours to as well. I am the lucky one here. Please believe that."

George pulled Annie's hand close and kissed the back of it. "So, my turn Miss Arnold. Tell me why aren't you married, like Claudette?

Annie was still giggling when the waiter came by to explain the menu that Johnny and George had agreed on earlier that day. Annie smiled at George, but the playfulness soon went missing from her voice.

"I like nice things. I grew up around the water with my father's tugboats. I saw the big sailboats and steamships that docked here. Lots of the people on those boats had nice clothes and had money to tip all the locals. Then they left, off to see the rest of the world, to experience more of life. I'm not saying I want to travel the world, but when I see how Claudette struggles, trying to make ends meet, well, it makes me think how much more there may be out there."

George had always put a lot of stock in common sense. In the brief time they had been together, Annie had displayed it on more than one occasion. George's attraction was growing in leaps and bounds. Even the cartoon over Annie's head of Fred waving an index finger at him was not dampening his emotions.

The evening was magical; Annie was having the time of her life. The conversation soon moved to George's upbringing as one of the world's richest young men. Annie sat there listening, trying not to be caught with her mouth open in amazement. She listened to countless stories of fame and incredible wealth.

They never let go of each other's hands, except to eat.

"I would not call my mother strict but rather overprotective. I never understood why really, until I was fourteen or so. She raised me until I was eight years old by herself, until Fred came around."

"Does she come here often with you and Fred?"

"She came a few times, but not too often. Funny, she will be here tomorrow. She's flying in on our sea plane for a few days."

It was getting dusky, and George, good to his word, suggested he get her home before dark. Annie leaned closer to George, and he reciprocated, so their faces were but a few inches apart. "I can't begin to thank you, Mr. Rausch, for this evening. The boat ride, the perfume, and dinner in our own private room; I feel like a princess. If I never see you again, I will remember this night for a lifetime. Thank you, George, thank you so much."

George kissed her hand again and said, "I hope this is only the beginning. I want to see you again and again. Thank you for accepting my invitation. You are so sweet."

They said goodnight to Johnny and strolled across the street to the boat.

They arrived back in Gore Bay in limited light. Annie lived in a small frame house at the end of a street, a two-minute walk from the harbor. She was looking at the ground as they walked up her driveway.

"This house would fit on your steamship, wouldn't it?"

George didn't answer. He put his hands gently on either side of Annie's face and kissed her lips so softly, he wasn't sure she felt it. Annie put her arms around his neck and kissed him with more intensity. He moved his lips across her face and bit her neck hard enough to produce an excited moan. He pressed her against the side of her house, and her hands moved down his back and pulled him closer.

"Annie, is that you?"

Annie's mother was leaning out the back door of the house. Annie, giggling, put her hand over her mouth. She whispered, "Do you want to meet my mother?"

George kissed her and smiled. "Not tonight, I think there will be a better time!"

He kissed her again, said goodnight, and walked down the street into the night.

The stars provided ample light for a smooth, uneventful ride home. Walking to the lodge, he smiled to himself, thinking how perfectly the night had gone. He sat on a log and watched the stars flicker, their reflection bouncing off the water of Mudge Bay.

He was preparing for Fred's questions in the morning. George knew he would hear about "keeping his guard up" and wanted his response to be honest. Knowing he would have to watch Fred's eyes roll back in his head, he would explain that this girl was different. It was too early for adjectives like "special," but he would tell Fred he intended on seeing Annie again.

And again.

The stars were electric, but their show was losing the battle against the call of his bed.

He was sure about one thing: he needed to phone someone tomorrow — anyone.

Chapter 12

Claudette was rocking the stroller with her left hand. Her other hand was waving over her head like the rotor of a helicopter. "Perfume from New York, a private dinner, and a boat ride under the stars with George Rausch? Geez Annie, you are sitting there like it was just another Monday night! What is wrong with you! I would be in the hospital on tranquilizers."

"I told you, I know what you are saying, but I didn't think about it that way. He is a real nice guy, so down-to-earth, just a normal person."

The baby was getting rocked like she was on a ride at Coney Island. "Save it, Annie, remember before the date? 'I'm so scared, I can't believe this is happening.' Remember all that?"

"I know, I know, but it turned out perfectly. He is not pretentious at all."

The rocking stopped. Claudette now had both hands on her hips, eyes opened wide. "Oh! I get it! I can't believe it, on the first date? You had sex?"

Annie jumped off the picnic table and grabbed her bag, "You think my name is Sue? I will pretend I didn't hear that!"

She walked across the street and into work.

*

Fred and George were trolling around Clapperton Island in search of a trophy pike.

Fred was watching his own reflection where his line entered the water. "Want to talk about your date?

"If you have an open mind, I do."

Fred laughed out loud. "Well, I guess that sums up the date. Not much else to talk about."

George laughed as well. "You are unbelievable. I thought I was ready for every question you could ask, and you give me that!"

"Let me have a go at this. It was the best date of your life. There is no way I would understand; she is 'different.' You can't stop thinking about her, and this is the start of something special."

Laughing harder, George put his arm around Fred's neck. "I'm not ready to use the word 'special' quite yet."

They laughed and laughed. Fred smiled at George. "I want you to be happy. That's all that matters to me. Your mother is coming for a couple of days. She will not be ready to listen to you go on about an island girl. Not yet, anyway; we will have to ease her into this. Just remember to be surprised when you see Trevor. Got all that?"

"Got it, but with one slight change. I am going to tell her I am dating someone, that's it."

"I would advise against that. She will want to know more. And when you clam up, she will start on me."

*

Fred and George stood, almost at attention, with Glenn a few feet behind. Mattie was at the end of the dock, arms stretched out, inviting a group hug.

"Mom, I'd like you to meet Glenn, our property manager and

jack of all trades. Glenn, my mother, Mattie Rausch."

Mattie held out her hand. "Hello. My family has given you good reviews. Pleased to meet you."

"Thank you, Mrs. Rausch. Let me get your bags."

While hugs and introductions were going on, Trevor had exited the plane and stood behind them.

"Ready for a good meal?"

George did a fair job of looking surprised and hugged his mother again.

"You must be tired, and you two need some time alone. Glenn will help you get settled. I have to shoot into town for a bit, I won't be long."

Mattie responded, "What on earth do you need to go now for? I just got here!"

Fred glared at George, anticipating the upcoming bomb. "The boat needs oil. The warning light came on when we were fishing. The marina in Kagawong doesn't have the right oil for *our* boat. I will be back in less than an hour."

Mattie seemed to believe the story. Glenn winked at Fred and led them to the lodge.

*

Annie jumped from her desk. George wasn't sure how to greet her in her place of employment. That decision was made when Annie took the lead and kissed him like the plane was going down.

George was embarrassed for the few people that were in the phone office.

"Wow, I'm happy to see you too!'

They walked outside. Annie was visibly excited. "I hope you don't think this is too forward of me, but Claudette and her husband asked us to come over to their place on Saturday, and I said I would ask you?"

George, still recovering from the kiss, hesitated. Annie picked up on it right away. Her face looked like she had lost a family member. "Oh no, I'm sorry. I've messed up, haven't I?"

George put his arms around her and said, "Not at all. My mother is here, and I'm just hoping she's gone by then. Yes, yes, of course we will go. That's three days from now. I hope the time passes quickly."

*

Fred could not get a double Jim Beam down his throat fast enough. He would have preferred a general anesthetic.

Mattie was in a mood.

"You have an unknown working for you? Referred by two people you never met. Fred, I think your drinking has clouded your mind. I am starting to believe you like being on your own here so you can drink! I do not approve of your hire."

Fred poured himself another bourbon. "And what, pray tell, are you basing that on? You have not said two words to Glenn. I can tell you he is bright, honest, and by the way, your son loves him."

"I get the feeling there are several things going on around here that I might not agree with!"

"Like what, Mom?"

George had entered the room, undetected.

"You startled me. I didn't hear you come in. Fred and I were discussing the hiring of Glenn, which led to my comment you just heard."

"What? You don't like Glenn? How can *anyone* not like Glenn?"

"It's not about liking. He is an employee, an underling, and we know nothing about him."

"He is the salt of the earth, someone I call a friend. He is staying as long he wants the job. So what else do you think is *going on*?"

"I don't think I care for your tone, George!"

"You come here for only the second time and start criticizing and bossing. We are quite happy here, your husband and I!"

"I'm sure you are! No discipline, drinking bourbon like it's fruit juice!"

George was pissed, and Fred could see where this was going — and that place wasn't good.

"Well, add this to your list, Mom: I have a girlfriend, a sweetheart, born and raised here on Spirit Island!"

Fred looked out the window, expecting to see the reflection of his lunch slowly rising upward from his stomach.

Mattie raised her hand to her forehead and closed her eyes. She took a few steps toward the fireplace. Shaking her head, and said calmly, "All I can say, George, is enjoy your time with these people. Try to remember you are a Rausch, for God's sake, and your real life is back in Detroit."

Mattie left for her room.

Fred was still looking out the window. George was sitting on the couch, his head in his hands. The room was painfully silent. A few minutes passed, then Fred walked out of the room to join Mattie.

The ensuing two days were chilly. The weather was warm, the atmosphere was frigid. Few words were spoken.

Despite Trevor's best efforts, preparing two exquisite pickerel dinners, Mattie could not wait to leave. Unfortunately for Fred, he was compelled to accompany Mattie back to Michigan.

*

"This is where Claudette lives?

George walked up the short, gravel driveway, doing his best to keep his thoughts to himself. The house was tiny and needed work. So much work that it would be difficult to choose where to start.

"No, George, come this way, around the back. Claudette, Frank, and the baby live in the basement apartment. Her mother and father live upstairs."

Once at the side of the house, Annie stopped and whispered in George's ear, "I can imagine what you must be thinking. I'm sorry, I should have told you. She is my closest, best friend. She is having a hard time right now, so I couldn't say no. She is dying to meet you. We won't stay long."

She kissed George, and the two knocked on the back door.

Claudette and a young, dark-haired man looked up the basement stairs. The piercing sound of a baby's cry bounced off the cinder-block basement walls.

"Come in, come in, thanks for coming!"

George watched Annie hug Claudette, then hug the young man he assumed to be Claudette's husband.

"George, these are my great friends Claudette and Frank Valentine. Guys, like he needs an introduction, meet George Rausch."

"We met briefly at your boat, but hello again, pleased to be formally introduced."

Frank held out his hand. "I really don't know what to say, George, gosh! I can't believe I'm shaking the hand of one of the richest people in the world!"

Claudette glared over at Frank, and Annie pinched the bridge of her nose.

"Nice to meet you both. Annie has told me all about you."

George looked in the direction of the annoying noise. There was little to see; it was one room with a double bed, a stove, fridge, and sink. There was a baby holding the rails of a crib, wailing as hard as possible. Behind the crib was a small room he assumed to be a bathroom.

George had to do something; he had never felt claustrophobic before. There wasn't even enough room or chairs for the four of them to sit down. He could not remember feeling more uncomfortable.

"It's a nice day. Why don't we take a walk down to the water? Frank can see my boat and I will get us some ice cream?"

To George's delight, Frank responded instantly. "I want to see that boat, let's go!"

They were sitting in the boat having ice cream, and Frank said, "I sure hope some of my friends come by right now. They won't believe it!!"

The comment prompted another glare from his wife and Annie to say, "Well, George and I are heading back to his place. He wants to show me around the property."

Claudette grinned at Annie then cast another venomous look at Frank.

*

The ride to the lodge was into a stiff breeze. The spray from the choppy water was making its way over the bow. George was happy to hold Annie under his arm, offering her shelter from the cool breeze.

"Thanks Annie, I was feeling out of place. Frank was making me nervous."

"I could tell. I feel sorry for him; he was just laid off from the mill. In his defense, he was nervous meeting you. He is the least worldly person you will ever meet. He really means no harm, and he's a nice guy. He has helped me out so many times. Boy is he going to catch it from Claudette. Did you see her looking at him?"

Glenn watched the boat dock and helped Annie out. "I know we have met before, Annie. I'm Glenn Long."

"I know your mother, and yes, you and I did meet years ago in Little Current."

George held Annie's hand and walked her into the lodge.

"Oh my, George, this is unbelievable. Look at that fireplace!"

George showed Annie around the family room. He turned to see Glenn with his hands on either side of his head, staring at the floor.

In an effort to keep Annie from watching Glenn's actions, he quickly said, "Have a seat. Can I get you a drink? Glenn and I need to talk to Trevor for a minute."

"No, I'm fine, thanks. Who is Trevor?"

"The cook. You will meet him shortly."

George and Glenn disappeared outside.

"Don't tell me you had another vision, not now?"

"I saw you again, in a nonhuman form, floating in front of the fireplace. The fire was burning, and I could see Annie, as she is now, in her human form, staring at the fire."

"Okay, more or less the same as the last time, right?"

"Not quite."

"What do you mean?"

"Annie wasn't alone."

"Who was she with?"

Glenn took a deep breath and put his hand on George's shoulder. "Fred, as he is today, alive, in a human form. I had to look again to be sure. There he was."

"Glenn, Fred and Mom left early this morning."

"I am aware of that, George. Why do you think I had my hands on my head? I couldn't believe what I was seeing."

"You could not have seen Fred alive. You saw him as a spirit."

Glenn looked at George. "Sorry, he was as alive as we are right now."

There were no further introductions required when George and Glenn reentered the lodge. Trevor stood smiling beside Annie.

"Where did you find this girl, George?"

Annie looked at George, giggling. "I'm not stupid. My father taught me to always make friends with the cook!"

George, a little frazzled, said, "Trevor, I expect you to outdo yourself this evening. Annie and I are going to have a quiet dinner on the veranda. Glenn, *before you leave*, would you make us some drinks? I need to change my shirt. I'll just be a minute."

Annie followed Glenn into the pantry. "This place is so beautiful, and George is such a nice man. You must be very pleased to be working here?"

Glenn hesitated before responding. He wasn't quite sure what Annie was saying.

"It was a fluke, really. George ran into my mother at the general store, and one thing led to another. What can I make you?'

"Just water is fine."

"I'm making George a bourbon and branch water. You want to try one?

"Bourbon? I've never had one; well, why not."

Annie took her drink and walked around the kitchen, taking in all the amenities. Trevor was busy, head down in the sink.

"This kitchen is bigger than the main floor of my house!"

Trevor turned, hands covered in potato peelings. "Funny, you could put the family room and this kitchen in the pantry of George's home in Michigan."

Annie said nothing, walking back to the main room.

"I can't get over this. I love this place, and that kitchen, wow!"

Glenn just looked at her with a quizzical expression as George returned, grabbing his drink from Glenn's hand.

"Bourbon, Annie? I had no idea. Welcome to my summer

home, cheers."

Annie took a sip and started coughing, looking for a place to put her glass down. "Oh my, that is awful, not what I was expecting at all."

Glenn laughed. "On that note, Annie, I will excuse myself for the evening. I'm off to Gore Bay. Enjoy your dinner."

Annie, still coughing, nodded and waved at Glenn leaving the room.

"I'm sorry, Annie. Jim Beam is an acquired taste. Can I get you something else?"

"No thanks, I think I need some fresh air."

They walked around the property, George detailing how the place was built, sharing the history he had learned of the native camp. He spoke with passion about his studies of the area and the Indigenous people, his fascination with the culture and his belief in the mystery the island possessed.

"George, how well do you know Glenn?"

"He's worked here for a month. He has exceeded all expectations; he's been great. Why do you ask?"

"No reason, I just wondered why you don't have someone from home, like Trevor."

"We decided someone from here would be of more use to us, you know, local knowledge. I don't want you running away from me, Annie, but I believe there is an 'energy' on the island. Glenn shares my belief. I have felt it here on more than one occasion."

Annie didn't seem phased by his comment at all. "Many here share your belief. I will say back to you, George, please don't *you* run away when I tell you I am not a believer."

George smiled and put his hands on her waist. "You and Fred will get along just fine, and by the way, there is zero chance I'm running away from you!"

Annie put her arms around George's neck and kissed him gently on the lips. "I love it here. You are so lucky.'

"I was hoping you would. We should get back for Trevor's feast. I want to get you home before too late."

Annie kissed him again and whispered, "I told everyone I'm staying at Claudette's tonight. I don't need to be anywhere until the morning."

Chapter 13

Trevor had removed the dishes and retired for the evening. The wind had gone down with the sun, leaving only the sound of the water slapping against the dock.

George sipped his third bourbon, trying hard to think only of the pleasure that lay ahead. It wasn't easy; Fred's gold digging warnings, combined with hostile images of his mother, hindered his focus. Just a week ago, he could never have imagined this evening becoming a reality.

It was upon him, and a decision had to be made.

"What are you thinking about?"

If honesty was to be the cornerstone of this relationship, now was the time to act. He had to put aside the physical attraction, bridle the hormones, and tell her what he had been told for years by family and friends. But wait — he was George Rausch. He had already had sex with a complete stranger, and other women were continuously knocking on his door. However, this was different. This girl was special to him, yes, the "special" word was now okay to use.

George reached over and held Annie's hand. He opened his mouth to speak, and Annie put her soft fingers over his lips. "I told you at dinner the other night that I like nice things. I told you I think there is more to life than this island has to offer.

What I didn't tell you was how shocked I was by how down-to-earth and normal you are. You are so nice. I think you are terrific. I am so blessed that you came into my life."

Annie stood, turning away from him. "It is impossible for me to tell you that your wealth and status have no effect on me. Your position in the world is so overwhelming, I'd be lying if I did. I don't blame you for questioning if my attraction is to you or your money. You are the only one that can answer that. All I can tell you is there is nowhere else in the world I'd rather be tonight than right here with you."

George tried not to let her see him tearing up. He wasn't sure whether his desire to make love to her made her words even more believable. But Fred and his mother had disappeared from his head, and all that was real now was Annie.

He walked around the table and held out a hand, motioning to her to stand. He turned her around so she faced the starlit water. Moving behind her, pressing against her firm rear, he kissed her neck while his hands moved over her hard, muscular stomach. He bit her neck aggressively. He could feel her hand move behind her, reaching for his hardening manhood. They moved to the couch at the end of the veranda. She pulled up her skirt, straddling him. He ran his hands up her legs, the legs that first attracted him, the legs he had dreamed about.

He unbuttoned her blouse as she pushed her tongue down his throat. He kissed her hard breasts; his hands caressed her ass.

"Take me, George, take me right now!"

He bent her over the end of the couch, entering her from behind. Each thrust was harder and deeper than the one before. Before he was about to climax, he rolled her over and went down on her until her screams scattered across the glittering waters of Mudge Bay. She straddled him again and watched his eyes roll back as he came into the night.

*

"I am asking you to talk some sense into our son! He belongs here and should be dating respectable young ladies with a proper upbringing from families we know!"

Fred was caught.

He thought what George was doing was okay. In fact, Fred was mildly jealous of George, envious of this time in his stepson's life, a time that he had not experienced.

"He's young, Mattie. Let him be. You have to trust his judgment. He is intelligent, a good kid. He knows who he is and where he is from."

"If he falls in love with this harlot, you will be singing a different tune, Fred! They have nothing to lose, these *people*. She will do *anything* to gain his love, and of course, his wealth!"

"She is not who you think she is. As a matter of fact, her father is a respected businessman in Little Current, a ship's captain, actually."

As soon as the words dropped from his mouth, he closed his eyes, knowing he had screwed up.

"Really? What else do you know about this tramp, Fred?"

"Nothing. That's it, that's all George told me. Other than she was very nice, holds a good job, and of course is quite attractive. Mattie, she is not a tramp or harlot. She is a young lady born and raised in another part of the world in a different set of surroundings. Agreed, she is not from the upper class, but that does not mean she is bad."

Mattie was not letting this go. "Well now, it seems like George has your support. Isn't this just lovely? Does this person have a name?"

"Annie."

Fred swore someone had opened a freezer door. The atmosphere was suddenly icy in the normally cozy library of the

Michigan homestead.

"This isn't over, Fred. I won't stand for it, I just won't! I'm not letting him ruin his life, and I expect your help!"

Mattie left the room, leaving Fred rubbing his eyes. The question foremost in his mind was not about Mattie or George. It was the location of the closest bottle of Jim Beam.

*

George opened his eyes. He was alone in bed. It was cold in his room, much colder than it was outside a few hours ago.

Where was Annie?

George opened his bedroom door. It was dark, almost black. He was moving, but he wasn't walking. He was breathing, but the air seemed thick, like water. He looked around, seeing nothing. He looked up. There was brightness above, but he could not move toward it. He heard a voice that he recognized, but it wasn't coming from anywhere — or it was coming from everywhere? He strained to hear the words. It sounded like the voice was saying his name at the end of a sentence, but he couldn't make out the rest.

He was experiencing that feeling of calm again.

He was confused, but in a euphoric state, none of the anxiety that normally accompanied a situation filled with unanswered questions. The voice wasn't identifiable; it wasn't Annie's, nor was it Mattie's, but he had heard it before.

Was it the spirit's voice from the "cabin"? It sounded different. It didn't matter; he couldn't make out the words.

He rolled so he was seemingly on his back, looking in the direction of some lighter area, maybe the sky. He could make out two figures, he thought a woman and a man. Was that Annie's face? He looked harder. It couldn't be; and the man's face was not familiar.

"George? George, are you okay?"

He rolled over. Annie was half on top of him, wearing nothing except a concerned look.

"You were running in your sleep! And you were breathing funny. I was worried."

George smiled and hugged her closely, staring past her across the room that looked as normal as ever.

"I'm fine, Annie. How could I not be with you on top of me?"

"What were you dreaming about?"

"I don't remember, to be honest. Nothing important, I guess. I better get you home. What time do you have to be at work?"

"In two hours!"

They laughed, scrambling to dress and get down to the boat.

*

For the first time in George's life, he was in love. Or at least he thought he was.

Annie had knocked him sideways. She was down-to-earth, honest, and her comments left nothing to the imagination. Annie's first words to George alluded to her fondness for "nice things" and how she wanted to see "what more life had to offer." He didn't think she was after his money; she had said numerous times, "I'd be lying if I said I wasn't amazed at your wealth." If she was anything she shouldn't be, she hid it perfectly.

George could never get the vision of his mother out of his head. Even when he was with Annie, he was attempting to justify the relationship to his mother's image that bounced around his mind. To a lesser extent, the same was true for Fred. His warnings about the gold diggers were always present.

George knew he had to talk about Annie with his mother and Fred sooner than later. The summer was short on Spirit Island, and he had already decided he was not going the long winter without seeing Annie.

Here he was thinking ahead while he hadn't even discussed this with his girlfriend. She had to feel something for him. Last night was as close to a religious experience as he had ever felt. There was no way Annie didn't feel the same way — he hoped.

*

It had been decided that the carriage house needed to be cleaned up. It was home to a lot of leftover construction materials from the lodge. George could see Glenn working as he arrived back home.

"How's it going?

"There's a lot of crap in here, some stuff worth saving, but most will get tossed. What's new with Mr. Rausch?"

George considered Glenn a friend, not a servant. He had no problem opening up about exactly what was new.

"Annie was here for dinner last night and left this morning. Enough said?" George was from the upper crust of society and was not one to kiss and tell, but Glenn would be seeing Annie around the place more frequently, and it was only a matter of time until he knew.

"I know. I was here last night. I wasn't feeling well, and Trevor was nice enough to make me something to eat. I took it to my room. I was in bed by seven."

George was praying he hadn't heard the noises from the veranda.

"George, there is something I want to talk to you about, but I'm not sure it's my place to bring this up."

George felt a rush of embarrassment. How much had he heard, *or seen,* on the veranda or the bedroom?

"Speak freely, Glenn."

Glenn walked through the door of the carriage house,

rubbing his head, looking at the waves smashing against the shore. Glenn was not himself, visibly uncomfortable.

"George, you and your family have been good to me. I love working here, you pay me more than you should, and I don't want what I have to say to put that at risk."

"Glenn, relax. There is nothing you can say. Please, what's up?"

"I said to you when I took this job I would do my best to be your information source about the island and its people. I would do this keeping the confidentiality of your family and looking after your best interests. You and I even shared spiritual beliefs about this place."

"You don't have to sell me on what you have done, Glenn. You are considered a friend — out with it!"

"I have concerns about your lady friend! There, I said it. I know I will live to regret it."

To say the ensuing moments were strained would be the island's greatest understatement. Glenn was staring at his feet like they were about to speak to him. George, in a state of shock, stared at Glenn with his mouth hanging open.

Glenn was shaking when he sucked it up enough to look at George in the eye.

"Can we sit for a moment so I can explain what's behind that comment that I'm sure has already cost me my job and a friendship?"

George walked toward the freshening waves that were now pouring over the dock. "I'm in shock, Glenn."

"I can imagine."

"But not for the reason you think."

Glenn loosened up slightly, starting to take deeper breaths. His heart rate was back down to an acceptable level.

"I'm in shock because I respect your opinion. Everything you have recommended or suggested since the minute I met you has been well founded and well thought out. Therefore, unfortunately, the pedestal I have Annie on just moved."

"George, Annie is a good person and is from a good family. Please revisit what I said. 'I have concerns.' They are centered around her circle of friends."

"What? Go on, please."

"They are not from the same upbringing and do not share Annie's work ethic, or overall ethics, for that matter."

"And how do you know this?"

Glenn walked past George and stood on the dock, hopping around, trying to keep his feet dry. "I told you I would look after your best interests. Some people might choose to call it something different, but I have done a little background work on Annie and the people she associates with. Again, George, for you, no one else."

"And what did you find that is a cause for concern?"

"First, you know Annie has only dated people with money or at the higher end of Spirit Island's community."

"I think that shows taste, and I actually admire that in her. She made her feelings about what she wants in life clear to me, right from the beginning."

"Please don't get defensive on me. Hear me out. Her friends, she has two couples that are quite close. Her best girlfriend Claudette, who you know, is a local girl who got pregnant with her boyfriend Frank at a young age. My concern is they are dirt poor. George, Frank has little education and is an unskilled laborer at the mill and hasn't worked in months."

"So, what does their misfortune have to do with Annie and I?"

"George, Claudette and Annie played with dolls together. They are as close as sisters. Annie listens to everything Claudette has to say. Claudette is the alpha dog in that relationship. Despite Annie's confident manner and better social position,

Annie thinks Claudette hung the moon! Further, people in town view Frank as — and I'll be nice — an underachiever. I'm asking you to keep that in mind, that's all. As for the other couple she spends a lot of time with, the jury is still out, but I am doing my due diligence."

George moved onto the dock and put his arm around Glenn. "I appreciate you looking after me, and I am relieved that is all that's creating your concern. I will park that in my memory."

George told Glenn about the dream or whatever from the night before. Glenn listened, making no comment, until he was done.

"That's interesting. I really have nothing to say other than what we have discussed many times. This place welcomed you. You are one of Maple Point's for eternity. Remember that visions, dreams, whatever, are all real. They are for you, so pay attention to them. Mom said you invited her to dinner here if I ended up working for you. You know, I think it may be a good time to have her over. A 'cleansing' may be in order."

"Cleansing?"

"Your studies. You must be aware of smudging?"

George looked at Glenn with his head tilted to one side, his mouth drooped open. "Your mother would do that?"

"I'm pretty sure, yes. George, remember because *you* choose someone doesn't mean they are automatically accepted by this place."

"You are referring to my choice of Annie. My turn now, Glenn. Do you not like Annie? Is there something here you are not saying?"

Glenn's feet were now soaked with the cool water of Mudge Bay rolling over his shoes.

"You are one of the richest people in the world, and I daresay one of the nicest. You can have anything in the world, and that includes the people you decide to share your life with. Annie is a nice person from Manitoulin Island. How many Annie's are there in New York, Chicago, London, or Rome? You get my point. I am not siding with your mother, but what do you think your wealth looks like to Annie? I'm saying, again, I have my concerns. Granted, not based on anything really tangible at this point. But George, your wealth, it sways my thinking, and I'm not sleeping with you!"

"And you never will!" George put his arm around Glenn's shoulders. "Let's change our shoes and have a drink."

Chapter 14

George heard the door of his pick-up truck close. Moments later, Glenn and his mother walked into the family room of the lodge. Angeni moved to George and kissed him on the cheek.

"Thank you for everything you have done for my son and the invitation to your lovely home."

"Your son is considered a friend, and I am the one who should be thanking you for coming here this evening. I am so sorry my father couldn't be here to meet you."

Angeni whispered something to her son, and Glenn walked her down the hall to one of the bedrooms.

"My mother is a bit nervous right now, but she will be fine."

Glenn and George were seated on the couch when Angeni reentered the room. She was carrying a small sachet. She kneeled on the floor and placed the sachet in front of her.

"Mr. Rausch, I am asking, *if you want*, to join me on the floor with Glenn. It is totally voluntary. Please do not feel you have to."

George moved quickly to sit beside Glenn, the three forming a small circle. Angeni pulled from the sack what looked like a shell and put it in front of her. In the shell she emptied the contents of a smaller sachet.

She looked at George with that angelic smile and said, "Cedar, sage, sweetgrass, and tobacco. Sage is to purify, cedar is to ward off sickness, sweetgrass is to attract positive energy. Tobacco is the most sacred, connecting people to the spiritual world. I am going to light these only long enough to produce smoke."

Soon, smoke rose from the shell, and Angeni rubbed her hands in the smoke. She asked the boys to do the same.

"The smoke cleanses, removing bad energy from you and the surroundings."

She took a feather and directed the smoke in the direction of everyone's eyes, ears, and mouth. She explained that for the eyes, it helped see the good in others. For the ears, to clearly hear the positive things, and finally, the mouth, so you would only speak good of others.

"George, my son has told me you have experienced things in and around this place that you cannot explain. I am afraid I cannot help you with that. You will figure that out on your own. What I can tell you is what I have been taught by my elders and knowledge keepers. Glenn told me you have started to study the culture of the first people. You should be proud of yourself for doing that. If you continue those studies, maybe you will make better sense of what you think you are seeing. The 'circle of life' is important to understand. Life continues after death, and death is as much a part of life as birth. It is believed that everything has a spirit. Everything.

"Boundaries between objects, animals, and humans and spirits become blurred in the afterlife. Your spirit just occupies your body during your lifetime. It moves on, possibly taking another form. Therefore, spirits of others would do the same thing, or these spirits may never be heard from again. My grandfather spoke of 'the land of everlasting happiness.' A place of eternal serenity. Many end up there."

George was riveted to Angeni's every word.

The smoke was gone. She packed up her belongings and

placed them outside the front door of the lodge.

"Thank you, Angeni. That was so gracious of you."

She kissed Glenn and George and sat quietly on the couch. The three enjoyed a fish dinner that Trevor had prepared with Angeni's spicing. The conversation went long into the night. George sat wide-eyed, listening to Angeni speak of the teachings of her elders, about Gitchi Manitou, the creator of the physical world and all the beings in it, and the animals and plants and what they represented to the Indigenous people. She spoke softly, with emotion.

She ended the evening by saying, "You are a good man, George. Respect your elders and their knowledge. Respect the gift of this land and all that it brings. Respect will always be the most important thing in your life."

It was a night that George never forgot.

*

The sun was sinking into the North Channel earlier every day. The days were cooler, with cold nights not far off. Some of the leaves had already decided it was time to say goodbye.

Summer was over.

Annie and George had been the talk of the island for the last month. Whether it was in the car or the boat, Annie was fashioning a more glamorous look, hallmarked by large hats. She presented herself as Spirit Island's Hollywood North. George was known for his perpetual smile. The islanders were in love with George, and he loved them right back.

If the monarchy had stretched to Maple Point, they were the prince and princess in waiting. George had not been back to Detroit in over nine weeks. Fred had been up once or twice, and Mattie had remained home the entire time. Annie and George had been inseparable, and a few of their island relationships had changed because of it.

George and Annie may not have been aware of the changes until George decided to have a farewell summer party at the lodge.

He spent a few bucks and dressed the place up. There were outside music, additional furnishings, and colorful umbrellas scattered around the property. If the guests were not crashing at the lodge, they would be shuttled home by people hired for the party. Trevor was preparing a BBQ feast, and Glenn had made the grounds look better than they ever had.

It was the social event of the year for Spirit Island. All of George's acquaintances attended, the owners of most businesses, and of course, Annie's friends.

Annie was dressed like she was scheduled for a photo shoot for a Hollywood gossip magazine.

The hat was white with a red border and was three feet wide. Her long, snugly fitting dress had to have cost four months' pay, the expense of which had tongues wagging all evening. George, well he was George, crisp collared summer shirt, nice tie, and looking like the millionaire he was.

Noticeably absent was anyone from Detroit, no Fred and certainly no mother. It was a pretty fair bet they knew nothing about their son's soiree.

Annie was all smiles, drink in hand, working the grounds, welcoming the guests. George was looking at the dock, which was now home to four or five boats. He summoned Glenn, concerned the boats were going to bounce into each other.

Claudette, with Frank nowhere to be seen, moved over to Annie and spoke in a very quiet tone. "There isn't a woman here that doesn't want to be Miss Annie tonight! You are the most famous girlfriend *these* parts have ever seen. To be in your shoes, the things some people might do, goodness gracious!"

Annie shook her head. "Claudette, do not let anyone ever,

ever, hear you say that, you got that?"

Claudette raised her eyebrows a couple of times, put her hands under her breasts, pushing them together, winked, and walked away.

Frank Valentine appeared from behind the boathouse, smoking a cigarette. He was in conversation with Brian Lloyd.

Brian was half of the other couple that were very close friends of Annie's. Glenn had expressed concern about Frank and Claudette but never expanded his take on Brian and his wife.

The two moved in the direction of some squawking seagulls that were going to town on the remains of a fish washed up on the rocks.

Brian took a long tug on his Export A. "I have yet to be introduced to George, nor has my wife. You and Claudette must be Annie's chosen friends. I guess we don't make the 'A' list!"

"I have only been with him and Annie a few times, all Claudette's doing. I don't really have a lot in common with moneybags either. I wouldn't take it personally, Brian."

Brian was a high school friend of Annie's. There had been rumors around town a few years back that they had dated for a while. Brian was a couple of years older and eventually dated another good friend of Annie's, Lillian Potts. It was love, or something, at first sight, and the two were married when Lillian was nineteen years old. Brian, like Frank, found work at the mill in Gore Bay. Brian lasted a little longer than Frank before he was laid off. Now, like Frank, he moved from part-time job to part-time job, scraping out a meager living for himself and his wife.

Claudette, Lillian, and Annie had been close since high school, which wasn't that long ago. Claudette was the leader of the three and was never backward about being forward. She always spoke her mind, while Lillian was more reserved. In comparison, Annie kept her thoughts to herself. All three were attractive and were the "boys' choice" in high school.

But Annie was the only single one. The early years of marital issues experienced by her two girlfriends only confirmed her belief that there had to be a better life.

It was looking like her decision was a wise one.

Glenn, looking extremely dapper, was helping Trevor work the crowd with trays of appetizers and cold drinks.

Annie moved to George and kissed him on the cheek. "This is marvelous, everyone is so impressed!"

George kissed Annie back. "I didn't do it to impress anyone. I did it to have a good time."

Annie appeared taken back by the comment, giving George a second look. She frowned and returned to the party.

Glenn saw George alone and moved over to offer him a drink. "I picked this up yesterday. Looks like Fred's writing."

A sparkle came to George's eye; he had been remiss in calling home and had not heard from Fred in weeks.

"This may not be the time or place, but there has been a complaint from one of the guests."

"Indeed."

"It seems that everyone else had more ice in their drinks than Claudette, and she mentioned it to Annie. Annie came over to me and told me to please freshen Claudette's drink."

Glenn smiled, shaking his head slightly, and walked away.

Fred's letter was one line: *When are you coming home, son? I miss you.*

George missed him as well. It was something he needed to decide shortly. That would be a difficult conversation with Annie.

The party was moving along nicely. Trevor had prepared a BBQ feast he called "Island Surf and Turf: fresh pickerel and beef tenderloin.

It was a huge hit.

George nursed a bourbon, watching the proceedings alone from the corner of the property. Brian had not left Frank's side, and both were doing their best to exhaust the lodge's liquor supply.

"A penny for your thoughts?"

Annie had sneaked around behind George and put her hands over his eyes. George took her hand and gave her the letter from Fred.

"That is to the point. Have you given anymore thought as to when?"

"I wanted to decide a date with you, but I'm thinking a couple of weeks."

Annie moved around and sat on his lap. "You know this is going to kill me. I just can't think about it now. I don't want to ruin such a great party."

"I told you, we are not going to be apart long. You will be coming to Detroit, and I will be here through the winter."

Annie rose to her feet, adjusting her dress. "The winters are long on Manitoulin Island, honey, very, very long."

She kissed George like it was their last time and went back to the party.

Brian could be heard from a considerable distance. The Jim Beam was taking over. He was pointing at George's boat as he and Frank made their way in that direction. Neither of the two were walking particularly well.

"George, I am trying to tell Frank that boat is worth ten thousand dollars, am I right?"

Brian wasn't slurring his words quite yet but was no more than one drink from doing so.

"Oh, I'm not sure, actually, my family had it made for me. It doesn't really matter, does it? It's a fun boat, a big person's toy, right?"

"A toy for you, maybe. It's worth more money than I will ever have in my whole life!"

George produced the world's most awkward laugh and said, "You guys want to see what she can do? The water's not too bad today."

Brian and Frank were sitting in the boat before George finished the sentence.

When George started the boat, the noise from the engine caught the guests' attention. Most turned to watch George tear away from the dock. In a matter of seconds, the boat was at full speed, screaming across the bay. George turned the boat sharply, sending Brian, who was in the back, flying across the seat. George turned the boat again, heading directly at the shore. Now the entire party was watching George's performance. The boat looked like it was going right up on shore until he turned it suddenly toward the North Channel, almost capsizing it. There were screams from a few of the female guests, the loudest of which were from Brian's wife, Lillian.

Moments later George docked the boat. "How was that, boys?"

Neither Brian nor Frank said a word. Both smiled at George and moved quickly back to the bar, in need of something to calm the nerves.

Annie ran down to George. "What are you doing! You almost flipped the boat!"

The look George gave Annie wasn't good. It was the first time any of her friends had put him on the spot about his wealth. He did not like that feeling.

"Oh, just having fun. They were asking me about the boat. Come on, let's grab a drink."

*

The party was winding down, and Glenn began to shuttle people back to Gore Bay and Little Current.

Annie and George were finally alone, sitting on the dock, dangling their feet in the water.

"I didn't mean anything when I said 'everyone was so impressed.' I was just making an observation."

"I know. I guess I took it the wrong way. Sorry. But in that vein, honey, a drunken Brian made me feel uncomfortable today, asking me about the cost of my boat. I'm sorry about the boat ride. Maybe I had one too many drinks as well."

Annie didn't look up. "Brian and Frank both had too much to drink. Claudette was so mad at Frank, and I'm sure Lillian was equally upset. But George, you have to expect that a little bit. These people have nothing. Geez, honey, you are one of the richest people in the world, and you are now socializing with some of the poorest."

George said nothing, kicking at the cool, still water.

Annie turned to him. "More importantly, I want to talk about the worst thing about to happen in my life."

George, with a heavy sigh, said, "We knew the day was coming. What do you want me to say? I will do anything. I want you happy; it's just as hard on me."

"I don't really want to come to Detroit. I don't belong. It will be awful for me. We can't sleep together, and your mother, oh my God, your mother, I can't even imagine."

George had no response. He knew he needed to say something, but he had nothing.

"I will have a few weeks to work on them. It will be fine. You will win them over in no time."

They walked back to the house and were heading to their room when Annie said, "Do you hear something?"

Sure enough, there were noises that could only be described as erotic coming from one of the bedrooms. The two stood outside the door, smiling, hiding their embarrassed faces in their hands.

George grabbed Annie's hand and led her down the hall. As they quietly opened George's bedroom door, they heard a door open and saw a naked Claudette run to the bathroom.

Annie, with an expression of total shock, said, "I thought Glenn took them home?"

George laughed. "I guess she wasn't that mad at Frank!"

Chapter 15

Lillian peered over her coffee at Claudette, wondering what she was thinking about. The two had agreed to meet that afternoon to rehash the happenings from the day before. Claudette had not, nor did she intend to mention, that she and Frank had been caught doing the "wild thing" at the lodge.

"Has she confided in you? I mean really told you how she feels about George, about this whole thing?"

Claudette opened her eyes wide, staring past Lillian's head. "Not really, and it's pissing me off. Sure, she said he's a great guy, really down-to-earth, but she has said nothing about her real feelings. Or more importantly, what she is really *thinking* about!"

"What do you mean?"

"Oh, come on, Lillian! Jesus, the richest man in the world, plane, boats, houses, millions of dollars? Wake up!"

"Maybe she really is in love?"

Claudette put her coffee down and leaned over the table close enough to kiss Lillian. "I know I would be."

*

Annie had agreed there would be no "scene" when George left.

This was a trip home for a while, but they would be seeing each other again, very soon.

It sounded good in theory.

There were tears rolling down George's cheeks as he watched the lodge get smaller and smaller out of the plane's window.

Annie was lying on her bed with tea bags on her eyes, trying to reduce the swelling from an hour of crying. For the first time in months, George was not lying beside her.

She had told George many times over this summer that she loved him. She had never told him that she was *in* love with him. For her it was a huge difference. She had said to previous boyfriends, "I love you."

George was different. She was sure this was the first time she was *in* love.

She should have told him before he left, thus the tea bags.

She had to call him tonight at the mansion.

*

It was hard to say who was hugging the hardest, Fred or George. Regardless, it was an emotional embrace. The two had missed each other terribly; they had a lot to catch up on.

Mattie held her son's face. "You look thin and you look tired. It's good your home. You need to get healthy again and back to your *real* life."

George did not want to get into it this soon, and for the sake of family harmony, he kept his mouth shut. The truth of the matter was the exact opposite. He had never been happier or felt more alive and healthy in his life.

Annie was working tonight, and he couldn't wait to call her after dinner.

The grounds were impeccable as usual. The Rausches had expanded the garage area of the property to accommodate several new cars. Seemed Fred had been a little bored over the summer and had acquired more toys.

"You are drinking out in the open now? No more flask? We have stepped it up, I see!"

"Your mother and I needed to find some religion, if you will. We opened up about a lot of stuff. You were of course a focal point, which led to other things, including my drinking. We agreed I would drink, sociably, never to excess, anytime and anywhere it was appropriate."

"Wow, that must have cost you!"

Fred laughed hard. "God, I've missed you! I agreed, in turn, to attend more of Mattie's charitable functions and to talk some sense into you."

"*What?*"

Fred looked at George and put his hand on his shoulder. "I kind of let some things I knew about you and Annie slip.'

"Slip?"

"Your mother is rather firm on her feelings about you and the island, and of course her boy being involved with a telephone operator. I didn't agree with her assessment. I came to your defense with information that had previously been between you and I."

"Is it Annie, or is it anyone that is not from here?"

"Great question, and I am convinced it is the latter. I would add the person's social status has a lot to do with it as well. The lady could be from Rochester Hills, but if she is not from society's elite, she would not meet your mother's criteria."

George shook his head and walked ahead of Fred. "This must be hell on you, Fred?"

Fred raised his glass and pointed to it with the other hand. "I negotiated well."

"Annie is wonderful. I am so happy with her. We have a problem, Father, she isn't going anywhere, in fact..."

"*Don't* say what I think you are going to say. Please, please don't."

George gave Fred a puzzled look. "I was going to say she is coming here to visit in a couple of weeks."

Fred's face was a picture of total relief. "I thought you were going to say you were getting married!"

George didn't smile; actually, he maintained a very deadpan appearance. "It may happen one day, I'm sure of that."

Fred took a healthy gulp from his crystal highball glass. "One step at a time. Annie's visit is going to be a major hurdle. Your mother is not going to receive this news well. Oh God, you have no idea."

"She has a choice. She accepts this and opens her mind to the fact that it is her son's life and his decision. Or she can expect me to be spending a lot of the winter on Spirit Island."

*

Mattie, Fred, and George were in the main dining room at a table that would seat twenty-four people comfortably. The three were huddled at one end of the table; for most normal people it looked absolutely ridiculous. Trevor had prepared a soup to nuts culinary delight.

Fred had a glass of bourbon in front of him that was comically large, and behind that was a bottle of wine with only *one* wine glass on the entire table.

He was expecting a bloodbath.

"I had a small party a couple of weeks ago. I'm sure Trevor must have mentioned it?"

Fred reached for his glass, acknowledging George's immediate move to the offensive.

"Yes, George, Trevor said there was a gathering at the lodge. No problems, I hope?"

"Why would there be problems, Mom?"

Fred tipped his glass so quickly, it was a wonder the ice cubes didn't fracture his nose.

"Well, George, please, you serve free alcohol to those people and you are asking for trouble."

Fred blurted out, "Mattie, why don't you tell George about the wing of the college they are going to name after you in recognition of your charitable contributions?"

"What do you mean by 'those people,' Mom? They are business owners and friends of mine."

Mattie put her cutlery down. "And, of course, 'Annie' and her friends as well."

Fred was moving around on his chair like it was electrified. There was no escaping; the floodgates were open.

"Yes Mom, Annie. My girlfriend and her friends were there. And if I may add, Annie was by far the classiest person in attendance. She would have presented well in Paris, London, or New York. You will see for yourself what I am speaking about. She's coming to visit for a few days next month."

Fred appeared in need of an immediate Heimlich maneuver. He was exhaling, but inhaling was not in the cards.

Mattie folded her napkin and slowly stood in front of her chair. "George, I have done my best to ignore your insolent attitude since you have returned home. This summer has certainly had an effect on you, for the worse, I'm afraid. That woman is not coming to visit next month, next year, or ever. When you want to have an intelligent, respectful conversation, we will sit down."

Mattie left the room, leaving George and Fred, who seemed destined for the emergency room — alone. Trevor entered the room and placed a mammoth sirloin steak in front of George. He looked at Fred, then looked at Mattie's vacated chair. "I see I will be eating well this evening."

*

"I can't begin to tell you how much I miss you. I'm so glad you called me. The thought of calling your house and your mother answering had my stomach churning all day. I have to talk quietly. You know how close I'm sitting to the other operator."

"I miss you too, Annie. The flight home was horrible. The only positive was seeing Dad; I missed him."

"Did you talk about me?"

"As a matter of fact, I just told Mom you were coming to visit in a couple of weeks."

"And?"

"You are coming in a couple of weeks, what more is there to say?"

"She wasn't happy, was she?"

"Initial shock, nothing serious. She will be fine."

"George, I have to go, damn it. There is something I want you to know, honey. I've always told you I love you, but I want you to know that I am *in* love with you. It is the most special feeling. Thank you for being so wonderful. God, I miss you."

The line went dead, cutting George off before he could respond. He tried calling back but could not get through. He walked down the west hall of his home, which took him past Mattie's office. He walked slowly to the office; thankfully, the door was closed. He scooted by and made his way down to the library, where Fred sat in front of the large bay window overlooking the tennis courts. Fred heard George enter and without turning around lifted his head from the evening paper. "That went well, don't you think?"

George couldn't help but laugh. "Oh boy, I stuck my foot in it now. Where do I go from here?"

"Whether you like it or not, you are going to have to sit down with your mother, and as Mattie said, 'have an intelligent conversation.'"

"But this is not negotiable. Either Annie visits and Mom is hospitable, or not. There is no middle ground."

"That approach will get all of us nowhere and probably find me in the hospital, drying out!"

"So how do I approach this?"

"Appeal to her intellect, her love for you. You are a bright young man, and Annie is a lovely girl. Sell your mother on that, for goodness sakes. You need to sell your upbringing, which she is responsible for, as the basis for making sound, intelligent decisions. Stay away from the class difference. You will never win that debate. Tell your mother that Annie is not after your money, and she really is fond of George Rausch. The person that Mattie created. You are personable and charismatic, and your mother knows that!"

"That sounds good, Dad. Let me sleep on that. You are not just a pretty face."

*

Lillian and Claudette exited Turner's Department Store and crossed the street to the Little Current post office. The wind was whipping off the harbor, and the clouds over the Cloche Mountains looked laden with the season's first snow squall.

"This time of year is so depressing. It's getting dark so early."

"It's going to be a long, bleak winter for us, Lillian. If it wasn't for my parent's house, I don't know what we would do. Frank hasn't made a dime in over a month, and there is nothing on the horizon."

"Brian's working at the garage changing snow tires, but that is paying nothing. Our savings are gone. We are all in the same boat."

The two made their way to the Anchor Inn for a coffee. Claudette pulled out a chair, screeching it across the barn-board floor.

"Then of course there's Annie, working, making money, still living at home. Oh, and that boyfriend of hers, I guess he's not stressing too much about milk money, is he?"

Claudette was in a foul mood, and her sarcasm was dripping all over the table.

"Claudette, you know me. I'm not one to make waves, and you know I love Annie to pieces."

Claudette's eyes lit up; a sparkle could almost be seen. "Why, Lillian, I don't want to get ahead of myself, but I am shocked! For you, this sounds like an act of war is about to take place!"

Lillian pulled her chair close, leaning into the suddenly smiling face across the table.

"I found out from Annie at the party what Mr. Rausch is paying 'handyman Glenn' a week. Keep in mind, darling, that's every week, fifty-two weeks a year, whether George or any Rausch is there or not!"

"Well, let's have it, Lillian!"

"You only wish you had it, Claudette: seventy bucks, cash!"

Claudette's mouth dropped open like her bottom lip suddenly weighed forty pounds. Her hand hit her forehead so hard, the noise made Denise, the waitress, look over.

"When Frank got laid off at the mill, he was making $32.50 a week!"

Claudette and Lillian stared at each other, speechless. The only thing that could be heard were the wheels turning in Claudette's head.

"You know, George could get *two* handymen for that price."

Lillian had one eye closed, looking at Claudette through the handle of the cup. "And Annie could keep her two best friends from ending up in the soup line."

Chapter 16

The skies had opened in Rochester Hills. It was raining hard, very dark, and at 11:45 a.m. on October 15, 1935, it looked like the world was coming to an end.

It was Mattie's birthday, and George had invited her to lunch, just the two of them. A more depressing-looking day you couldn't find, but George was committed to being positive and loving.

And more than anything else, at the top of his selling game.

He decided to have the family chauffer take them to the Statler. They were seated in the corner of a pretentious room with chandeliers the size of ice huts hanging twenty feet above the tables. Mattie, a teetotaler, made the first concession of the day.

"George, please feel free to have a drink. Don't feel you have to abstain on my account."

George smiled and said, "Thank you, Mother, that's nice of you. I think *I will* have a bourbon to take the edge off this awful day."

George raised his glass and toasted his mother's birthday. "I wish you all the best, Mom. To many, many more."

Mattie responded, taking the high road, "I may have overreacted the other night, dear. Let's start fresh and talk about things. I know you love the lodge, and of course the life that goes with it. But it is not the life I expected you to live. You must never forget, you are my son and whether you are nineteen or thirty-nine, I will always worry about you. That's what mothers do."

"Mom, you and Fred did a great job raising me. According to just about every one of your friends, business partners, and relatives, I turned out okay."

Mattie laughed and said, "Nothing like blowing your own horn!"

"My point is, I am the result of your teachings, loving, and mentoring. How can you worry about the choices I make in life? I base those decisions on what you taught me."

Mattie was silent, shaking her head, staring into George's eyes. "Sweetheart, it's not your rational thought I question. When emotions and hormones are not in the equation, I have total confidence in your ability to make the very best of decisions. Enter passion, love, and sexual desires, and your once sound mind may become clouded. Combine that with a person not from your financial or social background that may view you as an opportunity for personal gain, and that's when I get protective."

"Mom, if I brought a lady in here now and introduced her as 'Ruth from Long Island, the Hamptons, actually,' you would be your gracious, receptive self. And you would be thrilled with my choice of girlfriends. Wouldn't you?"

"Absolutely."

"Then how would you know after spending the weekend with us, it wasn't really Annie from Spirit Island?"

Without missing a beat, Mattie replied, "I would be able to tell, in double quick time!"

"Then let's put that to the test next weekend. Annie will be coming to stay at the house for a few days. I am confident she will change your mind. Mom, trust the choice of the person you created, please."

Mattie looked away, then down at the table. George sat motionless, waiting for his mother to say something, anything.

"I will allow her to come, as long as you fully understand my position. Annie or anyone from Manitoulin Island does not belong with us. I will never be convinced that she 'doesn't care about your money.' It is impossible. I will welcome her into our home and be hospitable. I am only doing this for you, George, because I love you. I will never accept her as your girlfriend. A friend, acquaintance, maybe."

George was amazed at how quickly his mother gave in. He couldn't help but think that dear Fred had softened her over the past few days.

"Thank you, Mom. She will change your mind, you wait and see."

*

Annie finished her shift at eight and made the cold, dark walk to Claudette's basement apartment. She opened the back door and went down the stairs. Claudette and Lillian were sitting at the *only* table in the apartment. Frank had gone out, and it was just the three of them, plus a sleeping baby. The basement was cold and devoid of any natural light, even moonlight; it made it a most depressing place.

"Coffee?"

"No, thanks."

"Something stronger, perhaps?"

"No, I'm fine. I told you I would drop in for a few minutes. I can't stay. George is calling at nine o'clock. What is so important anyway?"

Lillian walked the three steps to the stove and poured a

coffee. Claudette, looking a little put off by Annie's comment, said, "Well, I'm glad you could spare a few minutes for your oldest friends."

"Zip it, Claudette. I'm cold and tired, and I want to talk to George. You have a problem with that? Now speak up or I'm leaving."

"Now, sweetie, Claudette didn't mean that. It's tough times here, Annie. Life is not much fun right now, and with winter coming, we are all a little cranky."

"I know. What's the problem?"

Claudette walked around the table and hugged Annie. "I'm sorry. You know I love you. Lillian and I were talking the other day after the party. Well, there is no sense beating around the bush. You told Lillian that Glenn makes seventy dollars a week as George's handyman! Seventy dollars!"

Annie looked at Lillian with eyes on fire. "I knew I should *never* have said a thing! Damn it, Lillian!"

Totally out of character, and probably an indication of just how desperate the financial situation had become, Lillian yelled right back, "I'm not apologizing, Annie, not one bit. With all your good fortune, we thought you might, just once, think about your closest friends!"

Annie, looked confused. "What do you want me to do, tell George to start donating to the Lillian and Claudette charity? So what, if he pays Glenn seventy dollars, or he doesn't — what's that to you?"

Before Annie's words hit the floor, it clicked inside her head. She looked at both of them, squinting and shaking her head in disbelief. "I can't imagine you two would even think of asking me to talk to George about that! Do you have any idea how wrong that is, what ramifications that would have on my relationship with him? Did you even stop to think about that for one second?"

Annie was fuming. Lillian and Claudette said nothing, heads drooped, while Annie stomped around in the dank surroundings.

And to add to the mood, the baby started crying.

Annie stood with one hand on her hip and the other arm straight out, pointing right at Claudette's nose. "First of all, Glenn is his friend! Not just a handyman, his friend! Second, and more important than anything, and Claudette, you know this better than anyone, which is making me so mad, I could slap you! You know everyone in the world thinks I'm after his money! How do you think that would look — my friend's husband becomes his new handyman?"

Claudette looked up and said in a quiet voice, "We were thinking both Frank *and* Brian."

Annie let out a loud groan, almost a scream, grabbed her things, and ran up the stairs and out.

*

"This is a 1934 Dodge DRXX Coupe. I took delivery of it four weeks ago. What a beauty. I saw it and fell in love. The weird thing was, Mattie liked it too! Very rare that happens, George."

The two were driving through the country. A few remaining leaves bounced off the hood as they sped along in Fred's newest ride.

"Can I fly up and get Annie in the seaplane? The water is not frozen yet, and we can watch the weather. Annie has never flown before, and it would be a real thrill for her."

"I don't see why not. I will talk to our pilot tonight. No need to say anything to your mother."

Fred sped up on a flat stretch of road, and George put his hand on Fred's shoulder. "I'm going to ask Annie to marry me. If she says yes, I will give her the ring and make it official in the spring, in May, on her birthday."

The car swerved into the oncoming lane. Fortunately, the lane was empty. It swerved again to the right, Fred stood on the brakes, and the car skidded to a safe stop on the side of the road.

Both hands still gripped firmly on the wheel, Fred turned his head and in a very calm voice said, "You could have sprung that on me while I was on the couch, sipping a drink."

Fred smiled, put his hands on both sides of George's head, and pulled him close. "Are you sure, son? Are you really sure? You haven't known her very long. I want to know you have thought this out. A long engagement at least, I hope?"

"Dad, I am telling you this before anyone, including Annie. I am not asking her for another six months, and we will not be married for a minimum of a year after, and that's *if* she accepts! I'm that sure she is the most wonderful, loving person. You will see, you will love her as much as I do."

"So, nothing to anyone for another six months?"

"Relax, no! Nothing has changed, Dad. You are my best friend, and I tell you everything first."

Fred pulled the car back on the road. "Let's go see our pilot."

*

The weather on November 12, 1935, was cold. But there was a high-pressure front over Lake Huron and no snow in the forecast, so George and the pilot headed to Spirit Island.

It had been almost a month since their lips touched; the scene on the dock had a few onlookers wondering when these two were going to breathe.

Tears of joy were cascading down Annie's cheeks. "I've never been so happy and so scared at the same time in my life. I haven't slept in two nights thinking about this plane ride and your mother. I don't know which is scaring me more."

George laughed and held her close. "Both will be bumpy, but

Mom will calm down. The flight, well that's another story."

*

The Rausch limo picked them up at the dock. There was room in the back seat for ten Annies.

"Edward, meet Annie Arnold. Annie, meet Edward, the best chauffer in Detroit and a long-time member of our staff."

"Pleased to me meet you, Edward. I'm Annie."

"Indeed, my pleasure, welcome to Rochester Hills, Miss Arnold, and if there is anything I can do to make you feel more comfortable, please do not hesitate to ask."

Annie whispered in George's ear, "Could he take your mother for a three-day drive?"

"Sorry I missed that, Annie, what would you like?'

"Oh, nothing Edward! Nothing at all!"

Annie was mortified and buried her head in George's shoulder. George, grinning widely, whispered, "I forgot to mention, Edward has exceptional hearing."

The two were sitting on top of one another. They had not been intimate in over a month, and the hormones were bouncing around the back seat like tennis balls. George slid the privacy screen across, separating them from Edward — about as subtle as asking him to find a hotel. Annie wasted no time and kissed George while unzipping his pants. She had him in her hand and was down on it seconds later.

"Annie, honey, for God's sakes!"

Annie didn't flinch and worked her magic. Not too surprisingly, it ended in a very short period of time.

"Oh my God, honey, you are incredible."

Minutes later, Edward pulled in the driveway, and Annie watched the eighteen-foot iron gates swing open. She enjoyed her first view of the Rausch estate. Edward stopped the car in front of the massive entrance and held the door open.

"Annie, welcome to the Rausch home. I hope you enjoy your stay."

George, his normally combed back hair slightly in disarray, and looking like he wasn't sure whose house this was, slid out behind Annie. "Thank you, Edward, please take Annie's bags to the front lobby."

Edward grabbed the two bags from the trunk, giving George a curled eyebrow and a smirk on the way by. Annie looked collected as she took in a vista that she could only have seen in magazines. Acres of manicured grounds, fountains, and statues reached to the sky. A home that was twice the size of any hotel she had ever seen pictures of in her life. The front doors were twenty feet high, their handles larger than the front door to Annie's house on Spirit Island.

She turned to George. "Oh my God, I am trying to do what you said, honey. I'm trying not to be that star-struck country hayseed, but this is beyond anything I was imagining."

Before George had a chance to respond, Mattie and Fred were standing five feet away.

George held Annie's hand so tight, her fingers were getting red at the tips. "Hi there, we made it!"

Being, the saint he was, Fred stepped up and broke the ice. "I have heard so much about you, I feel like we are old friends. Welcome to Rochester Hills and our home, Annie."

Annie shook Fred's hand, and despite all the rehearsals she had practiced at home, she found her voice cracking as she replied, "Annie Arnold, I am pleased to finally meet you. George has told me so much about you."

George moved Annie in front of his mother.

The time had come.

"Annie Arnold, my mother Mattie Rausch. Mom, meet *my girlfriend*, Annie."

Mattie extended her hand, but the smile ran from her face after hearing those two words. The smile vanished at the same time as Fred's eyes could be heard rolling back in his head.

"Welcome, Annie, welcome to our home. I hope the plane ride wasn't too harrowing for you?"

To Annie's credit, she shook Mattie's hand and in a clear, confident tone said, "Thank you for having me to your home, Mrs. Rausch, and yes, the flight had its moments, but all is fine, thank you for asking. You and Mr. Rausch have a beautiful home, magnificent."

Mattie gave the most manufactured smile possible, turned to George, and said, "Why don't you show Annie to her room? I will have the bags sent up."

The guest bedroom Annie occupied was bigger than her house. A sitting room furnished to the nines opened into another room, housing a king-size bed that could sleep six people. The walk-in closet was larger than Claudette's basement apartment and was filled with robes and nightgowns. The en suite was appointed at a level of opulence that could not be described. Annie wanted to spend an entire night in the bathtub that had ten types of bubble soap placed at the end.

She began talking at eighty miles per hour. "I'm not going to make it, George, this was a bad idea. I feel so awkward. No matter what I say, it's going to look bad on you. And *why* did you say 'girlfriend'?"

"Sorry, I had to. I know, not the best choice of words. But you are! So be it!"

George spent the next couple of hours showing Annie around the house and grounds. They were alone, and if Annie said "Oh my God" once, she said it fifty times.

There were several occasions where she made no comment out loud. She thought of Claudette and Lillian and the topic of their last meeting. What would they think of all this? She knew what they would think and tried to put it out of her mind.

She found herself siding with Mattie. She was in love with George, not his money, but no one would believe it. No one should.

The lodge, the plane, the boat, and *The Rose* had boggled her mind. And now this? The home and property were so over the top. How could anyone in the world not think about the endless wealth? Many times, when walking through the home, she forgot George was there, it was so overwhelming.

If she were Mattie, she would have the same concerns — maybe more! Who wouldn't?

Maybe that was the conversation she should have with Mrs. Rausch before she left.

What did she have to lose? Agree with Mattie about her concerns, tell her they were well founded. Mattie would always think the money was the real motive for her wanting the relationship, and nothing would ever change that. That might be the smartest thing Annie Arnold ever did.

The question was, should she tell George her idea or just wait for the opportunity with Mattie? Woman to woman.

It was a big risk.

Chapter 17

Dinner was served at seven.

Annie looked stunning in a dress George had purchased for her earlier that summer. It was deeply cut in the back and fitted snugly to just below the knee. Fred admired the selection, silently, from across the dining room table. George had surprised her with two dresses in July; one was worn at the summer closing party and the second debuted this evening.

The dresses were expensive, far outside Annie's snack bracket. It didn't take Mattie long to get things going.

"Lovely dress, Annie."

Mattie was looking directly at George, not Annie, when she made the comment.

"A Madeleine Vionnet, if I'm not mistaken?"

"Yes, Mrs. Rausch, George bought it for me earlier this year. I just love it!"

Fred smiled and raised his glass. "Well, whoever picked it out, full marks! You look beautiful, Annie."

"Thank you, Mr. Rausch, that's sweet of you to say."

Mattie looked at Fred out of the corner of her eye. "I daresay it's the only one on Manitoulin Island!"

George kept the conversation light, discussing his mother's charities and talking about growing up in Rochester Hills. Mattie was great, and the evening went on without any tense moments. Fred was Fred, steering the conversation to safe waters the minute it looked like it may be going off course.

Annie was tired from her long day, and George picked up on that, suggesting she turn in early.

"I will be back later. Don't lock the door!"

"You will not! There is no way that is happening. Are you kidding, in your mother's house?"

Annie ushered George out of her room and closed the door behind him.

*

The visit had come to its last night. All in all, a visit that exceeded expectations. Annie had presented well, very well, according to Fred. However, his appraisal was surely based on different criteria than Mattie's. It was clear from the beginning that the best Annie could do was not cross Mattie. She was not going to win her over or change her mind. Not this visit — not ever.

There was one final hurdle before Annie headed back to the great white north. A small cocktail reception had been planned at the Rausch home to acknowledge the dedication of a university wing. It was to be known as the Matilda Rausch Center for Advanced Studies, dedicated to Mattie for her considerable charitable contributions and countless hours of volunteer work. Mattie had done her best to have this reception moved or canceled because of her son's house guest, but it was too late.

"I would appreciate if you would introduce Annie as your 'friend' and not your 'girlfriend,' George. I do not want the rumor mill going about my son. People will gossip about anything, and that would be prime fodder."

George was not happy about the request. "I will be holding her hand. Let them think what they want. I won't know one of these people anyway."

*

Annie was dazzling again, wearing the low-back number she wore a few days before. George looked as proud as any man could as he strolled past his mother with his "girlfriend" on his arm. Fred winked and said, "You are one great-looking couple. Are you two boyfriend and girlfriend?"

A handsome couple in their later twenties appeared out of nowhere. "Excuse me, Mr. Rausch. I'm Dr. William Langer, and this is my fiancée, Joyce Stewart. I just wanted to thank you and your family for inviting me this evening. I haven't been able to get near your mother, and I'm afraid we must leave. I graduated from the university a few years ago and sit on one of the committees."

George couldn't help but notice, Dr. Langer hadn't taken his eyes off Annie the whole time he was talking.

"You are welcome. This is my girlfriend, Annie Arnold. Too bad you have to leave so early."

George looked at Annie, who was smiling at the doctor when she said, "Pleased to meet you, Doctor. I hope you and Joyce have enjoyed your brief time at the party?"

The four talked for a few minutes, and the doctor and his fiancée left.

"Nice-looking couple, weren't they?"

For the first time in their relationship, Annie had commented on another man. George said, "He sure liked looking at you!"

"Why, George Rausch, is that a hint of jealousy I detect?"

George forced a smile. "Let me get you a drink."

George left for the bar, and Annie moved to the side of the room. She looked at the front hallway and saw the doctor saying goodbye to a few people. The doctor looked at Annie, smiled, and waved in a fashion that no one else would see, especially his fiancée. Annie smiled back and returned the small wave.

*

The next few months were cold and bleak, as one may expect in Gore Bay. They weren't much better in Rochester Hills.

Annie was miserable.

George was miserable.

One trip to the island, six weeks ago, was the only highlight for both of them. George had set a new phone bill record for the State of Michigan, calling Annie every day, and today was no different.

"It is March first. Six more weeks and I'm back to the lodge for the season!"

"I'm supposed to be happy about that? Six weeks is an eternity!"

"What do you want from me, Annie?"

The tone was as icy as the weather. There was silence on both ends of the phone. Annie spoke up, "I think its best we just hang up. Nothing good can happen from this conversation."

No words from George, just the click.

*

"Annie, I've got to say, you are no fun to be around. Just call him, for heaven's sakes."

It had been three weeks, and neither had budged.

"I am not calling. He hung up on me, and that's that. He's probably out with some rich bitch and couldn't care less if I fell into the North Channel!"

"Rich *and* wearing a backless dress cut down to her ass!" Claudette sat back from her coffee, laughing.

"Shut up, Claudette. I'm ready to lose it on someone. I'd close your mouth if I were you!"

"Why don't you go out, maybe on a date, even?"

Annie looked at Claudette, then looked away. "It has crossed my mind."

Claudette spat out her coffee, choking and hacking. "Are you out of your mind? Seriously? You are playing with the crown jewels, and you want to date some stiff from here because you're having a lover's spat?"

Annie sat back, oblivious to Claudette's verbal barrage. "I've been in the presence of a whole room of George Rausches. I love him, Claudette, don't get your knickers twisted. I would never date anyone else. I'm just mad and missing him. But you know, I think I fit with those people."

Annie put her coat on and threw some change on the table. "And you know what's the best part? I think *they think* I fit as well."

*

"Slow down, George, Jesus, I want to see the spring!"

George was putting Fred's new Dodge to the test. Fred liked speed as much as the next guy, but when the tires hit the shoulders on most of the turns, enough was enough.

"I am compensating for what is going to happen tonight. I'm going to call Annie and apologize. Don't say it, I know what you're thinking."

George slowed to a normal speed.

"I'm thinking I'm going to live to see another day! As far as commenting on what you should or shouldn't do regarding Miss Arnold? You are on your own there. I support any decision you make. How's that, diplomatic enough?"

"Yes! And, I *might* add, of no help whatsoever. I should never have slowed down!"

*

George was nervous, lying on his bed listening to Annie's phone ring.

"Hello?"

"I'm sorry for hanging up on you three weeks ago. This has been the worst time of my life. It has confirmed how much I love you, and I also learned how stubborn you can be!"

"I'm sorry, who is this?"

"Not funny, Annie!"

Annie was laughing and crying. "Oh George, please let's promise never to let this happen again. I have been voted Gore Bay's biggest bitch! Oh God, I've been miserable, and it's all your fault!"

George was laughing too. "I have decided to freeze my ass off and move into the lodge earlier. I will be there in seven days!"

Annie let out a shriek. "I am so happy! You better rest up, sweetie!"

*

A few days later, George asked Fred to go for another drive, this time in the city, at the speed limit, normal blood pressure would be guaranteed.

"Where are we going?"

"Engagement rings."

Fred dropped his head into hands. "You know everything is in your mother's name? I will get nothing when she throws me to the curb. She will do it, you know, the minute she knows I was in on this! Couldn't you do this on your own? Now I'm an accomplice!"

George laughed. "No. Now tell me where to go!"

"How do I know?"

"You gave Mom a ring!"

"I bought it in Chicago."

"That's helpful!"

"Try Roman's, it's been there for twenty years."

There was no one in the store. Not a big surprise, since diamond shopping in the Depression was not a popular pastime. They looked at rings, they looked at each other, and finally decided on a style that would be made for George Rausch: a two-carat solitaire diamond, set in 22-carat white gold.

Simple, elegant, expensive.

A new car in 1936 was eight hundred dollars.

The same as the ring. A year's pay for Annie.

*

On April 1, 1936, a beautiful, sunny day at Maple Point, snow drifts were still piled high, but the daily temperatures were above freezing; there was light at the end of the tunnel. The car and boat were still tucked away. George was motoring around in the pick-up that had been there since they first broke ground a couple of years before.

The road into the lodge was slow at the best of times. Add ice and snow, and it was an hour from the main highway. Annie was all over George. Not that he minded but felt his bed would be a better venue.

"Honey, Glenn has the place up and running. Fireplaces are raging, and more importantly, he has left for the day. We will be there in twenty minutes."

Annie pulled her coat open and slowly dragged her skirt up, exposing the clasps of a black garter belt.

"Not interested?"

George did his best not to miss the driveway.

After the lodge door closed, he pushed her against it and

began fumbling with the buttons of her blouse. She already had his belt undone as they bounced off walls on the way to the bedroom.

She was face down on the bed. He ran his tongue up the inside her legs, and she arched her back, shoving her firm ass into his face.

He rolled her over and entered her slowly. "I can't go another winter without you. I want you every day."

Annie groaned and pulled him closer, sending him deeper inside her. She was on top now, smiling, moving quickly up and down. Groans culminated with a scream, raking her hands across his chest.

She collapsed on top of him, gasping for breath.

A few minutes later, she looked at him and whispered, "Sorry, sweetie, that was all about me. It's been too long."

George pulled away the sheets, lying limp in every sense of the word. Smiling, he said, "I hate to tell you, it wasn't *all* about you."

The sun smashing through the window wouldn't allow them to fall asleep.

"I am planning another party here, my dear."

Annie was now wide awake.

"Great! Exciting! Are you sure you want to have a party inside? The last one was so wonderful on the grounds."

"It's not until next month. I'm thinking May 20th?"

Annie rolled on top of George. "Really? My birthday? A birthday party for me?"

"How often do you turn nineteen?"

Annie kissed him and kissed him again. His hands moved down her back, and the exhaustion they both experienced minutes ago had vanished.

For the second time, they made the most of the midday sun.

Chapter 18

"No, I will not be at the party!"

Fred was very clear on his position about Annie's birthday festivities. He was more concerned the waves of disaster would soon roll down Lake Huron to Rochester Hills.

"You are giving Annie a ring, and you don't think your mother will hear about it? George, you are George Rausch, maybe Manitoulin Island's best-known resident! May 20th will be here very soon, one week to be precise. You better come up with a better plan!"

George knew Fred was right. "I will call you later. Annie and I are having dinner at the Anchor tonight."

Johnny Griggs was happy to see George walk in. "Mr. Rausch in the flesh! It has been a long winter. I've missed you! How are you?"

"I'm great, and I'm hungry! I have missed your whitefish. Bring it on, Johnny."

"Annie, what can I get you?"

"Whitefish sounds good, sweetie, thanks."

George was not himself; he did not look comfortable. Annie took his hand. "What is it?"

"I was talking to Dad earlier today. I have to go home for a day or two, papers to sign."

Annie sat back with a look of disgust on her face just as Denise arrived with two plates of fish. "You were just there!"

"What can I tell you, business. Dad is sending the plane."

"I will go with you!"

"*No!*"

Annie's head snapped back. "*Okay*, geez."

"Sorry honey, I didn't mean to say it that loud. I'm as put off as you. I will be back before you know it."

George did not like lying to Annie, but the thought of ruining the biggest day of his and her life justified the fib.

*

Fred watched the plane land on Lake St. Clair. George waved from the window as they taxied to the dock.

"Are you telling your mother alone, or with me?"

"With you, of course!"

The long-forgotten flask reappeared. "Okay, you bought the ring on your own! I am hearing all of this for the first time, the same as Mattie, right!"

"Yes, relax. I'm giving her a ring. No date is planned, at least a year or two away. I'm doing it because we spend half the year apart. I love her, and I want to show my intentions."

George took a swig that had to empty the flask. He looked at George and smiled. "Your mother may pass out. Good luck, son."

*

Mattie, Fred, and George were having lunch. It was a nice day, and they were seated in the screened-in terrace overlooking the tennis court.

Mattie looked tense, unsure why George was home only a couple of weeks after leaving. Fred was talking about the Tigers' chances in the upcoming season. It was falling on deaf ears.

George reached in his pocket and slid a small jewelry box across the table in front of his parents. "Mom, Dad, I'm giving Annie this on her birthday next week."

Mattie looked at the box. Then she looked at George and slowly reached across the table. Fred, not looking at anyone, said, "A birthday present, George?"

Before George could answer, his mother opened the box then closed it faster than she opened it. She looked at George, her face reddening at an alarming rate.

"Over my dead body are you marrying that woman."

George looked at his father and stood up. "I am giving her that ring next week. One day she will be my wife. I thought you had opened your mind, Mother, but I see I was wrong."

Mattie was now openly weeping. "You are ruining your life, George! This is wrong! This won't happen. I won't allow it." She wiped the tears away, "And when were you planning this godforsaken event?"

"There is no immediate plan. We want to have fun and live life. But we will marry in a year or two, and I hope I will have your blessing."

Mattie stood slowly, folded her napkin, and placed it over her plate. She looked through swollen eyes at George. "You will never have my blessing, I'm afraid. My only hope is you will come to your senses before this travesty occurs. Come, Fred."

Mattie exited the room with Fred a few steps behind, looking over his shoulder, George slumped in his chair.

*

George looked down at the beauty of Spirit Island, the water as blue as the sky he was flying through. The white caps broke over the shoreline of his property. He could feel the stress drain from his neck and shoulders as they started their descent. God, how he loved this place; the emotional hell of Rochester Hills was melting away.

He was meant to be here. For now: forever.

He looked around on his way to the lodge, yelling "Glenn" every few steps. There was no answer. Once inside, he called Glenn's name again. Apparently, he was alone.

He sipped his bourbon, watching the North Channel roll onto his shore. He was amazed at the calm he was experiencing, given the emotional torture of the day before. Then he realized the calm had taken over completely. He turned, or at least he felt he turned and witnessed his own image facing the fireplace. He tried to move closer but was unable. His image was white, like all the blood had been drained from the body. Yet the image was smiling, moving around the room. He noticed the clothes; they were not familiar to him. He tried again to move closer, and again his efforts to move failed. He watched his likeness pull his hand from his pocket. The image was wearing a wedding ring.

"George! George!" The image was gone, and he was alert, listening to Glenn's voice calling from outside the lodge.

"In here, Glenn!"

"Welcome home, George."

George was carrying bags loaded with party supplies for this weekend's birthday bash.

"I just watched myself float around the family room."

Glenn, put the bags down and looked at George. "You sure it was you?"

"Positive."

"Can I ask, did the image seem older than you are now?"

"No, I'd say it looked like I do now. Why?"

"No reason, just trying to make some sense of this."

"What are you saying, Glenn? Come on, what are you thinking?"

Glenn walked toward the door to get more bags from the truck. "Some people believe spirits take the form of their last earthly appearance. I don't subscribe to the belief. I think it's because that's the only presentation you are familiar with. You don't know what you will look like fifty years from now."

"Goddamn it, Glenn! Sign me up for your belief! What the hell, I'm going to die tomorrow?"

"Relax, boss, it was a vision. You aren't going anywhere."

*

The Maple Point spirits responsible for the weather on May 20th did a terrific job. It was pristine, like a mid-August day. Birthday presents covered one table, and balloons and streamers were everywhere around the property. Annie looked very summery in a bright yellow dress with a matching yellow hat. Thankfully, there was no wind that day, or the hat would have lifted Annie out over Mudge Bay.

Annie's mother and father were in attendance. George was thrilled they were there. A week earlier, he wasn't convinced they were going to show at all.

George had asked Annie's father, John, to meet him at the dock in Gore Bay. He said he was planning a surprise for Annie at her birthday party, and he wanted his help.

George had made no mention of his plans to give her a ring.

George and John had met several times before. George always had the impression Annie's father didn't like him. Whether it was because of his fame and fortune, or it was because he spent so much time away from Annie in the winter, he wasn't sure. Annie had always explained that it wouldn't matter who he was, sleeping with his little girl. Regardless, Annie said the idea of her father not liking George was all in his head.

They walked along the boardwalk of Gore Bay. George talked

about the party, some problems he was having with the well at the lodge, and how he was assured by Glenn that all would be fixed for Annie's birthday. The topic soon turned to Annie and how their relationship had continued to grow and how much he really cared for her. It didn't take John long to see where this was going. John slowed his pace to a crawl, turned to George and said, "Annie is too young to be married. I want her to see the world. You are a nice man, George, but no, I don't want her getting married. Not to you or to anyone."

George replied, "John, she will see the world, with me. We have no plans to get married now, not for a couple of years. But I want to give her a ring on her birthday. I love her, and I know she loves me. I will always take care of her, John."

John walked a bit more. "You two are very young. I love Annie more than anything in the world, and I will support whatever decision she makes. But you two are from different worlds, George. I don't see how this will work."

John shook George's hand. "I'm afraid you are not going to convince me otherwise, not at this point anyway. Don't get me wrong, George, you are a good man, and I like you."

George was disappointed for sure, but at least it wasn't the hell he would experience in a few days with his mother.

John thanked George for the courtesy and said good day.

*

The party was gearing up. The alcohol was flowing, the music could be heard for miles, and people were dancing. Claudette and Frank were chewing up the grass with the new dance craze called the Jitterbug. Brian walked past the two and said, "Try and keep your clothes on later, will you?"

Claudette punched Frank on the arm in recognition of Frank having spilled the beans about the horizontal gig at the last party.

George pulled Annie to the side and said, "Meet me by the birches on the other side of the lodge in five minutes. There's something I want to show you."

George ran into the lodge.

It was late afternoon and the water was like glass. The outline of Clapperton Island looked like a painting against the brilliant blue water.

Annie had her back to the lodge, taking in the magnificent view. She heard a noise and turned to find George on one knee, smiling up at her. In his hand she saw the ring, and she put her hand over her face.

"I have been thinking of the appropriate things to say at this moment for a long time. Annie, I came to the conclusion there are no words that would do justice in describing my love for you. I want to spend the rest of my life with you. I want you to be my wife when you are ready to become Mrs. George Rausch. I love you."

He held the ring out in two of his fingers.

She moved her left hand out, and he slipped the ring on her finger. Annie still had her other hand over her mouth, tears of joy running over it.

"I'll take that as a yes!"

Annie threw her arms around George's neck and kissed him deeply. Wiping the tears away, she said, "I never expected this now, not today. Oh, George, you have made me so happy. There is nothing I want more than to be with you, today and forever."

Annie was speed-talking again. "What are we going to say? Are we telling everyone? My parents? Oh, Lord Jesus, what did your mother do? Oh my God! Does she know? When are you thinking we will get married? This year? Next year? Am I ever welcome in your home again?"

George was laughing, holding Annie in his arms. "Slow down, honey, baby steps, baby steps! First, I think we should say I have given you a ring, we have no date to get married, we are going to enjoy life for the next while. How's that?"

Annie walked in a tight circle, looking at the ring the entire time. "Yes, yes, I think that's good. I agree."

George tried to make eye contact. "We will talk about all the rest later. Okay? We have the rest of our lives to talk."

Annie hugged George again. "Oh George, I'm still shaking. But we better get back. Please, let's go see my mom and dad first, all right?"

George thought, *Well, might as well get the toughest thing out of the way right now.*

The party was hopping. It was a safe bet no one noticed the two were missing.

Annie walked toward her mother. Twenty feet before she got there, the tears started flowing down her face. She held her ring finger out, and her mother started crying as well. George, a step behind, was looking directly at Annie's father. John moved to Annie and hugged her tightly, whispering something in her ear. He moved to George and shook his hand.

"Those are tears of joy running my daughter's face. I am shaking your hand because it's the right thing to do and it is what my daughter would want me to do."

George said nothing as John rejoined his wife and Annie in a family hug.

Minutes later, Annie and George started making the rounds.

Annie walked over to Claudette with George on her arm.

"George gave me my birthday present."

Claudette let out a scream that was louder than the music. There was no need for an announcement now; people who were not at the party had to have heard that scream. People came running from all parts of the property. The news was out. George stopped the music and stood in front of the table of presents.

"I would like to thank everyone for coming to Annie's

birthday party. I guess most of you are now aware I gave Annie a ring a little earlier today."

There was a burst of applause and yelping.

"I have asked Annie to marry me, and she has accepted. I want everyone here to know that Annie and I will be having a long engagement. We have no immediate plans, not for at least a year, probably two. We are going to love each other and enjoy life. We are going to have fun!"

There was more applause, and people were asking Annie to say something. Annie stood up beside George.

"Thanks everyone. By being here today you have made the greatest day of my life even more special. George is the sweetest man, the love of my life, and I couldn't be happier."

George raised his glass and toasted his bride-to-be. The two looked around and saw Annie's mother still crying. Her father was not smiling; in fact, he was just staring at George.

Claudette and Lillian were arm in arm, twirling each other around. It was if *they* had just announced *their* marriage. Or won a jackpot.

Chapter 19

Glenn tripped over Brian in the poor light provided by a sun that had not quite broken through. He had to be uncomfortable with an arm on the couch and the rest of his carcass on the hardwood floor. Lillian was on the couch, on her back, passed out. Her mouth was wide open, and the noises coming out of her were not good.

A disgusting sight, actually.

Glenn's foot to the side of Brian's head did not wake him. He didn't budge.

Glenn continued outside to start on the carnage from the night before, and it was considerable. The contents from two garbage cans were spread evenly around the grounds, compliments of the Maple Point Raccoon Association. They did a fine job, most artistic, leaving nothing in either can.

Through the early dawn, Glenn saw one lone person sitting on the dock, a tiny column of smoke rising over his head. Glenn, garbage can in one hand, a shovel in the other, worked his way to the dock.

"You scared me. I thought I was the only living creature here!"

Frank had a line in the water, slowly reeling it in.

"Catch anything?"

Frank pointed to a stringer off the corner of the dock with a few good-size fish attached.

"Where's Claudette?"

"The last I saw her, she was being sick out the back of the lodge. I couldn't watch it anymore. I said to her, 'No wonder, with the amount you had to drink.' Probably not a good thing to say at the time. She told me to take my poor excuse for a husband and leave her alone! I'm lying, she added a lot of profanity, but you get the idea."

Glenn was chuckling and sat down beside Frank. "I have only met your wife a few times, but it seems she excels at getting her point across!"

"You said a mouthful there, Glenn, she can be a brute!"

"I've had the impression from the first time I met her that she doesn't care for me too much."

Frank packed his rod away and took a long drag on the smoke. "Take it with a grain of salt. Claudette and Annie are the closest of friends. She wants to know everything that is going on all the time with her and George. Between me and you, she knows you and George are friends. She's jealous of anyone that is going to keep her from knowing everything. She wants Annie to tell her everything, and if he tells you stuff, maybe Annie is not hearing those things, then neither is she. That's just her."

Glenn picked up his shovel and can started walking. "There's coffee on inside. Nice talking to you, Frank."

*

Annie rolled over and opened one eye at a time. She was hoping the second eye would be less painful than the first.

Wrong.

George was face down. There was some concern he was still breathing with his face buried deeply in the pillow.

"George?"

A faint grunt was the reply. At least he was alive.

George got up to go to the bathroom. He opened his bedroom door and heard a thud, followed by, "Ouch! You ass, wait!"

Some rustling was heard, and he could now open the door fully. The first attempt had opened the door into Claudette's head, who was passed out on the hall floor.

Claudette quickly crawled to another bathroom and shut the door. The noise that followed sounded like she had launched most of her internal organs.

George climbed back into bed. "I don't think Claudette will be drinking for a day or two!"

Annie, still with only one eye open, said, "I am never drinking again, ever. Oh George, I don't remember anything from last night. I remember midnight and dancing and laughing, and then nothing."

"Do you remember I gave you that ring?"

She held her hand up in the air, looking at it through one eye. "Oh yes, I sure do!"

"Do you remember dancing with Lillian and Claudette on top of the table?"

"No."

"So, you don't remember Lillian pulling her dress up and revealing the results of her decision made earlier in the evening?"

"Oh my God, no, don't tell me?"

"I guess she felt undergarments were overrated."

Annie had both eyes open and sat straight up in bed, holding her forehead. "Oh no! Brian must have flipped, he's so protective of her!"

"Lillian was the hit of the party! She left nothing to the imagination. Brian pulled her off the table — quickly. I didn't see them again after that."

George looked at Annie, who was not in very good shape.

The alcohol and excitement had taken more than their toll. Regardless, George wanted to talk and threw out the first question.

"Your father was less than enthusiastic about the news. He just glared at me the rest of the night."

"Mom was so happy, that's all that matters. Dad will come around. Look, we've talked about this. He's worried you are a global playboy going to hurt me one day. And I'm his little girl! Honey, he will be fine. Speaking about mothers … you have yet to tell me if she even knows."

George got out of bed, realizing his head was still not its normal size. "Mom freaked out. She is dead against it … right now."

Annie looked at George with as sad a face as anyone human could muster. "So, what do we do? What happens?

"*We* have fun and keep our distance from Mom for a while. We do all the things we want to do, and in a year or so, hopefully Mother has mellowed. Or at least has come to the conclusion we are a couple, and not her or anyone else is going to change that."

"That will be hard on you, won't it?

"As long as I see Dad regularly, I will be okay."

There was a loud crash from outside, moving them to finally get out of bed.

Glenn had dumped all the glass bottles from the party into two forty-gallon drums.

"Sorry, there was no quiet way to do that. But boss, it is almost noon!"

Glenn had been busy. The grounds were getting back to normal. Claudette had joined Frank on the dock, and they were sharing a cigarette.

Annie tried not to laugh, "Claudette, sweetie, you don't look well."

Frank chuckled too. "Brian offered to take us home in his

boat, but Claudette didn't think she could make the ride."

Glenn came over and said, "I'm taking the truck to the dump. Come on, I'll run the two of you home."

Claudette, who still hadn't uttered a word, tried to smile at Annie as she walked away. She was hunched over, indicating another event could soon take place.

The party was over.

It was just the two of them now. They sat on the end of the dock. The splashing water of Mudge Bay and a chainsaw on the far shore were the only sounds to be heard.

The emotions lingered, but the major hurdles had been jumped. The parents knew, the friends knew, and soon the whole world would know. The heir to the Rausch fortune, the nineteen-year-old millionaire, George Rausch, from Rochester Hills, Michigan, was engaged to a fifteen-dollar-a-week telephone operator, Annie Arnold from Gore Bay.

If Annie and her friends pooled all their money they would make for the rest of their lives, it would not equal what George kept in the Little Current bank as "mad" money.

Two kids from different classes of society, as far apart as Rochester Hills and Spirit Island, were now under the world's microscope.

From this day forward, Annie Arnold would live with the knowledge that most of the world would forever view her as a gold digger. An opportunistic girl who came from nothing and jumped on George and his money.

Their backgrounds and their friends had nothing in common.

How was this supposed to work? How were these kids with their feet dangling in the frigid water going to make it?

Well, millions of dollars were sure to help.

Glenn pulled the boat into the dock. Annie and George were still there. George had one arm around Annie, the other waving at Glenn.

"I never got a chance to *really* congratulate you guys yet! I want you to know I wish you years of happiness. You are nice people, and you deserve each other. I have something for you."

He reached into the boat and came out with a small package wrapped in brown paper and a bottle of champagne.

Annie lost all the color in her face. "Thank you, Glenn, but the thought of alcohol right now, not a chance. We will share a glass with you some other time."

George was busy unwrapping the other gift. It was a tiny hand-carved figurine of an Indigenous women, well into her nineties, sitting by a camp fire. The whole carving was no larger than a golf ball. The detail was incredible. The woman's face looked real; the flames seemed alive.

George could not stop looking at it. He was spellbound.

"Legend has it this was carved over a hundred years ago. My grandfather gave me this and two other pieces on my eighteenth birthday. George and Annie, it was found not far from your lodge, here on Maple Point."

Annie showed polite interest in the story but nothing more. George was beside himself.

"Why am I only hearing about this now Glenn? This is incredible!"

"To be honest, I never planned on parting with any of the three pieces. But as our friendship has grown and we have shared a *few things*, I decided it would be a nice gift for your engagement."

George hugged Glenn. Annie stood, seeing it was the thing to do, giving him a hug as well.

"I will leave you two alone. Again, congratulations to both of you."

George was silent, staring at the piece like it was about to say something.

"Shared a few things? You want to tell me anything, George?"

George said nothing, still in a trance.

"The spiritual stuff — really? I mean, I know you have mentioned dreams to me, and you have told me about Glenn's beliefs. But you, George, you *really* believe? You are not native; you are a white man from Detroit."

George looked at Annie and said, "I believe there is a power, for those who are accepted, I really do. I believe, actually, that it had *everything* to do with you and I."

"Really? You are serious?"

"If I didn't feel the way I do about Spirit Island, and specifically Maple Point, I never would have stayed. *Something brought me here*. Therefore, there would be no Annie and George."

Annie looked at George for what seemed like an eternity. She looked so deeply into his eyes, it started to spook George.

"What?"

"George, I hope this isn't turning into an obsession. We have all read about people doing weird things because a 'voice' told them to."

"Annie, please, I am nowhere near that."

Annie stood and kissed George so erotically, it was a wonder George stayed in control.

"Well, thank God or *whoever* for making you stay here, because I'm so happy there's an Annie and George!"

Annie grabbed George's hand. "I'm feeling much better. We need to consummate our engagement!"

George picked up the carving and the bottle of champagne and ran to the lodge.

*

It was May 21, 1936, the day after Annie's nineteenth birthday.

And it was the beginning of an eighteen-month party.

George and Annie would never be apart. Annie gave her

notice at the telephone company and officially became a kept woman. It was a big issue in the Arnold house that John never came to grips with.

That summer was nothing but good times. George showered Annie with more clothes than she could wear in five summers. Annie's passion for hats increased, if that was possible. She was known around the island for them. Annie could never sneak up on anyone; even in calm conditions, her hats would make a noise. Each hat seemed larger and brighter than the one before.

Claudette remained her best friend, although the jealousy was apparent. Annie, to her credit, took both Claudette and Lillian to as many places as she could and of course always paid the bill.

One time, Annie was picking up some dresses George had ordered from Detroit. They had shipped six dresses instead of the three. Annie gave the other three to Claudette and Lillian rather than returning them.

This happened with other purchases as well. Annie was very generous to her friends — with George's money. But she always told George what she had done. George never seemed to mind. Perhaps twenty-five-dollar mistakes when you are receiving a thirty-thousand-dollar-a month allowance are looked at in perspective.

Fred came to the lodge a few times that summer, mainly to fish with George. The last time he came in September, he cruised up on *The Rose*. Mattie and a few friends were on board.

Annie asked George if she could have lunch with Mattie, just the two of them.

"Are you crazy, girl?"

"We are going to be married one day, George, wouldn't you like her there?"

"Yes, but I don't see it happening."

Annie got her wish, and the lunch was arranged.

Again, both George and Annie knew they had Fred to thank. George drove Annie over to *The Rose*, where a private lunch was served on the aft deck.

The two talked cordially for over an hour. Annie's position from the beginning was to agree with Mattie's concerns on the wedding of her son to the "commoner."

"If I were you, I would feel the same way. Of course, your wealth makes my head spin. It would make anyone crazy. All I can tell you is, I love your son. I'm sure the whole world thinks I'm a gold-digging woman. I can't change that. I will prove those beliefs wrong, trust me."

Mattie was polite and said very little. Annie thought, after the fact, that it had been a waste of time. In the long run, it was the best thing she could have done.

Mattie mentioned to Fred that evening that the lunch was a pleasant surprise. Mattie said, while Annie was still a little rough around the edges, she carried her herself in an acceptable manner.

Mattie had softened — a little.

Whatever happened at that lunch was a good thing for the future Mr. and Mrs. George Rausch. Whether it was Annie's sincerity or Fred's plea to Mattie to think about George's life, no one would ever know. More than likely it was a combination of both.

But that winter, Annie and George spent weeks at a time in Rochester Hills. Overall, Annie did well selling herself to the Rausch family. There was just one incident she wished never happened. And of course, George was to blame.

Hormones.

They got the best of the young couple one evening. George assured Annie that his parents were gone to a fundraiser. Annie made George watch the limo leave, making sure Fred and Mattie were in the back. Annie did not feel comfortable even kissing

George in the Rausch home, at any time, regardless of whether they were alone or not. So off to the stable they went for an old-fashioned "roll in the hay." George was enjoying himself to the utmost, but Annie's nerves prevailed.

"Forget it," she said finally.

The two dressed, much to George's dissatisfaction, and made their way back to the house. They were walking up the stairs when the front door opened, and in walked Mattie and Fred. Annie, thankful she had cut things short in the stable, turned and said, "Wow, you folks are back early?"

"We got all the way there, and I realized I'd left my speech at home," Mattie replied.

Annie noticed a smirk on Fred's face. He was staring at George's crotch! Annie looked over, and her eyes rolled back in her head.

There were three strands of straw sticking out of George's pants.

Fred was amused, Mattie was not.

Nothing was ever said, at least not by Mattie or Fred. Annie, on the other hand, had a few choice words for George.

Mattie had not changed her opinion about her son marrying Annie. She would never be on board. But she had eased her position, and her mind had opened. Mattie had resigned herself to the fact that this marriage was going to happen.

Chapter 20

It was the spring of 1938.

Another summer had come and gone at the lodge. More parties, more of Annie and George tearing up Manitoulin Island. The latest craze for the two of them was how fast they could travel by boat from the bridge in Little Current to their dock on Maple Point. The best they could manage was twenty-eight minutes. That was in perfectly calm conditions and the speedboat at full throttle. It was never clear if George had made a "contribution" to the Ontario Provincial Police. The speed limit in the harbor was ten miles per hour. George and Annie had to be doing four times that speed on numerous occasions. They were never stopped.

More importantly, another winter had also passed. Another winter spent between the island and Rochester Hills. Mattie was by no means ready to adopt Annie, but the two were cordial to each other, and the once visible tension had gone. Let there be no mistake, she was still not in favor of the marriage. She was doing this for George.

The winter, however, was not without a dash of drama.

Fred turned fifty-five that year, and Mattie decided to break up the gloom of the Michigan winter with a party for her husband.

A surprise party, no less.

The plan was for George and Fred to attend the Detroit Car Show during the day and meet at the Hilton for dinner with a few friends, Annie included. Except the catch would be George would fall ill at the show and tell his dad he was in no shape to go out that evening. The two would be forced to return home. Naturally, to a house filled with people ready to celebrate Fred's big day.

The idea went off without a hitch, and Fred was surprised. In fact, when the throng of people screamed the word, Fred was so startled, he flung his arm out in a natural act to retain his balance. His hand landed in the bosom of Hazel Vanberg, the wife of the Republican senator.

Fortunately, Mattie and Fred were big financial supporters of the Republican party.

The party was a big event. Black-tied waiters and cocktail-dressed waitresses served trays of champagne and hors d'oeuvres to Michigan's upper crust.

Annie was in her element. Soon to be twenty-one, she had a good figure and selected the perfect dress. George and his bride-to-be mingled all night, showing off Mattie's ring but making no mention of a firm date. The night was George's father's, and they did not want to steal any of the attention that was Fred's due.

It was getting late, and for a crowd predominantly in their forties and fifties, it was resembling a party from *The Great Gatsby*.

Mattie was dancing. Unheard of.

George was talking to a group of people, Annie chatting to a different group.

A few minutes later, George noticed Annie being danced across the floor. The smile dropped from George's face faster than Fred was drinking bourbon.

It was Dr. William Langer! Half of the "good-looking couple" described by Annie from a party a year or two before.

George didn't even realize he was in attendance. A "few" dances later, Annie caught up with George at the bar.

Annie could tell George was not amused.

"You remember William, don't you?"

"'William' now, is it? Not Dr. Langer?"

"Oh, George, he asked me to dance, what was I going to say? He complimented me on my ring and *our* engagement. He wanted to dance some more, no big deal."

"I'll bet he did. Where is his wife? It was Joyce, wasn't it?'

"No wife, they broke it off."

"Stay away from him, please. I don't trust him."

Annie stepped back, took a drink, and said, "Please, don't use that tone, and *please* don't tell me what to do!"

George gently held Annie's arm and pulled her closer. "I think you've had enough to drink tonight."

Annie took a deep breath, put her glass down, and walked away.

*

It was an abnormally warm spring.

For a change of pace, the two decided to fly to the lodge, stay for a week, then, weather permitting, drive the car back to Michigan for a much-needed overhaul.

Of course, the week at the lodge necessitated a party. The regular crew attended this affair, but there was no glitter, no special food, just loud music, alcohol, and good times.

George and Glenn were in deep conversation, sitting on the shore.

"I have not had a 'visitation' or 'event' in well over a year. You know, the more that I think about it, I haven't had one since you gave me that 'artifact.' And that will be two years next month!"

"No explanation, my friend, sorry."

"I think Annie and I are going to get married this summer."

Glenn stood up like a Massasauga rattler was on his lap! "What? You are?"

"Shush your face! Sit down! I haven't said anything to anyone! Not even Annie!"

Glenn sat as quickly as he had stood.

"We have been engaged almost two years. There have been a couple of small bumps, but I'm still very much in love. I couldn't imagine her not in my life. It's time."

"Is she in the same frame of mind as you?"

"Why do you say that?"

"No reason other than the obvious. It would be better if she was, don't you think?'

They both laughed and clinked their glasses.

*

Annie and Claudette were watching Frank make an ass of himself, trying to skip rocks across Mudge Bay. He was feeling no pain, so it was a wonder he was hitting the water at all.

"Tell me about this doctor again! This guy was *that* forward, right in the Rausch home?"

"Keep your voice down! If George knew the half of it, he would go wild. First of all, he has got to be ten years older than me. Second, I was talking, actually talking, to other people and he interrupted them to ask me to dance! I didn't have time to respond, and he had me on the dance floor."

"He's good-looking too, isn't he?"

"Dreamy good-looking. He said to me, 'I am so happy to see you again! I hear congratulations are in order?' Claudette, he was holding me very close! If George had seen, oh my God! He then said, 'I broke off my marriage plans, too many beautiful women in the world, like you'!"

Claudette had to steady herself on the chair. "What a cad! What am I saying, I wish it were me he was dancing with."

"Claudette! Really!"

The two sat drinking, continuing to watch Frank tripping over himself.

"Claudette, it's a world so close to here yet so far away. Those people are so different, yet so much the same."

"Annie, you are drunk. You are talking in circles."

"No, I'm not. Listen to me. I could be born there or born here. I could be with Frank, George, or even William. It's not the person, it's the place. Now that I've been there and socialized, I could get by there in a minute! And so could you, or Lillian, or anyone, for that matter."

"You are getting married to George someday, remember?"

"I know. I'm just looking at the bigger picture. You know how many doors to the world existed at Fred's birthday party?"

"Annie, I will say it a different way. Do you still want to marry George?"

Annie reached in her pocket and put something in Claudette's hand.

It was a card that read "Dr. W. Langer, Plastic Surgeon." Claudette's eyes fell out of her head. Annie snatched the card back and tucked it away.

"Of course, I love George to death. Nothing has changed or ever will."

*

George and Annie arrived at the Rausch home by car, safe and sound.

George found Trevor and arranged a private dinner for himself and Annie that evening. He asked Annie to put on a dress and meet him in the garden at 7:00 p.m. He had a surprise for her.

Annie was ravishing, as always.

"Tonight, Annie, I will be in your bed. No questions asked."

"The door will be open, honey, but when your mother or Fred walk in, it's your fault!"

George raised his glass. "I want to get married soon. Like in the next few months. There, how's that for a final proposal?"

"It's perfect, the sooner the better!"

"I will ask Mom and Dad to have breakfast with us. We will start the planning then."

Annie and George spent the rest of the night walking the grounds, organizing their thoughts for the morning.

"Do you think your mom will want the wedding here, at the house?"

"I'm sure she will, are you okay with that?'

"This is where I want to be married, honey. It will be the first day of the rest of our lives."

George looked at Annie, somewhat confused. "That's an interesting way to look at it." He kissed Annie. "You look tired, get to bed."

George winked, and the two made their way inside.

*

"The time has come, dear parents. Annie and I want to wed this summer. We are more in love now than we were two years ago, when I gave Annie the ring. I'm asking for your blessing."

Mattie did not take long with her response. "You have my blessing. George, you are my son, and I will love you unconditionally until my dying day, as I have since you were born. Annie, I hope you will love my son and be a good wife to him. He loves you very much."

Annie hugged Mattie and then Fred. Mattie started crying when George put his arms around her. She whispered in his ear, her voice cracking, "I love you. I hope you are sure?'

George pulled back, looking deeply into his mother's eyes. "Thank you. I love you too. Please put your mind at ease. I've never been more sure about anything in my life."

Fred yelled for a servant, and moments later champagne was flowing. He raised his glass. "To my son, my best friend, you are a lucky man. Annie, you are a kind, loving person. I wish you both a long, healthy and happy marriage, God bless."

Later that day, the details were being discussed. The date of the wedding was to be August 2nd, 1938. The announcement would be made in two weeks, on May 23rd. The ceremony and small reception would take place at the Rausch home in Rochester Hills.

The honeymoon would comprise of a trip to Lake of the Woods for a few days, then a few weeks celebrating with friends and family on Maple Point.

It was getting late in the day, and George and Annie had just shared the news with the staff. Trevor and Annie were laughing and drinking champagne with Fred. George and his mother had gone for a walk to the stables.

"George, there is no easy way to broach the subject, so here it is. Have you and Annie given any thought to financial arrangements?"

"What do you mean? You want Annie's father to pay for the wedding?"

George was laughing, trying to get the last part of that sentence out of his mouth.

Mattie was not smiling. "I mean the larger financial picture, George. You receive tens of thousands of dollars a month. You are to receive almost ten million dollars when you turn twenty-five. George, you can't tell me you it hasn't crossed your mind!"

"It has, but I figured it would look after itself, you know, governed by the law of the land."

Mattie stopped in front of one of their prize horses, stroking the side of its face. "Who will get this horse, *your* horse, George, should you die prematurely — or divorce! The infinitely more likely scenario!"

"Mom, this is an awful discussion on this day, of all days. Can we do this later? With Dad?"

"It needs to be discussed now! George, let me guide your thinking. You need things to be spelled out to your wife. Clearly, in a document. A legal document."

"What, like a contract?"

"Yes, exactly!"

"And how do you think Annie will take that news?"

"I don't care how she takes it. I really don't! This will be done! If need be, I will bring in my own legal team to make this happen. For God's sake, George, this can't be coming as a surprise."

Mattie walked away.

George thought the horse had climbed on his shoulders.

Chapter 21

"I have to agree with your mother on this one."

It was not the answer George was expecting. Annie was already in the car, looking at her lips in the rear-view mirror.

"Dad, she is going to flip when I say, 'But I do love you more than anything! Just initial here and here and sign here. Now, how about we make love?'"

Fred couldn't hold back his laughter. "Never lose your sense of humor, son! Listen, I think she will understand, I really do. You have told me many times, and so has Mattie, that Annie admits she is amazed at the level of wealth we enjoy. You wait. I think it will go better than you think. I even think she will be expecting it."

George hugged his dad and picked up his bag. "Mom is mailing me a 'draft.' I can't wait."

They waved goodbye, starting their long drive back to Maple Point. Annie told George she was going to sleep for the first part of the trip. That was perfect for him. He needed to think about how and when he would toss this contractual grenade at his future wife. He ran through countless scenarios with endings ranging anywhere from screaming and tears to a kick in the groin. He was a wreck; he felt his palms wet on the steering wheel. The whole time, he watched Annie, sleeping like she was drugged.

*

"I have to choose between new overalls for Brian or a pair of shoes for me. We can't afford both! You think Miss Annie has to think about that?"

Lillian and Claudette were pushing the baby stroller along the boardwalk. Claudette smiled at Lillian.

"After August 2nd, I don't think you will have to worry about that anymore."

"Why? I'm not becoming Mrs. Rausch."

"Lillian, I swear, darling, you must have been absent the day they were handing out the brains! You think Annie Rausch is going to forget about her two closest *poor* friends? She has a fifty percent say in things the minute he says 'I do!'"

"Sure, Claudette, I can hear Annie on the honeymoon, 'Okay, honey, let's give my friends some cash today!' You are the one missing the gray matter, not me!"

"There's more than one way to skin a cat, Lillian, you will see. She will look after us — she has to!"

*

Annie was still asleep. George was in the kitchen having morning coffee. He was focused on the middle of the table, a note from Glenn: *Picked this up yesterday, looks like it's from home.*

It was from home, alright; he had been dreading this day for weeks.

George read through the legal jargon quickly, trying to get to the punch line: $250,000.

That was what his marriage, or failure thereof, was worth to the future Mrs. Annie Rausch. George was twenty-one. If the marriage ended, for whatever reason, prior to George turning twenty-five, Annie would receive a lump sum of *a quarter of a million dollars*. It was vague and steeped in legalese about what was to happen after he was twenty-five. But that was years down the road and at this point of no interest to George.

The average wage was around two thousand dollars a year. Annie had been making fifteen dollars a week. A new waterfront house on Spirit Island, done to the nines, would be ten thousand dollars So, $250,000 was nothing to sneeze at. But it didn't matter what the amount was. This would turn a love affair into a business arrangement.

At least that was where George's head was at. And he was convinced Annie's head would be in the same place.

*

It was hot. June had come in scorching after a rather cool May. George had his heart set on finding a trophy pike that had to be waiting for him in one of Clapperton Island's bays. Annie was not ready to fish, but today baking herself in the northern sun appealed to her. She had purchased a few bathing suits in Detroit, one more revealing than the next, and she was ready to give them a test drive.

Clapperton Island was massive. It was also isolated. It would be rare to see another boat there all day. Each bay, each turn, offered a spectacular vista. George slowed to trolling speed, and Annie stretched out in the back, wearing a white suit.

"Where did you get that? I must say, the manufacturer must be doing well — he sure didn't spend much on material!"

Annie was in a playful mood. She smiled, reached around behind her, and undid the straps. The bathing suit fell to her waist, and she settled in, putting her hands behind her head.

"It's time my girls see a little daylight."

George smiled. "Don't burn now, honey, I'd hate to hurt you later!"

The day was a Chamber of Commerce tourism ad for Manitoulin Island. The fishing, not so much. A few little pike that George released off the side of the boat.

"What day are we heading back to your mom and dad's?"

"Sometime middle of next month, around July 15th."

All George could think about was Annie handing the signed document to his mother. What a disaster; George's stomach was in knots.

"I have to give my dad lots of notice. He is so nervous about going to your home. Mom can't sleep now, thinking about it!"

"You buy her a nice dress. The nicest one you can find. And buy your dad a new suit at the same time."

"Thanks, sweetie, they won't want to accept it, but I will make sure they do."

George had been more generous than usual lately, which was saying a lot. He had been overcompensating, anticipating the inevitable.

George couldn't fight the temptation of Annie's perky breasts any longer. He reeled in his line and hopped into the back of the boat.

"I thought you had lost interest. Not a good thing with our wedding around the corner."

As things were heating up and wondering how this was going to work, George pulled back.

"I can't do it! I have something to tell you that has been killing me for a month!"

There were tears in his eyes, his face so red, he looked like he was having a stroke.

"Sweetie, relax. Whatever it is, we will deal with it."

"I want you to know this is not my doing, this is the business of my family, and their demand."

George was shaking.

Annie did herself up. She held George's hand and wiped the

tears from his face. "Relax George, I'm pretty sure I know what this is about."

"*What?* You do? I don't think so! You couldn't! They want you to sign a financial release. It states a sum of money you will be paid if our marriage ends before my twenty-fifth birthday. I think it is an insult to you! I'm so sorry!"

Annie hugged George. "You are one the richest families in the world. I did expect this. I did."

A smile came to George's face. "You are wonderful. I love you so much."

Annie moved him back. "How much?'

"What?"

"How much do I get?"

There was little or no discernable expression on Annie's face. "You get $250,000."

Annie moved to the passenger seat in the front of the boat.

"Annie, honey, say something."

"I am not hurt or shocked that your family wants this agreement before the wedding. It is totally understandable. Don't be upset or take this the wrong way, but I don't think it is very generous. Your family sold the business for well over a hundred million dollars."

For the first time since he had met the beauty from Gore Bay, he heard words he didn't want to hear. He was reminded of the numerous talks with Fred and his mother. Talks that never pertained to Annie until now. They were about gold-digging women. Women that he had been able to avoid his whole life. Time stood still for George. He was looking at the woman he loved, the woman he was marrying in a matter of weeks. But those words; she was different now. So much had changed in a matter of seconds.

Annie smiled, put her arms around him, and said, "But, we will never have to worry about it, will we?"

George hugged her back, looked into her eyes and said, "We never will. Let's put this out of our minds. We will be happy and have fun the rest of our lives."

*

The wedding announcement had gone out. The plan had Fred standing up with George and Annie's mother standing up with her. The wedding would take place on the grounds and be attended by a small group of relatives and friends. It was July 10th, and they would be heading to Rochester Hills in less than a week.

Johnny Griggs poured coffee for the three ladies. "On me today. I guess the next time I see you, it's Mrs. Rausch! You still going to talk to me?"

Annie winked. "How long have we known each other? Since I was five? I think I'll still say hi."

Claudette and Lillian looked across the table, waiting for Annie to open up.

"I have been doing some thinking, girls. I will be married in less than a month, and I want to give you guys a wedding present!"

Claudette kicked Lillian so hard under the table, it moved her chair. Annie shook her head and rolled her eyes at Claudette. "Subtle, darling, very subtle. I am going to ask George to hire Frank and Brian."

The two were bouncing around on their chairs, clapping their hands silently in front of their faces.

"Before you wet yourself, there is one big thing that has to happen. I need to move Glenn out of the picture. That won't be easy."

Lillian looked like she lost a family member. "Won't be easy? Annie, how the hell is that going to work? They are tight! You get us all excited and then you drop that?"

"I didn't say it would be easy, but trust me, I promise you I will look after you two. Your husbands will be the new caretakers before I say 'I do.'"

Lillian saw Brian walking in front of the Anchor.

"Damn, I got to go. Fill me in later, bye."

She ran out the door.

Claudette had remained quiet, taking all this in. "Okay, girl, let's quit cutting bait. It's time to fish. I have a bunch of questions. You ready? You know as well as I do that George will never get rid of Glenn. Why are you so sure that will happen? But the much bigger question is the three of us sat at this very table and talked about this exact scenario. If I remember correctly, you were 'appalled' at the idea! Remember? So why the change of heart? Come on, out with it!"

Annie looked around the room and took her time responding. "I am not going to expand on this answer. You are lucky you are getting a response other than 'you need to trust me.' Let's just say for now that I plan on having more of a say in things after we are married."

"I need more about Glenn. How are you going to get rid of him?"

"I told you, Claudette, don't ask for anything else, not now!"

"It's the doctor, isn't it? He's got you thinking about all sorts of things, doesn't he?"

Annie's pause wasn't timed well; Claudette tilted her head and raised one eyebrow.

"It's not the doctor. It's the whole thing, the whole lifestyle. I love George, but I'm barely twenty-one. What will I be thinking in five years? In three years? I'm young, and so is he. This whole social class thing, maybe it will be too much for me to handle."

"Sweetie, you are preaching to the converted. You don't think I'd like to start over?"

Annie stared down at her coffee. "Maybe I'm just getting cold feet so close to the date and everything? It happens, right?"

Claudette had an awful grin on her face. "Or maybe you are just starting to think in a different direction, a better direction."

Chapter 22

Wealth is a strange animal.

It affects the people that have it more than the people that don't.

Mattie's acceptance of her son's wedding turned 180 degrees when George informed her Annie would sign the release. Annie the person had nothing to do with Mattie's mindset. Her son maintaining his share of the estate had everything to do with it.

Annie was stressing over her ability to fit into a class that wealth had created. The wealth itself was not an issue — the people were.

Fred felt bad for what his son had gone through with Annie. While his position had not changed, he knew it would have an effect on the kids' relationship. Mattie's mood had improved to the point that she had planned a small party, even though the wedding was but two weeks away.

George and Annie were swimming. The pool was eighty degrees, at least fifteen degrees warmer than the water they were used to at Maple Point. Annie said, "Your mother is a different person, any idea why?"

George was toweling off. "You are not amusing, Annie. I thought we agreed we were moving on from that?"

"I am — we are — I am sorry. It's so blatant, geez!"

Things were tense. It was only natural. A lot had happened, and the wedding date was closing in. Annie's parents were due in a couple of days, in time for Mattie's impromptu party. For John Arnold and his wife, it would be a different universe. There would be no talk about tugging barges up the Wabano or how the price of lumber was killing the island's mill business. It would be opinions on the Republicans' position on state corporate taxes. Or how Hitler's sword-rattling was good for the export business to Europe. John was a successful captain and well respected at home. He would be fine. Annie's mother would be a nervous wreck, and Annie knew it.

Annie had two mothers that were the source of most of her stress. Of course, there was another source, but it was complicated. She tried to explain it to Claudette, but all she did was give herself even more to think about.

And think about it she did.

There were thirty people invited to the party. That was in addition to the family members staying at the Rausch's.

In Annie's eyes, the initial meeting between the parents went better than expected. George and Annie did the introductions, and Annie remained glued to her mother's side. Fred, being the class act he was, immediately invited John into the smoking room.

"Why don't we let the kids get the misses settled while you and I have a chat. There are some pictures in the smoking lounge I think you would find interesting."

*

"Mom, this is your room for the next ten days."

The room was more like a "mini-wing" of the house. You entered a sitting room that was as large as the Arnolds' entire main floor. From there, two large doors that rose to the ceiling opened to a bedroom twice the size of the sitting room. There were two bathrooms and two walk-in closets on either side of the room. The window across from the king-size bed provided a panoramic view of the property where the Arnolds could see the pool, stables, and most of the grounds.

Annie watched her mother's expression. Annie was near tears. "Isn't this something, Mom?"

George saw this was a moment for Annie and her mother. On their way out, the servant said, "Mrs. Arnold, my name is Mary, I will be here twenty-four hours a day for you and Mr. Arnold. Please, if there is anything you want, anything at all, just ask."

"We will be down in a bit, George. I'm going to get Mom settled and let her catch her breath. It's been a long trip."

George winked at Annie and exited the room.

"Annie, I don't think I can do this. I am in shock. This can't be real. What are we doing here? We don't belong! What am I going to say to these people? At a party no less."

Annie opened one of the walk-in closets where only one dress was hanging. She placed it on the bed. "Mom, you get that out of your head right now! We *do* belong! You are the bride's mother. You and I and Dad have a new life, starting right now. Remember last month, we bought the suit in Sudbury for Dad to wear, and I told you that your dress was being ordered special? Well, here it is. It's from New York City, Mom! Please try it on, I'm dying to see it!"

*

"John, I want to welcome you to our home. I am embarrassed we haven't spent any time together at the lodge, but that's all going to change after the wedding!"

Fred had poured John a drink.

"Thank you, Fred. I really don't know what to say. My wife

and I spent our lives on Manitoulin Island. Sure, I've spent time in the big cities with my haulage business, but this is really overwhelming. I have to congratulate you on your success."

John laughed to himself. "My poor wife, she must be in quite a state. Thank goodness Annie is with her!"

"I want you to know, John, I'm very fond of your daughter. You did a wonderful job raising her." Fred raised his glass. "My stepson is everything to me. He is my boy, even though the records will show different. He loves Annie and will take care of her, I promise you that."

John clinked his glass. "It's such a different world from what she knows."

"They will be fine, John. They are two good kids. And the most important thing is love, and those two are in it! I know!"

*

Annie's mother looked like she belonged. Not a Gore Bay housewife — she was a Michigan socialite, and, of course, mother of the bride.

"Mom fell on the bed like a little kid when I told her the dress from New York cost eighty dollars!"

George was not smiling, barely listening. "What the hell is *he* doing here?"

Annie looked where he was looking and hoped her gasp went unnoticed. "Dr. Langer! Who invited him?"

George left Annie with her mother and father and made a beeline over to Mattie. "Mom, you invited Dr. Langer?"

"Yes, he is going to be the university board president, and his *new girlfriend* is also on a committee at the school."

George looked somewhat relieved. "He is not on the wedding invitee list, right?"

"No, he is not. What is the issue, George?"

"Nothing."

George was approached by another couple and pulled away.

Minutes later, Annie's mother and father were being introduced to Dr. Langer. Annie had one eye out for George; luckily, he was in another room.

"This is my girlfriend, Olivia. Olivia, the bride to be, Annie Arnold and her parents."

They chatted briefly, Annie's eyes scouring the room, dreading that George would appear.

"Well, very nice meeting you, Olivia, but we have to go. I promised the Flemings I would introduce my parents to them before they leave."

Dr. Langer gave Annie a hug and discreetly pressed a small piece of paper into her hand. Annie tightened her hand and moved away.

Annie's father commented. "Very nice man. You seem to know him well?"

"No, met a couple of times at Rausch functions. He works with Mattie at the university. He can be a little forward."

Annie's mother whispered, "He looks at you differently, darling."

"Oh, he does not. Come on, there are some people I want you to meet."

*

Annie hadn't dared look at the note.

She lay in bed, feeling her heart beating as she unraveled the paper. She folded it back up before seeing what it said. Her marriage to George was days away; this feeling of excitement was wrong. She could see a cartoon of Claudette's sly grin, and it wasn't good.

Then she thought about the papers she had signed. They

were now in the possession of the Rausch's lawyers.

She opened the note.

I changed my mind about my fiancée because I wasn't sure. You still have time. There is a spark between us, I know you feel it. I'm here for you.

There was a knock on her door. Annie pulled on her housecoat. Walking to the door, she thought even Dr. Langer couldn't be this bold.

Annie's mother, still in her new dress, was looking quite flustered.

"Mom, what's wrong?"

"I'm so embarrassed, Annie. I'm lost!"

Annie laughed. "Oh, Mom! You are on the other side of the house! Come on, I will take you!"

*

The wedding day had arrived.

Intimate. Classy. Tense.

Annie's parents looked the part. John, the captain, dressed in a dark blue pinstriped suit, could have been Detroit's most successful marine merchant. His wife, in her New York-designed, floor-length dress, was indeed casted correctly. She looked the bride's mother.

She was escorted to her position at the front of the great room, passing some forty guests who smiled politely, muttering whatever people mutter when they are at weddings.

Mattie had taken her place in the front row. She had the perfect seat to watch the wedding she had never wanted to see.

Fred and George strolled in slowly from the back of the room. They took in every step, smiling at every guest.

It was their moment.

The stepfather. The man who had assumed the responsibility

of loving and raising a child who was not his own. A task that he cherished and excelled at. It was his proudest moment, walking beside his stepson, who had turned into a better man than he could have hoped for.

The stepson whose best friend, also known as "Dad," was standing up for him. The person that taught him the important things in life, that guided and mentored him each step of the way. The man who had realized his wife, George's mother, was not allowing the boy to breathe. Not presenting the opportunity to see the world as it really was.

The two stood proudly, focused on John and Annie as they entered the room. The guests turned. Annie was in a white gown, holding white and yellow flowers. Her beautiful face beamed under a large yellow hat, which had become her trademark.

A gorgeous young lady, a bride whose picture would be in thousands of newspapers the following day. All eyes in the room were on her.

All eyes except Mattie's.

She remained focused on her son, not looking directly at Annie until John gave her hand to George.

"You may kiss the bride."

The two embraced, and in an instant Annie Arnold from Gore Bay was Mrs. George Rausch. A twenty-one-year-old telephone operator, the daughter of a tug boat captain, had married into one of the richest families in the world.

That scenario, for better or for worse, was captured in the expression on Mattie's face. It was neither happy nor sad. It is best described as nondescript, lacking emotion of any kind.

One might say businesslike.

The honeymoon started the following morning. The two were to fly to Lake of the Woods, where they would spend several days, hiking and sightseeing.

It was August 2nd, 1938.

Mr. and Mrs. George Rausch had made it official.

As Annie said, "Today is the first day of the rest of our lives."

Chapter 23

Annie paced around their honeymoon cabin on Lake of the Woods. George was still snoring — loudly.

They could have been eating cracked crab in Marseille, but Kenora was chosen over the French Riviera. Yet there are still some that say there is no power, no spirit, that attracts its own to the north. These two chose deer flies that draw blood by the quart over satin sheets, beluga caviar, fine wine, and the Mediterranean Sea.

Two days of hiking had taken their toll on George. Or maybe two days of "honeymooning." Either way, Annie was awake, with a new thought to stress over.

They were scheduled to return to the lodge tomorrow. Annie had yet to discuss the whole "Glenn out, Frank and Brian in" staffing change. It was headed for an argument you could sell tickets to see. One that Annie would prefer not to have.

But she had given her word to her two best friends.

Besides, she was his wife now. She wanted a say in things moving forward. What better way than to ask your husband of two days to fire one of his closest friends?

This wasn't going to end well.

They had decided to take a final canoe around the bay. Annie and George were both paddling, so they weren't facing each other.

Good thing.

"George, I have been meaning to talk to you about something for a long time. But with the wedding and all that went with it, well, here we are."

George said nothing.

"Honey, Claudette and Lillian are really struggling. Frank and Brian haven't had steady work in months. I would like to do something for them."

"Like what?"

Annie couldn't believe how quickly he said those two words, and his tone wasn't too exciting either. She was afraid he would see her neck muscles tighten as she prepared to deliver the *big* line.

"Well, maybe we could give Glenn's job to the two of them? We would get two people for the price of one and be helping out people that really need the money."

Annie cringed in anticipation of his response. Expecting everything from, silence, to screaming, to possibly the tipping of the canoe.

Whatever the action, George was now fully aware; he had a *wife*.

"And what will Glenn do?"

"You have been paying him so well for almost three years now, I'm sure he has enough to last him until he finds something else."

The heated part of the conversation had entered from the rear of the canoe.

"I can't do that! Not only has he become a good friend, I would rate his job performance an eleven on a scale of one to ten!"

Both had stopped paddling. Annie turned around, facing her new hubby. "It's what I want, George. You have to start thinking as *us*. Frank and Brian are our friends, Glenn is your friend."

"They are married to your friends, Annie, they are not *my* friends. Glenn is my friend, and you are asking me to do something I do not want to do!"

Annie took her time, turning completely around to face her husband. "You mean like signing a marriage contract? Something like that?"

George put his paddle back in the water, splashing water into the canoe. "Let's get back to the cabin. It's time to go home."

*

Flying home a day early from your honeymoon is bad enough. Not saying a word to each other for twenty-four hours is priceless.

Adding to the marital bliss, Claudette and Lillian had a party waiting for them at the lodge. They had solicited Glenn's help. A dozen or so people, including Annie's parents, were waiting to greet the *loving* couple.

Claudette, jumping up and down, put her arms around Annie. "Congratulations, Mrs. Rausch! Welcome home! We are so happy for you!"

Claudette pulled back, picking up on the mood right away. Annie's neck and shoulders felt like cement. Annie was sporting a smile that looked to have been attached with a nail gun.

George grinned at everyone and filled the nearest glass to the four-finger mark.

John hugged his daughter and raised his glass for all to hear. "From all of us, congratulations! We are glad you arrived here safely. I trust Lake of the Woods was good?"

There was a spattering of laughter, then George responded, "A few surprises, but wonderful, as I knew it would be. Thank you all for being here. Annie and I are very fortunate to have such great family and friends."

Annie hugged her mother, and her girlfriends gathered around. George, drink in hand, grabbed Glenn and walked toward the bar.

He poured Glenn a healthy drink.

"Everything okay around here?"

"Perfect. What's wrong?"

They walked to the boat. Glenn could read George's body language better than anyone, even Annie.

"Since I was old enough to date, Mom and Dad never let me forget that I was from massive wealth. They warned me that every girl I met would be after my money. Only recently did I realize how much that has affected me emotionally. It has been a load to carry, and I never realized the weight. It could be argued they were saying, 'You will not be loved, your money will overpower any feeling that a person may have for you.' Then I met this guy on Spirit Island, a person I listened to very closely. He said the same thing: 'Be careful, the people here have no idea of the depth of your wealth.' I listened to all of you, and I *was* careful. Glenn, I am starting to believe I wasn't careful enough."

"Get in, I'll drive."

Glenn took off from the dock and headed toward Gore Bay.

"What happened, George? I need details if I'm to help."

"My mother wouldn't let us marry unless Annie signed a paper limiting our financial exposure should the marriage end before I'm twenty-five. I thought she understood, I really did. But she's playing it against me, Glenn. She wants me to replace you with Frank and Brian."

Glenn slowed the boat to a crawl. "I know you have bigger issues, but please don't worry about me. You need to keep your marriage on solid ground."

"There are many more issues. I don't want to get into them right now. But none are bigger than you. Glenn, I don't want to replace you. Forget the job, you are my friend."

"And I always will be your friend too, George, here and after. George, I will be fine. I have made more money in three years than I could have made in six years anywhere else. I will never be able to repay your generosity. I will get my things together tonight and will be out in the morning. Please believe me, I am okay with this."

George couldn't look him in the eye. Not now, anyway. "I will pay you one year's severance. You will have it by the end of next week. Glenn, I am sorry, you are a special friend, forever. As you said, on this earth and after."

*

"Sweetie, you haven't been married a week. Your husband is worth millions of dollars, and from what I've seen, a pretty decent guy. That combination should have you as bubbly as champagne. Instead, God, Annie, what is going on?"

Claudette poured the bride another drink and sat back with her hands clasped behind her head.

"*You!* You are what is going on, you ass!"

Claudette unclasped her hands and slapped them down on the picnic table. "Me? I wasn't at your wedding, and I sure as hell wasn't on your honeymoon!"

"I told George that Frank and Brian needed work! Remember, you ditz? He has to fire his friend to make that happen! Holy, Claudette, did you have a lobotomy while I was gone?"

Claudette tried everything, but the sly grin broke through again. "You did? You mean it's going to happen? Yes, yes, yes!"

"Shut it! It's not for sure. I think he will, but it's not a hundred percent."

Claudette poured herself a drink, and it was gone like her stomach was on fire. "Come to think of it, Annie darling, they left in the boat!"

"They did? Shows you where my head is at. I didn't notice."

"So, girl, I've heard lots of little stuff from your mom and dad, but let's have the real scoop. Tell me everything! His mom, parties, wedding, honeymoon, all of it!"

Annie looked at her parents and her other friends chatting and walking around. "Where is Lillian?"

"She and Brian should be here soon. They had boat trouble. What else is new. I'm shocked that scow still runs."

"Let's walk a bit, Claudette. I saw the doctor again. He slipped me a note at my so-called engagement gathering!"

"Nothing like easing a person in! Holy crap, what did you do? What did it say?"

"He called off his wedding, planned a year ago, told me if I wasn't sure about mine that he was there for me."

Claudette now had one hand on a birch tree, steadying herself, shaking her head in disbelief. "What happened next?"

"Nothing. He left."

"Annie, don't leave me now. What happened, really?"

"I'm telling you, nothing. At least nothing with him. What happened with George and I before that is a whole other thing. Claudette, what I'm about to tell you goes in the vault! You got that?"

Claudette put her arm around her best friend. "We have plenty between us. That vault is getting full, and I'm sure there will be a lot more."

"George's family demanded I sign a marriage contract. If the marriage ends before he's twenty-five, I get $250,000."

Claudette suddenly looked light-headed, again reaching for the birch tree. "Fuck! $250,000? Oh my God, what a ton of money!!"

"Are you serious? Really, a ton of money? Mattie probably has that much cash in her purse. Regardless, I signed it. I'm not going anywhere, and neither is he. When he turns twenty-five in three and a half years, the contract is void."

Claudette was sitting on the ground beside her tree, looking across the North Channel. "The contract was Mattie's idea?"

"Totally. George was embarrassed by it. I believe he was. I know he loves me."

"The question is, what did it do to you?"

Annie sat on the grass beside her friend. "My mother, who has never stepped foot off this island, spent over a week in the Rausch home. Servants, stables, dinner parties, the whole show. She put on that New York dress and walked around on the arm of my father, and you know, Claudette, she could have been Mrs. Rockefeller, no one would have known. When she got there she was in tears, fearing she couldn't handle the change. She said she didn't belong. By the time she left, she was a new woman.

"Claudette, *I* am a new woman, and I love it. I am never going back, ever. So, to answer your question, it didn't change anything. It only reinforced what I realized a year ago when I was first exposed to that life. That elite class of people enjoy incredible wealth, and they protect it, as will I. I belong there, I know that now more than ever, and I'm staying there."

Claudette agreed with Annie's words without adding any of her own. That devilish grin was all that was required. "You have the best possible scenario. You have a guy you love. If indeed it is the life you want, you live happily ever after with wealth beyond your wildest dreams. If something happens, God forbid, you get an amount of money that will keep you in that league until you find what or who you want."

"You don't believe I love him, do you?"

"Annie, for the money that's in play in this game, I will believe anything you want me to believe."

Claudette hugged Annie and whispered in her ear, "Frank will be working for you soon, and we will do or say anything you want. You have my word."

*

George walked up behind Annie. She was sitting alone by Claudette's birch tree.

"I guess we should talk, but I don't quite know where to start."

The party was over. George and Glenn had been gone a long time. Annie stood up with her empty glass. "Why don't you sit. I will get us a drink. We do need to talk, honey."

George hugged her, and the two kissed like they hadn't seen each other in months. Make-up sex was imminent, but both had to bridle their lust. Glenn was inside, only yards away.

"Annie, I am sorry. I can't do anything about what has transpired. We have to decide how we will deal with it. I am afraid we will have a big problem, if you can't get over it."

"I am sorry too. I have had time to think about how unreasonable my request was to you. I am sorry, George. I will get over it, I promise. Did you tell Glenn?"

"The hardest thing I have ever had to do."

"How did he take it?"

"Like the stand-up guy he is. He will be my friend for life."

Annie kissed him. "Did you tell him it was my idea? He will hate me forever."

George kissed her again, his hands on her butt. "No, of course not. You didn't say anything to Frank or Brian. Did you?"

"No!"

"What about Claudette?"

"Honey, I have said nothing. I didn't even know if you were going to do it or not."

The wind picked up out of nowhere. The trees that were still moments before were swaying wildly.

Chapter 24

Glenn loaded the last bag into his pick-up.

Annie leaned against his truck, drinking her morning coffee.

"I want you to know this isn't goodbye. You will be missed. You are a special friend to my husband. I hope you come by, often."

Glenn smiled at her. "That's the first time I've heard you call George your husband. It's nice to hear."

Annie squinted. "Is that supposed to mean something?"

"Not at all, Annie. I like George very much, and I only want to see him happy. He really loves you. I hope you love him as much. I don't want to see him hurt."

"And you think I'm going to hurt him?"

"You are putting words in my mouth. All I said was it's nice to hear you call George your husband, because that's what he is. You seem a bit defensive? I best be going."

Glenn closed the door, his arm out the window, backing out.

"You are wrong about me, Glenn. I know what you are thinking, and you are wrong."

Glenn edged the truck forward. The look he gave Annie would stay with her for a long time. He was inside her head, and she was sure he could see her thoughts. She felt vulnerable, like he knew everything that had happened.

Or was about to happen.

"I hope Frank and Brian work out for you. Take care of your husband."

She watched the truck bounce down the driveway. The chill of the morning air felt colder than it should. It went right through her.

Frank, Brian, and the wives were expected around noon. It was a business meeting, or as close to one as possible. Annie was in agreement with George's plan of how he saw this complicated relationship moving forward.

He was to pay each thirty-five dollars per week. That was comparable to what both had made at the mill and way more than either had made at any time during the year.

He was very clear to Annie: they would be expected to put in a full day's work, and for the initial few weeks their performance would be closely watched. Annie had told George that Lillian would be helping around the lodge, cleaning and cooking. Lillian's services would be free as a thank-you to George for offering her husband work.

Claudette would not be contributing; her time taken up with her two-year-old.

Annie was falling all over George. She knew how hard this was for her husband and was going out of her way to let him know how grateful she was. That morning, George was in the bathroom shaving. In the mirror, he could see Annie's smiling face behind him, then it was gone. He could feel her hands undo his pajama bottoms, and seconds later, the shaving cream was all he had on. Annie was naked, and he watched the top of her head slowly going up and down. He asked her to get into bed; she said nothing, moving her head from side to side. He assumed that meant no. The top of her head moved faster and faster, and in a few minutes the reflection of his face blurred in the mirror and he grabbed the sink to steady his rubbery legs.

*

Frank stood at the door of the carriage house. Brian, inside, was opening the lids of some crates.

"I see several trips to the dump in my future."

George had arrived and put his hand on Frank's shoulder. "Glenn had started cleaning this out but got sidetracked with landscaping. This will be your *second* focus after you cut and stack cords and cords of wood."

George pointed at three small plies of firewood. The long winter had taken its toll. Frank said, "A few days' work for sure. Okay, let's get at it Brian."

George headed to the boat. "I will be back in a couple, banking to do."

*

Lillian had her head in the oven. Annie and Claudette, drinking coffee, watched their friend scrub.

"There was a guy and his wife at the wedding. I had never met either. He was some big shot at an insurance company that the family did business with. She had a necklace on that you couldn't imagine. I knew she saw me staring, so I complimented her on it. She said her husband 'surprised' her with it after he returned from a weekend in New York City."

Claudette put her coffee down. "Either he was really bad in New York, or she was really good the night before he left!"

Lillian bumped her head on the top of the stove while laughing.

"Exactly! Claudette, you hit it right on the head. Sorry, Lillian, no joke intended. I am sure there are so many affairs going on in that society, it would boggle your mind."

Lillian's muffled voice came from the oven. "Why do you think that?"

"What else do they have to do? All those people do is pamper themselves, trying to be as attractive as possible. And it's so social, party after party."

Lillian couldn't see Claudette's mischievous grin. Claudette said, "I know I'd sure like a taste of that life."

Lillian appeared from the oven. "Claudette, you are all talk. You wouldn't leave Frank and the baby for anything."

"Who said anything about leaving? Just a little excitement, change things up around here. You know what I mean?"

Lillian's mouth fell open. "You are awful. I could never do anything like that!'

Lillian grabbed her dirty towel and headed outside to take laundry off the line.

"Annie, honey, I hope this is understood, and I'm wasting my breath saying it out loud. I want a better life too. I would love to be in your shoes, but timing is everything. I will do whatever I have to to get ahead. You know that, right?"

"Sweetie, I don't know what else I can do for you. Frank is working now. There are none of Detroit's elite here for you to mingle with."

"Money!"

"What?"

"Oh, geez Annie, you have $250,000 for starters. You have millions more ahead of you. If and when you decide you want it sooner than later, I am here for you! Just like Dr. Langer said to you!"

Annie shook her head, looking at Claudette in contempt. "You are bad. I am starting to think you are bad for me as well. I told you, even though you don't believe me, I love my new husband. I should never have told you all the other stuff. I'm afraid it's turned you into a crazy person!"

"You kept that doctor's note. You didn't tell George about it. Why not? You have changed since you signed the contract,

Annie, and don't tell me you haven't. You know yourself — admit it! It's not George *and* the money, it's the money *and* George!"

Annie walked out of the lodge saying nothing, leaving Claudette sipping her coffee and smiling. Claudette's work was done for the day.

*

George had not seen Johnny Griggs for a month.

"The married man in the flesh! Congrats, George! Let me buy you a drink. How are you and your beautiful wife?"

"We are great, Johnny."

George shook Johnny's hand and continued past him to look at a familiar painting.

Johnny toasted George. "That painting does something for you, doesn't it?

"I actually thought about it last night, funny enough."

Johnny took it off the wall. "From me to you, have a long and wonderful life with Annie."

"Oh, Johnny, I couldn't."

"Too late, it's yours."

George handed Johnny twenty dollars. Only if you take this to replace it." The painting, showing two men in a boat, pointing at something on Maple Point, was always somewhere in George's mind. It would now hang over the mantle at the lodge.

He wasn't sure why he'd walked to that painting today, or even why he walked into the Anchor Inn. But he did, and the painting was now in the back of his boat screaming across the water to Mudge Bay. He turned left toward Maple Point; his mind was on Glenn. He was the only other person that would appreciate that painting. It would mean nothing to Annie; he would tell her it was a wedding present from Johnny and leave it that.

*

Brian and Frank were earning their pay. Both looked like a cardiac event could happen at any time.

"Warm today, George! Brian was commenting on how out of shape we are! You can't tell, can you?"

Brian was laughing, choking, trying to catch his breath.

"George, Frank and I want you to know how grateful we are for this opportunity. We know how close you are with Glenn. Please be assured we will work hard. You won't be disappointed."

"I am not going to lie to you guys, I love Annie to death. She asked me for a favor for her friends. That's the story, no sense putting any other spin on it. But listen, I like you guys, and we will be fine."

*

"What is that?"

"A wedding present from Johnny!"

Annie watched George step down the ladder. "That old thing off the stained back wall at the Anchor Inn? That's it? Not exactly breaking him, is it?"

"I love this painting! Look, it's called 'Maple Point'."

She kissed George on the cheek. "As long as you like it!"

She smacked him on the butt and went outside to have a drink with the girls.

*

"I want you to tell Lillian how much you paid for your mother's dress."

"Eighty bucks."

Lillian nearly inhaled the ice from her glass. "Holy, Brian

would drop dead if I told him my dress cost that."

Claudette lowered her sunglasses. "Really? Maybe I should tell Frank!"

Annie laughed out loud. Lillian just glared at Claudette and left to attend to more chores.

"Are you ever going to tell her about your doctor admirer?"

"No! God, no! Claudette, you are starting to bug me. Would you get off this whole thing!"

"Not to beat this to death, but I'm going to let you in on something, Annie. I am twenty years old, I have a baby and a husband that I've been with since I was fourteen. I have never slept with anyone else. He will never amount to anything, and I will never get off this island. I am sitting across from my meal ticket and my only hope to change that. I'm not asking for anything right now. But as sure as hell, an opportunity for both of us might materialize in the near future that will get both of us what we *really* want. So, when you are ready to talk to me, I mean *really* talk to me, I am ready to listen."

*

Two days had passed, and the wood was piled. Frank had moved to cleaning out the garbage from the carriage house. George sat outside, reading the paper, listening to the description of everything. Frank was walking out to the truck.

Brian and Lillian were in town, grocery shopping and doing a mail run.

"George, you better have a look at this."

There was a box with the lid open.

George walked over and looked inside.

Frank grabbed his arm. "Don't touch."

"Dynamite?"

"That's what it looks like to me."

*

Lillian handed Annie four envelopes addressed "Mr. and Mrs. G. Rausch." Claudette, looking over her shoulder, said, "That's you now, girl. You don't need permission, open them!"

Annie proceeded to read the congratulations from people she didn't know. She got to the last envelope and by this point was paying no attention to who it was from. The card was hand-painted on parchment paper, delicate, a real work of art. The picture was of a young girl in a long white wedding gown. She was crying in front of a fountain, preparing to throw something into the water. The card was not signed. Annie handed it to Claudette and Lillian.

"Beautiful, isn't it? But they forgot to sign it."

The girls acknowledged its beauty and handed it back to Annie.

Annie picked up the envelopes and walked over to the trash. She noticed the envelope of the unsigned card.

No return address, except on the flap, in tiny type: *President, Board of Directors, Michigan University.*

Chapter 25

"I wonder how old that is?"

"George, I'm no expert, but I remember a guy at the mill telling me it can become unstable after a while."

"Unstable?"

"You know, ignite before it's supposed to or the fuse doesn't work right. I think we need to get someone from Gore Bay or Little Current to get rid of this."

"Amen to that. Close it up. I will talk to someone in town in the next few days."

*

George sipped on a Jim Beam, studying the expression on the man pointing at Maple Point. He wasn't paying any attention to the cards Annie placed in front of him.

"I don't know any of those people. And what, pray tell, are you looking for? You have been staring at that old painting for twenty minutes."

"Do you not wonder what they are pointing at? What do you think they see?"

"I don't know, and I really don't care. Who are the McGraths?"

George picked up the cards. "They are friends of the family.

Oil-rich, own thousands of acres of land in Texas."

He sifted through the other cards, holding one up to Annie. He laughed. "Well, isn't that a sincere wish? They couldn't take the time to sign it? And who would send a wedding card with the bride crying?"

Annie felt her heart skip a beat. That card was not supposed to be there.

"I was thinking the same thing! I couldn't believe it either!"

George shook his head and went back to his painting. Annie cleaned up the cards and left the room. She looked at the bride on the front of the card. She knew exactly who it was from and the message it was sending. She carried it to her room. Claudette was screaming, sarcastically, inside her head, *Why, are you keeping the card? You love your husband, throw it out!*

Annie didn't have an answer. Claudette was right. Why did she keep his business card? Why wasn't she telling George? Why was she keeping this unsigned message of an unhappy bride?

She had everything a girl could ask for, a loving husband and life's highway paved with gold. What was missing? Maybe the taste of the upper class was just a tease, and she wanted to see more. Maybe she really didn't love him. She was only eighteen when they met. Or maybe it was Mattie? She would never be able to meet expectations. She would never be Annie; she would be George's wife.

*

"You tired, honey?"

She hadn't heard George come in the room. She tucked the card under the pillow.

"No, just daydreaming, I guess."

She hopped up, hugged George, and said, "I'm late honey, I said I'd be at Mom's by now."

They walked out of the room arm in arm. George looked at the bed behind him. Enough of the card was out in the open for all to see.

*

Everyone had gone home.

George watched Annie push the throttle down, turn around the point and out of sight.

He sat in front of the painting. This time his mind wasn't totally on the men in the boat. He was also thinking about the lady in the boat that just left to visit her mother. Why did she keep the unsigned card of a crying bride? And who would send that?

He poured himself a drink, his face six inches from the canvas. He was reminded of the old man in the Anchor who said, "*When they look for it again, it won't be there.*"

Look for what again? The cabin and the spirit that George experienced years ago? That was his best guess. He thought about the crying bride. He thought, when *he* looked for the innocent eighteen-year-old girl he fell in love with, *she won't be there.* He felt a chill come over his body. Maybe he was thinking too much, freaking himself out. But the chill was soon replaced by a feeling of calm. A feeling that was all too familiar.

He turned to see the same thing, present in the corner. It was looking out the window at the glassy water of the North Channel. He heard words, but they didn't seem to be coming from the figure. It sounded like, "You will never leave here." Words he had heard years ago.

He said, "Who are you? What does that mean?"

He looked at something rise above and turn to him. He thought he could make out an animal's face, skeletal in appearance.

"You will be happy, George, at peace forevermore."

He tried to move toward it but could not move his legs. George screamed, "How do you know my name? *What are you?*"

The feeling of calm was gone, and so was the vision. The sun shone brightly through the window, illuminating the men in the painting, pointing at Maple Point.

*

It was the first time Annie and her mother had been alone since the wedding. They sat in the backyard, drinking lemonade. The swing set Annie played on as a kid was rusting quietly beside them.

"A little different look than the Rausch's, eh?"

"When you were first married to Dad, I mean a week after, did you ever question what you had done?"

"I still do!"

"Seriously!"

"Honey, every woman does. It's a huge change; it's only natural. Are you stressed, honey?"

"Yep. I'm thinking about things I shouldn't be."

"Like?"

"Life on my own."

Annie's mother's body language said everything. She shifted in her chair, adjusting her dress, and made an unnatural hand movement toward her face. "Something happen you want to tell me about?"

"It's the whole class thing, the money. Mom, I really feel comfortable there, and I want to experience more, I think. Maybe just more life!"

"That isn't what I meant. I was asking about George?"

Annie took her time in answering. So much time that her mother didn't really need to hear what she had to say. "I have got a lot going on in my head, Mom. I love him, but it is confusing right now. I wish I could make sense of it."

"Let things play out, honey. Newlywed jitters, it will all work out."

*

George slept late. He rolled over; his wife was gone. Frank was loading the truck for another run to the dump.

"Have you seen Annie?"

"Went for a walk with Claudette. You going to find out about this dynamite? Pretty soon it will be the last box to be moved. Remember, Claudette and I are leaving at noon today. The baby is going to the doctor this afternoon."

"I remember. Brian and Lillian are arriving when you guys leave. I won't be going anywhere today. Brian has the truck and the water looks ugly."

"George, I heard high winds, four-foot rollers for the next few days."

*

The two girls were standing on the western extremity of Maple Point. Their hair was straight out behind them, and the waves were smashing the shore.

"I am a wreck. I talked to Mom yesterday for hours, I'm sure she thinks I'm losing my mind. I don't know what end is up."

"What do you want, Annie? What do you *really* want? When you figure that out, I will help you get there."

An extra large curler hammered the rocks in front of them, sending spray over their heads.

"Okay, Claudette, hear me out. I meet the richest man in the world and fall in love with him at nineteen years old. I sign a marriage contract, me, a hayseed from Manitoulin Island, a marriage contract, so his mommy can protect her little boy's money. As this is transpiring I'm introduced to a class of people that I fall in love with: parties, limousines, endless cash. Then there is an older doctor that I am *very* attracted to, chasing me down in front of my new husband!"

Annie took a deep breath and put her wet head in her hands. Two seconds later, her head popped up and in a much softer voice she said, "You know, I think I want my cake *and* I want to eat it to. I love George, or at least I think I do. But I want it all. I love the money, and I love the life those people live. The doctor, well, he is so handsome and he makes my heart race. There, best friend, does that answer your question about, 'what does Annie want'?"

"Annie, I think that does answer my question. You answered it by telling me what you *have* is not what you want. You want more!"

Another wave crashed the rocks, drenching the two of them. They didn't seem to mind. As a matter of fact, it became rather funny. They sat, lost in thought, while the spray from numerous rollers soaked them to the skin.

"Have you talked to a lawyer?"

Annie wiped the water from her eyes. "No. About what?"

"You signed the marriage contract and didn't seek legal advice?"

"Claudette, I wasn't buying a house. I was marrying a man that I love whose mother was protecting their money."

"Exactly! You even told me when you heard the amount was $250,000, you thought it wasn't enough."

"I didn't say it like that. What are you getting at anyway?"

"Maybe the contract isn't fair. Maybe you can do much better?"

"I've signed it. I'm married."

"Go see a lawyer."

"Behind George's back?"

Claudette laughed, getting a mouthful of spray from the crashing surf. "Behind his back? This from the lady who has a horny doctor's card under her pillow?"

Their hair soaked, water trickling down their faces, they started back, walking slowly, arms around each other's backs.

"You can always divorce him. That option is open at any time."

"No! Did you not hear one word I said? I care for him, Claudette. Geez, I'm young; I'm not sure I even know what real love is! But I think that's what I have with George!"

They were now stopped. Claudette, arms around Annie's neck, looked directly at her like they were about to kiss.

"There is another possibility."

Annie looked at Claudette, waiting to hear the idea. Claudette dropped her arms, looking past Annie toward the wild water.

"Let's say a situation presented itself where *no one* would ever find out and..."

Annie screamed, "Claudette, shut your fucking mouth!"

Annie pushed her so hard, Claudette fell on her ass. Brushing herself off, she rose to her feet. "Well, isn't that what we are talking about?"

"No! God, no! It never crossed my mind!"

"Then divorce him."

"I am not divorcing him."

"Listen, it won't be tomorrow, it may be never, or maybe it will. You will never know. Situations may present themselves. You say he believes 'something' is talking to him? Who knows what that could mean?"

Annie looked away, tears in her eyes. "I love him, Claudette. It's not his fault I want more. And *never, ever* talk about his visions out loud again! You promised me! *And* quit talking about that other stuff. You are scaring me to death. What's gotten into you?"

Annie was now crying. "Oh God, I can't believe we even talked about that."

They stopped, Claudette looking wild-eyed. "Annie, you will look after me. I *will* have a better life, a life like yours, and you will have the life you really want. You will never know, if and when anything ever happened. Promise me you will see a lawyer?"

Annie said nothing the rest of the way back to the lodge.

*

Frank was in his normal trance, not talking, trying to avoid the potholes.

"Frank, you need to listen to me, and what is to be said never goes outside this truck."

Claudette slid over, their faces, inches apart.

"You and I are going to be rich beyond our wildest dreams, but we have to do something to get there."

Frank pulled the truck to the side of the gravel road.

"If George were to have an accident or be in a situation where an accident could be staged, we need to try to facilitate that. It may be tomorrow, it may be three years from now, or it may be never. If the opportunity presents itself, we cash in."

It was hard to tell what was open wider, Frank's eyes or his mouth. "Are you out of your mind? Who the hell are you? Do you know what you are talking about?"

"I do, Frank, and you better be hearing me."

"Oh, I hear you alright. You are sick! Now you listen to me. I will never do anything of the sort, and neither will you! Now let's forget this talk ever happened. Geez, Claudette! What the hell has gotten into you?"

Claudette slid over to the passenger door, still glaring at her husband.

Frank pulled the truck back on the road and headed home.

Chapter 26

The sun was just rising out of the water. George was sound asleep, alone, in bed. Annie was already two hours into a four-hour ride to Sudbury in George's truck.

She had told George she was taking her mother to see a gravely ill friend at the hospital.

Mr. Christopher Mahon was the highest-profile lawyer in Northern Ontario. He had recently won a large divorce settlement for the wife of the CEO of Falconbridge Mines.

She had called only the day before, but once she identified herself, she was told to come in at her convenience.

Annie felt her heart racing and short of breath as she handed the marriage document to Mr. Mahon. He was seated behind a massive desk, making him look like a child playing in his father's office.

"You have been married but a few days. Is there something other than this document you would like to discuss? Please, Mrs. Rausch, our relationship is and always will be totally confidential."

Annie cleared her throat, praying words would come out unimpeded. "No, I discussed this contract with close friends, and they suggested I seek a legal opinion."

"A wise suggestion. A woman in your social position, globally recognized, should have legal guidance."

Annie had never heard herself described as "globally recognized.' She was calming, her heart back to normal.

"I know you have traveled from the island and plan on returning later today. A long day indeed. Why don't you relax in the boardroom? I will have a brunch brought in. My assistant and I will go over this contract for the next couple of hours and get you on your way as soon as possible."

Annie read the paper, drank a gallon of coffee, and paced around the room for over two hours. She heard the lawyer more than once talking on his phone. *He is still taking calls? He is supposed to be working on my contract!*

She had been in the office over three hours when Mr. Mahon opened the door.

"My apologies. It took longer than I expected. I solicited the opinion of two colleagues from Toronto, and the calls were long-winded. I guess that should be expected; lawyers are paid to talk!"

The faintest of smiles appeared on Annie's face.

"The contract, as you would expect, is well done. But it is not air-tight by any means. My opinion, which is shared by both colleagues, is it would not hold up should you decide to contest. God forbid, Mrs. Rausch, that day should ever come."

Annie responded, "In words I would understand, please, why would it not hold up?"

"We would make the case that you signed it 'under duress,' a young girl, hopelessly in love, then at the last minute told she must enter into a contract to make the marriage happen. Furthermore, you were not privy to the magnitude of your husband's wealth. We feel the publicity this case would receive would be cause enough for the Rausch family to agree to a substantially larger amount."

The drive home went by quickly. It took over four hours, but Annie was consumed in thought.

The next morning, Annie told Claudette about the visit to Mr. Mahon. The days were long gone where Claudette tried to hide her real feelings from Annie.

"You see, Annie, nothing but money awaits. You said yourself, $250,000 was a joke!"

"I did not! You are driving me crazy. It's a good thing I'm not seeing you for a few days. I need to get my head screwed on straight."

*

Frank's weather forecast was accurate. The winds around Manitoulin Island were at a summer high and had been for almost a week. The trees around the lodge had a different sound. The sound was an invitation to listen more intently, possibly sending a message or even a warning. One of them had to come down sooner or later; it was wild.

There was a different feeling in the air, a feeling of insignificance. The islanders were spectators at best, incapable of changing what was in store. Nature was in control, reminding everyone where the real power of the north resided.

The three guys looked at the box of dynamite from a distance.

George moved toward it slowly and cautiously opened the lid. There were six, maybe eight sticks. He pointed at the bottom few that actually looked wet. "I wouldn't touch those ones."

Brian took a step back. "I wouldn't touch any of them, thank you very much."

George closed the lid. "I'm not going into town until tomorrow. Let's have lunch and a beer."

The wind gusted, and there was a noise after the three left the carriage house. George looked back. The door had blown open. He walked back and noticed the lid to the dynamite box was open.

He knew he had just closed it.

"Frank, you saw me close the lid on the box, right?"

Brian added, "We both did, why?"

George looked back again. "No reason."

*

Lillian looked at the food on the picnic table, hoping it wasn't going to blow away. Annie placed a tray of beer in front of the group.

"Too bad Claudette stayed home today. This looks like a party in the making!"

Frank unconsciously put his head in his hands when he heard his wife's name.

"The little one's not feeling too good."

George lifted his beer. "Cheers, everyone. Lillian, thanks for the lunch. And honey, here's to lucky thirteen!"

Annie looked totally lost. "Lucky thirteen?"

"We have been married thirteen days!"

Brian applauded. "What do you want Frank and I working on this afternoon?"

"You guys have been working hard. Let's enjoy the lunch, have a couple of beers, and see what happens."

George drank two beers while the rest were still on their first. There was a devious, playful sparkle in his eye.

"Too bad it's so rough. I feel like taking the boat on a tear! What do you guys feel like doing?"

Not a word.

"Come on, we have to do something!"

Annie smiled at him and shrugged, not knowing what he wanted to hear. She thought about her husband's toast to thirteen days. Why would he think of that? What possible special meaning would that amount of days have to him? A part of her felt like it had been thirteen months or even thirteen years. Another part felt like the wedding was yesterday. If everyone only knew about the marriage contract, the lawyer's visit and everything else in her young mind.

Lillian had settled on her husband's lap. She was laughing and looked like the happiest person on earth. It struck Annie as funny; here was Lillian, the same girl who sat at the Anchor Inn complaining about having no money. Now, thirty-five dollars a week later, not a trouble in the world. George had a thousand bucks in his dresser drawer! Why wasn't she that happy?

It had to be something other than money. Or maybe the *amount* of money. That might be it; enough money to move off the island and up to that class, with no strings, no contract! You didn't need fifty million dollars. Not anywhere near that; $250,000 would be enough — or a doctor's income. Annie shook her head. That wasn't a good thought.

Lillian pinched Brian's leg, and the two started gathering dishes. Annie stayed put, enjoying the wind blowing her hair all over her head.

"Frank, let's take another look in the carriage house."

Frank downed his beer and grabbed one for the road. George was ahead when there was a huge crack. A limb fell to the ground, narrowly missing the two of them.

George laughed. "I'm glad I got up when I did. A few seconds later and I would have had some kind of headache!"

"I will grab the saw, boss. I will have this put away in a few minutes."

George was pleased to see the carriage house door was closed. He entered and couldn't believe his eyes. How in hell was the lid open again? He looked around, expecting to see a spirit or vision of some kind.

There was nothing.

The dynamite didn't seem as scary as it did before lunch. Or before the two or three beers. But George still had all his senses. He was by no means diving into the box, despite the lid lying open, twice.

Frank looked at the explosives. "I used this once. I was at the mill, I had just started working there. Me and the foreman were asked to move some rock to widen the road for the loggers. Have you ever heard this stuff go off?"

"No. Well, once, but from miles away. Fred and I were on *The Rose*. They were building the highway, here on Spirit Island."

"It is loud! We were behind cover, about fifty yards away. The rubber tires they laid over the rock weren't done correctly. A piece of rock the size of my ass flew over my head from fifty yards away! Powerful, George, mighty powerful."

The thought of the power excited George.

The exhilaration of the unknown. He remembered the first time he was alone in his boat on Lake St. Clair. He was thirteen. He watched the needle on the speedometer pass forty. He felt the wind in his air, the roaring of the motor, full-out. He was on top of the world; he felt so alive.

He looked at Frank, his eyebrows raised. "Let's light one."

If the residents across Mudge Bay were outside, they heard Frank.

"*What!* Are you kidding?"

George stepped a little closer, reaching into the box.

Frank grabbed his hand. "Don't do that!"

"The ones on top look okay, fuses are there."

"Why do you want to do this?"

"Why not? I hold it, you light it, I throw it out the door. Simple."

Frank scratched his head, leaning closer, inspecting the two sticks on top. "Are you sure?"

"Get your matches out."

George reached in the box, lifting the stick gently out. Frank looked like he was going to puke, fumbling with the match. George moved the fuse and looked at the door, positioning himself for the throw.

"Okay, Frank, you ready?"

"Don't wait around, George. You toss it the second it's lit, and for God's sake, don't miss the door!"

Frank struck the match.

Nothing happened; in fact, the match snapped in half and fell to the ground. Frank was breathing heavily. His hands were not working well, like it was the first time he had used them.

"Frank, come on!"

He tried again, this time a flame. It touched the fuse, and a thin ember ran toward the end of the stick.

"Throw it!"

George took half a step toward the door and hurled it at the water.

The crack from the dynamite rolled over the choppy waters of the North Channel like thunder. Frank was crouched, hands tightly clasped over his ears, facing the corner of the carriage house.

George was laughing hysterically. "Holy shit, Frank! Could you believe that bang? It blew a hole in the ground. Look, the water from the bay has already filled it up!"

George was smiling, giddy, and in a matter of seconds he grabbed another stick. "Stand up, Frank. Light it!"

Frank slowly rose to his feet, trying to ignite another match on his way up. This time the match lit on first strike. George was ready, the fuse inches from the flame. The ember caught, only this time it moved more quickly toward the stick. He turned to the door, and his heart stopped.

Brian was standing in the doorway. "What the fuck happened? What was that explosion?"

Annie was ten feet behind Brian, panic-stricken, crying,

"What is going on?"

Both Brian and Annie saw the lit dynamite in George's hand.

With the door blocked, George turned to the open window and threw the stick.

It didn't make it.

The dynamite hit the frame of the window, dropping to the floor inside.

Frank was still crammed in the corner of the house as George dove away from the window behind some boxes.

The ensuing screams of terror never made it to the North Channel. They were lost in the towering pines of Spirit Island.

The noise from this blast was many times louder than the first. The explosion shredded the side of the carriage house. Broken glass and splintered wood sprayed in all directions.

Lillian ran down from the lodge. Her husband was unconscious on his back, where the wall used to stand. There were growing pools of blood under his head and under his arm. Lillian screamed his name and threw herself on the ground beside his body.

Annie was just getting to her feet, crying. Blood ran down her leg, and her arm bled from above her elbow. Her vision blurred, pain shooting into her hand.

"George, George! Where are you?"

She went inside what was left of the garage. She put her hand over her mouth. "Oh God, Jesus no!"

The first person she saw was Frank, squirming on the floor. He was trying to stand. Blood ran down his forehead, he was wiping his eyes, trying to see.

"Annie? Annie? Is that you, are you okay?"

Annie was in shock, shaking uncontrollably. "Are you alright? Where is George? My arm hurts, my hand is numb, but I think I'm alright."

Lillian was screaming, a few feet away. "Help me! I think

he's dead! Oh God no, help me!"

Frank ripped his shirt and wrapped it around his head. He stood and felt a sharp pain above his knee. He saw a foreign object coming out of his leg. He pulled at it, screaming in pain. Another inch of wood came out. He took the rest of his shirt, wrapped it around his thigh, and moved to Brian.

Annie heard George moaning under a pile of wood and glass. She pulled away the debris and saw his face looking up. It was a smear of red. Blood trickled from two small cuts on either side of head. His eyes were open but fixed, and they weren't focusing on anything. His left arm was trapped awkwardly under his back. He was bleeding from the same shoulder. It appeared the force of the explosion had blown him into the air, landing on his back, with his arm underneath. He was conscious, obviously in shock.

"Where is Dad? Is he okay? Was he hurt?" He grabbed Annie's shoulder with his good arm. Annie, talk to me, where is Dad? Is Frank okay?"

Annie, her face soaked in tears, said, "Your dad was never here, George. Tell me what happened? Yes, Frank looks okay."

"My shoulder hurts, my head, my head is..."

George passed out.

Frank yelled, "Brian is breathing, he is mumbling."

There was a big gash on the back of Brian's head, and blood was pumping out of his arm.

"Someone, get me a towel or rag, fuck, something."

Annie got up and yelled at Lillian, who was huddled over husband.

"Move! Get, towels, shirts, whatever you can find. We have to tie off Brian's arm and pack his head. Fuck, move Lillian, move!"

It was an unbelievable scene. Like a war zone. A very bloody one. There was glass and wood everywhere. A portion of the carriage house wall was gone. There was a hole in the roof you could climb through. A chemical stench from the exploding TNT hung in the air.

Brian had turned his back against the blast, and wood and glass had carved a hole in the back of his head. A large splinter was still in his arm, and he was losing massive amounts of blood. Lillian was the only person spared from the explosion. She had arrived a minute after the second blast. The horror of the moment and the dire state of her husband had rendered her useless. She, like everyone else, could make no sense of what had happened or what was going on.

Annie moved back to her husband, who was trying to get up. His arm hung in an ugly manner from his left side. Annie held him up the best she could. Her leg was cut in several places, some glass still embedded in the skin. She leaned right into his face. "We need to get to a hospital! I don't know if Brian is going to live, George!"

George started weeping. He screamed, "What have I done? I'm so sorry! Oh, someone help us!"

Lillian handed Frank some clothing and a few rags. He packed the back of Brian's head and wrapped a towel over that. He tied it off with the belt from his own pants. He stood, looking around. "Where the fuck is the truck? We need to get to Little Current, now!"

Lillian finally spoke, "The truck? It will take way too long! Brian has no time!"

Annie screamed, "The boat, we will take the boat!"

Frank looked at Brian, then at George. He looked up at the swaying trees, which were making a howling, awful sound. Frank looked past the pines to the massive, churning water of the North Channel

"Annie, look at the wind, look at the size of those waves."

Chapter 27

Shock is a result of the body not getting enough blood flow. There was no lack of blood flow on Maple Point. Everyone was covered in it.

Even Lillian, who was spared the blast, was drenched in her husband's blood.

The lodge sat on six hundred acres of land — a private, reclusive setting. What George and Annie would give now to have neighbors close by.

There was no one. They were on their own, wracked in terror, all in various degrees of shock.

Brian was the most seriously injured. The tourniquet on his arm was not doing the job. It had to be redone or he would bleed to death in short order. He was awake, moaning in horrible pain. His sounds were muffled by the towel tied around his head.

George was in and out of consciousness; his shoulder looked to be separated. But miraculously, he was not bleeding to any great extent. The shock or blow to his head had him asking about people that weren't there, but then in the next sentence he was totally coherent.

Other than Lillian, Frank was in the best shape of the group. He was injured and needed medical care but was able to move and looked to be taking control.

He continued to stare at the water, uncertain about taking the boat. But time was up; Brian was near death, and they had to act.

"Annie, can you walk?'

Annie had wrapped her leg. She had little strength in her right arm. The bruising was already showing below the elbow, and blood trickled from the glass in her skin.

"Yes, get Brian to the boat. I will help George."

Lillian, still screaming, was more of a hindrance than anything else but tried to help her husband up.

Frank lifted Brian to his feet. "Lillian, get the fuck out of the way. Go to the dock, make sure everything is cleared from the boat."

George was standing, walking around in circles. "Annie, I can walk by myself, take care of yourself."

"You can't walk! Put your arm around my neck."

Annie put her good arm around George's waist.

Lillian was on her knees. The wind and the waves hitting the dock made it impossible for her to stand.

Frank was bearing so much of Brian's weight that only Brian's toes were dragging on the ground.

"I don't know, Annie, the waves are big in the bay. What's it going to be like in the channel?"

Annie looked at the bay then toward the east. Frank was right; the water was awful, and the wind felt like it was increasing.

"We'd be well over an hour in the truck, and people would have to ride in the back. I still say we take the boat, forty-five minutes tops, to Little Current."

"Annie, not in this water. We will be way more than that. I think we should go back to the truck."

"Frank, we are here, let's go, we are taking the boat!"

Lillian undid the bow, trying to keep it steady while Frank loaded Brian into the back seat. His arm was pumping out blood;

the tourniquet had completely loosened off. Annie put George in the opposite rear seat. Frank sat in the middle and started working on the tourniquet. Annie moved in behind the wheel. Lillian sat beside her in the front passenger seat. George's eyes were glued to the blood gushing from Brian's arm. Tears flowed down his face.

"What have I done? Oh Brian, I'm so sorry. Oh God, please save him. I'm so sorry!"

Frank watched Annie holding her arm, her head moving up and down from the pain.

"Are you sure? You are okay to drive?"

"I'm okay right now. Let's see how it goes."

With the tourniquet repaired, Frank moved to the front passenger seat. Lillian took her place in the back between her husband and George.

They pulled into the bay. The boat was rocking crazily. Annie looked at Frank. "It's not to late to take the truck," he said.

Annie looked into the North Channel, having second thoughts.

When she was a little girl, she rode on her father's tug, towing a barge to an outward island. She remembered the water being as rough as it was today. They were in wide-open water, the tug's bow disappearing from time to time into the breaking waves. The cable snapped and the barge went adrift. They tried to catch the barge, but by the time it was safe to do anything, the barge was being hammered against a rocky shoal. She remembered she and her father being helpless as the barge took on water and eventually sank.

She looked at Brian and Lillian, then back at Frank.

"We have to go now!"

"Annie, keep the nose either with or against these breakers. If we go sideways, this girl is going to capsize."

Mudge Bay was forty minutes in good water from Little

Current. Back in the day, Annie and George had made it in twenty-nine minutes, on water as smooth as glass, with the boat pinned the entire way.

That wasn't happening today.

Annie had only been driving fifteen minutes, and her arm had deteriorated considerably. The waves were relentless, jerking the boat, trying to tear the wheel out her hand.

George was telling Lillian how to maintain pressure on her husband's wounds. He was yelling to his wife and Frank where to steer the boat. With the sound of the motor, wind, and crashing waves, no one heard a word he said.

The trip was well into its second hour, and they were only at Honora Bay. They had forty minutes more to Little Current. They had not achieved a speed of more than ten miles an hour since leaving the lodge. The normal wind pattern was from the west, which would have at least made the trip downwind. But as luck, or lack of it, would have it, the stormy weather was brought in by high winds from the east. They were bucking four-footers the entire way.

Annie started weeping. Her head was drooped down over her chest. "Frank, I can't do it anymore. My arm is killing me, I can't hold the wheel!"

Frank looked back at Lillian, then Brian, who appeared unconscious. George's eyes were glassy, but he was awake and yelled, "Frank, take over for Annie. Brian is not going to make it!"

Frank grabbed the wheel, and Annie slumped into the passenger seat.

The sky was purple black. It was from another world. No one should be on the channel today, in any size boat. It was walls of water, no shoreline to see. If anything, the wind had increased again, the rollers getting larger.

Annie looked back at her husband of thirteen days. He was

staring at Brian, his face drained of blood. George looked at Annie and started to cry more. Annie had never seen that face before. She saw a small boy that was scared, ashamed of what he had done. Fred was not there for him, like he had been most of his life. George was alone, having to live with what he had done. His eyes, filled with tears, were asking Annie to make some sense of this. Annie heard Frank groan loudly, watching him put his hand over his bloody eye.

Frank was suffering.

His injuries were taking their toll.

"Annie, I can't drive any faster, or we will be swamped. We may be another hour!"

Lillian heard Frank's words and screamed, "Brian might be dead already! He can't last an hour. We have to speed up!"

Frank's hands were frozen white from the death grip he had on the wheel. He peered ahead, trying to squeeze out another mile per hour in an effort to save his friend. Another thirty minutes passed. It felt like they had gone nowhere.

Then hell broke loose.

Lillian screamed hysterically.

Annie turned. George was standing, one foot on the side of the boat. Annie could not believe what she was seeing.

"George!"

The rollers were higher than ever. The boat heaved from side to side. A huge wave rocked the port side of the boat, and Frank turned the wheel sharply, trying to keep the boat from being swamped.

Annie was thrown against the side of the boat. She looked back again.

George was gone.

He had plunged over the side of the boat, disappearing under an enormous wave.

"Turn the boat around! Turn it, turn it!"

Annie was pointing behind the boat. Frank made a wide turn, trying not to flip the boat.

"There, I see him! Do you see?"

Frank yelled at Annie, "Sit down or you will be next!"

"Frank, there! See him?"

George's head appeared for a brief second and was gone. Moments later, his head appeared for the second time. The wind was insane, and the waves could not get any bigger. Frank was having a hard time keeping the boat from flipping; he couldn't keep it in one place.

Annie, on the verge of a breakdown, was screeching, "I don't see him! Frank, I can't see him! He has to be here, keep it right here!"

She threw herself to the floor of the boat, her hands covering her head, screaming. Lillian tried to help her up. Frank circled the boat again and again.

They looked for ten minutes.

Nothing.

The waves crashed against the boat, tossing it like a toy. The wind maintained that horrible drone, sounding more ominous than ever. Annie looked in the water, then looked at Lillian holding her dying husband.

The floor of the boat was soaked in his blood.

She looked at Frank. A mix of blood and tears ran from his cheeks, into the corners of his mouth. He stared at her, saying nothing, wondering what do next. She looked in the water again, expecting to see George come up.

This was so surreal, unexplainable. She continued to look at each roller, hope fading and reality creeping in more with each passing wave.

Her husband had to be there. They were just married. How could this be? This was a nightmare. It couldn't be real. Then she heard the crushing words.

"We need to go, Annie. Brian is still alive. We can save him."

With a blank look, in a beaten, solemn tone, she said, "I can't leave George."

"He's gone, Annie. No one could last in these waves. He drowned."

Her head didn't move. The spray from the water that had consumed her husband pelted her face.

Frank turned the boat back into the pounding waves and headed toward Little Current.

Annie sat in the passenger seat, her eyes open, facing forward and seeing nothing. Frank held the wheel, his eye now swollen shut, blood dripping from his chin.

Annie turned her head toward Frank, "He's really gone, isn't he?"

Frank didn't move, nodding.

She continued to look at him, trying to make sense of this cataclysm.

Frank had done everything humanly possible in this disaster. Actions beyond heroic. If Brian was to live, it was because of Frank and Frank alone. He was a train wreck, but he was hell-bent on getting everyone to safety.

But he didn't save George.

He saved everyone else.

Why did he turn the boat so suddenly when George was standing up? Was it really because of a wave?

Claudette.

No, there was no way.

Frank was the one insistent on driving the truck to Little Current. He didn't want to take the boat; he was worried about everyone, including George.

Annie continued to stare at him, but he didn't notice. His eyes were straight ahead, water smashing off his bloody face.

Chapter 28

It was dusk.

Annie had arrived in this harbor hundreds of time in her young life, most of those times with her father in one of his tugs.

Many times with George.

She would never do that again.

It looked the same, exactly the same. People on the boardwalk, enjoying the boats, oblivious to the hell she had gone through. Of course, they had no idea, why would they?

Strange.

A crowd quickly gathered, horrified by the scene unfolding at Little Current's dock.

People, yelling for medical help, tried to get Brian up to the boardwalk, his head wrapped in a blood-soaked towel. There were expressions of disbelief as the locals viewed the injuries sustained by Annie and Frank, screaming women and children, having never seen such misery and pain.

Frank had his arm around Annie, blood running down his face. Two men grabbed each of them and moved them toward a waiting truck.

Frank collapsed a few feet later.

Others had loaded Brian and his wife into a medical vehicle and were gone.

Annie was the last to be put in the car. As the door closed, she recognized a familiar face, and she could hear his voice over the bedlam,

"*Annie?* What the hell happened? Where's George?"

It was Johnny Griggs. He had just arrived at the Anchor Inn. He jumped back in his truck, following them to the hospital.

*

Annie lay on her back, one eye closed, the other being pulled open by the doctor shining a blinding white light.

"Can you hear me? Do you know where you are?"

"I'm in the hospital in Little Current."

"Does your head hurt at all? Is your vision clear?"

"My head feels okay. I can see fine." Annie started weeping. "There was a dynamite explosion at our lodge. It was awful."

"Do you remember being hit on the head at all?"

"I don't think I was, no."

"You have sustained lacerations to your leg and arm. There are splinters of wood and glass in your skin we need to remove. The explosion happened in a building?"

"Yes."

"You are fortunate. Your injuries do not appear to be severe."

Annie tried to sit up, but the doctor wouldn't allow it.

"What about the others?"

"I don't know anything. There is another doctor working here. As soon as they are stable, they will probably be moved to Mindemoya Hospital. You will be going there as well; we need to get an X-ray of that arm."

The doctor left the room. A nurse continued to work on her wounds. Minutes later, a Provincial Police officer entered the room.

"The doctor said you were okay to answer a couple of

questions. If you are not able, I will come back."

Annie looked at the officer and started crying.

Reality hit her like a brick. It was dressed in a uniform.

George was gone.

Annie's husband of thirteen days, heir to millions, had drowned after a horrific dynamite accident. Annie Arnold, the fifteen-dollar-a-week telephone operator from Gore Bay, was there and knew all the details.

Or did she? The world was about to find out.

"Mrs. Rausch, I'm Officer Fleming. We just spoke to Lillian Lloyd a few minutes ago. The doctor said 'she is probably in shock.' I would like you to verify what she said."

Annie put her hand over her face, trying to wipe away the tears.

"Perhaps I should come back?"

Annie looked at the officer. The nurse was still tending to her leg. "No, I can answer you."

"Mrs. Bryant said your husband was injured in the dynamite blast. On the way here, he fell overboard. She said he wasn't seen again."

Annie's screams brought the doctor back into the room. He held her still on the table. He turned to Officer Fleming. "You have to leave, right now."

Annie woke up two hours later. She had no idea where she was. Her thigh and arm were bandaged, and she had a piece of gauze on the back of her calf.

"It took five stitches to close that gash." The nurse pointed at her lower leg. "It was glass, and the cut was deep. Mrs. Rausch, I will let the doctor know you are awake."

Annie was trying to recall her calf injury. She had no recollection.

The doctor entered. "How are you feeling? I gave you something to calm you down."

"I'm fine, a little groggy."

"Your parents want to see you. Are you all right?"

Annie's parents entered. No words were spoken for minutes.

"Annie, the doctor said he thinks Brian is going to make it. He is being moved to Mindemoya to have surgery."

Annie forced a smile. "What about Frank?"

Her mom took Annie's hand and said, "He's great. I heard him tell Claudette to quit fussing over him."

Annie went quiet, gazing at the ceiling. The drug had calmed her to the point that the mention of Claudette's name went over her head.

"It was horrible. I had no idea he was playing with dynamite. After that it was just survival, it all happened so fast."

John got on his knees so he could hold his daughter's head and look into her eyes. "What happened to George?"

Annie took her time, doing her best. "He went over the side of the boat. He was standing, I don't know why. He had not been totally coherent and was preoccupied with Brian. He looked in shock. Dad, the water was big, the waves were as big as I have ever seen with you. I don't know why he stood up. Why would he do that? Dad, help me please, why? Why did he stand up?"

Annie lost it again. Her mother was crying as hard as her daughter.

John got up and walked towards the door. "The Rausch family hasn't been told. Frank told the police it happened in Honora Bay, but they don't have any detail to tell the family. I'm sorry, darling, but he hasn't been recovered. The police need to talk to you first."

Annie thought, *The police are going to tell Fred and Mattie their son is dead?* She had to do it. She owed that to Fred.

She asked for a few minutes alone before Officer Fleming returned. She needed to remember everything that happened. So much in such a short period of time.

She didn't have answers to inevitable questions. It was the cross she would bear for the rest of her life. She didn't know the extent of George's head injury. Did he even have one? His other injuries, amazingly, didn't seem that serious.

Why did he stand up? If he hadn't, he would be in Mindemoya with Brian, alive.

He went overboard in heavy water. He was standing, like he was inviting death. *Did he see something?*

"Mrs. Rausch, your husband fell overboard?"

"Yes."

"How long did you look for him?"

"Not sure, exactly. Ten minutes? We were afraid of tipping the boat. The water was severe."

"Lillian Bryant said he was bleeding from the head and shoulder. His arm 'looked funny.'"

"Yes, that is correct."

"But he was talking to you, coherently?"

"Yes, he was."

Officer Fleming folded his notepad. A pained expression went over his face. "We will be informing the family within the hour. I'm sorry you have to hear this; we will start the search for your husband in the morning, weather permitting."

With that, he left the room, leaving Annie staring at nothing.

*

Annie could see Claudette standing behind the nurse.

"If you are up to it, your friend Claudette wants to visit for a few minutes."

Claudette looked at Annie's face and went to pieces. The two girls who years ago talked about their first crush and shared their first cigarette behind the ice cream shop were now all grown up. There was no more grown-up situation than the one they were in. They held each other for a long time, neither one wanting to let go.

The sobbing and crying were the easy parts. Now they had to look into each other's eyes.

"My dad said Frank is doing well?"

"He's got a lot of stitches in his head, but he is great. He is going to be fine."

Annie sat up in bed and took Claudette's hand. "Frank was amazing. None of us would have survived without him. Claudette, he is the reason we are alive. He was a hero."

Claudette held Annie tightly. "I'm so sorry about George, sweetie. Frank said he stood up in the boat. Why would he do that?"

Annie pushed Claudette back and looked deeply into her eyes. Claudette did not blink or look in any other direction.

She was trying to figure out which Claudette she was looking at.

"Frank turned the boat sharply to ride a huge roller so the boat wouldn't tip. That's when George went overboard."

"So, Annie, what are you saying?"

"I'm not saying anything."

Annie continued to look for something in her friend's expression. Claudette kissed Annie on the forehead and turned to leave the room. "I'm going back to be with *my hero*, Frank. I'll check in on you in a little while."

*

It was just after 9:00 p.m. Officer Fleming and another constable were standing beside Annie's bed. Annie's father sat in the corner.

"We have informed the Rausch family that their son is missing and presumed drowned. We spoke to Fred Rausch directly."

Annie's face went red, her eyes welling. "Oh God, no."

"Needless to say, Mr. Rausch is in shock. No one can ever be ready for that devastation, so he is in bad shape. He has called back twice since our initial call. He wants to talk to you."

Annie went sickly pale, appearing ready to pass out. "I couldn't, I can't, not yet."

Annie's father moved to her side. "I will call Fred back."

"No, Dad, I will do it. It's my place, I just need some time."

Annie asked to be left alone. There was a phone in another room where she would be moved when she was ready to make the call.

Where would she start with Fred? What about the questions she couldn't answer?

And what about Mattie? Oh God, what about Mattie?

Annie lay on the bed, staring into a blank ceiling. She was reminded of Kenny Morris. Kenny had been a friend of her dad's, a different sort who lived on a tiny island under the Cloche Mountains. In a terrible thunderstorm, Kenny's little fishing boat capsized in huge water two miles from the nearest land.

Kenny had no family, and Annie's father was really the only person that called him a friend.

There was a brief service for Kenny at the Anglican church. A minister, Annie, who was seven, and her dad comprised the entire gathering.

Three weeks later, the police called on Annie's house. It was raining and cold. Annie and her dad answered the door and standing between the two officers was one Kenny Morris.

What if George wasn't dead? Maybe he didn't drown. Stranger things had happened; Kenny was over fifty and out of shape. He would start breathing hard doing up his shoes.

And he made it.

*

The operator put the call through to Michigan.

Fred picked up before it completed one ring. The operator said, "Go ahead, please."

The voice was hoarse; it could have been anyone. "Annie?"

Annie had rehearsed this for forty-five minutes lying in bed. It was of no help; she burst out, wailing and crying. "Oh Fred, oh Fred!"

"My son, my sweet George, oh God, Annie, tell me this isn't true! Tell me he's not gone!"

Fred was beyond hysterical. Annie could hear voices and commotion on the other end. Then her heart stopped, hearing Mattie scream in the background, "You killed him, you, miserable whore, you killed my baby!"

There was silence. Someone had covered the phone or hung up. Annie sat in the chair, trying to catch her breath, trying not to faint.

"Annie? It's Fred. I'm sorry, are you okay? What happened?"

Annie did her best keeping it together and told George the details to the best of her ability. Her voice cracked, and she had to pause on numerous occasions but eventually completed her story.

"Why did he stand up?"

"I don't know, Fred, I have asked myself that over and over."

"I will be there sometime tomorrow. I want to control the search for George. I will be bringing some people. I will stay at the Anchor Inn."

"Fred, I am being moved to another hospital for a few days. Dad will be at the Anchor with Johnny Griggs; they can help."

There was a long pause. Fred had obviously closed the door and seemed to be alone.

"Annie, he's really gone, isn't he? My boy is gone forever,

isn't he?"

Annie was a mess, sobbing, trying to speak. "Yes, no one could have survived in that water."

There was a longer, painful period of dead quiet.

Then a screaming, crying, hysterical female voice: "Murderous slut, you won't get a dime. You are going to jail!"

The line went dead.

Chapter 29

"Frank knows these waters as well as most. If he said Honora Bay, that's where I suggest we start the search. Keep in mind, the water there is over a hundred feet deep and the currents are strong. The body could be miles from there by now."

Johnny Griggs looked over the table at three men, all from Detroit.

The one with his head in hands was Fred Rausch. He raised his head, took a deep breath, and said, "Mr. Griggs, can you put an ad in the paper and get the word out that I will pay twenty-five cents an hour to anyone that will search these waters? If there are three men in a boat, they each get the hourly rate. Furthermore, I want it posted everywhere. The person who recovers my son will receive $1,500 cash!"

Johnny left the hotel and ran across the street to the post office. In less than two hours every boat in Little Current was headed west to Honora Bay.

"I want to drive out to the lodge. Let's go."

Fred and one of his associates jumped in a truck and headed to Maple Point.

*

Annie opened her eyes to a coffee and newspaper in the Mindemoya Hospital. Her mother was asleep in the chair across the room. The headline read, "Newlywed Heir to Millions Drowns after Dynamite Blast."

She was awake now.

The article was full of pungent phrases like, "$15-a-week Gore Bay girl" and "foul play has not been ruled out."

Later that day, a nurse presented Annie with a few telegrams. One was a sympathy and get-well message from Trevor, the other expressing similar sentiments from Glenn.

Annie read the final one and looked up quickly to ensure she was alone.

Annie, words cannot express my shock about the news. Please know my thoughts are with you. My expertise is cosmetic surgery. I read you were injured. Dr. Langer.

Annie folded up the telegram as Lillian walked in the door.

"Brian is in the recovery room; the surgeon said it was a routine surgery. He said Brian is a strong man and will be fine. Annie, he also said if the towel had not been wrapped around his head tightly, he would not have made it. Brian owes Frank his life."

Annie looked at Lillian and smiled. "We all do honey, we all do."

*

Fred had a difficult time looking at the charred wood where the wall to the carriage house once stood. A couple of police officers were sifting through the glass and boxes.

"Mr. Rausch, please stay clear of this area. There is still dynamite buried in the remains. Please step back."

Fred's associate shook his head. "Amazing anyone in this area survived."

Fred started crying and walked back to his truck. He said in a broken voice, "Everyone survived, except one."

A truck pulled in behind Fred's. Glenn jumped out and threw his arms around Mr. Rausch. "I'm so sorry. I wish I had been here, maybe I could have done something."

The two hugged tightly, weeping. "Why George, why him?" Fred looked at Glenn, his hands on his shoulders. "Let's you and I go for a walk. I think it would be good for both of us."

*

Lillian sat on the edge of Annie's bed, hoping to say the right thing.

"Honey, do want to talk about it, or not yet?"

"I'm fine, I don't want to wake Mom up."

Lillian leaned closer. "The surgeon said that some of Brian's pain came from the chemical burns from the dynamite. When I asked Frank how he felt this morning, he said the same thing. He said he felt better, but his head and arms were really sore and stinging. The doctor told him it was from chemical burns as well."

Annie had a blank look. "Are you expecting me to say something?"

"Sweetie, we really don't know how much pain George was in or what caused it. He had a few cuts, and his shoulder looked bad, but that's all we know. I'm suggesting maybe, just maybe, he couldn't take the burning from the dynamite anymore."

Annie looked at her friend with raised eyebrows. "Huh, now that's a thought. Maybe."

"Annie, honey, he stood up for a reason. I'm grasping at straws, like we all are."

*

Fred still had his arm around Glenn's shoulders. They stood silent, looking across the channel at Clapperton Island.

"Funny, it can look so peaceful."

Glenn nodded then looked back in the direction of the lodge. "The water wasn't the reason, Mr. Rausch. If there was no dynamite accident, there was no reason to be in the boat."

Fred walked closer the water in a vain attempt to hide his tears. "Why did my son let you go?"

"Oh, Mr. Rausch, I don't think that's important now. He treated me so well and gave me a large severance."

Fred turned quickly, the tears all but gone. "I think it is very important Glenn. I'd like an answer, please!"

Glenn was startled by Fred's tone. "Well, Mr. Rausch, this is hard for me. I promised George it would remain between the two of us."

"My son is gone, Glenn, please."

"George told me that Annie wanted to help out her friends, so George gave them the job."

"And that was it? George just did it?"

"Oh, Mr. Rausch, I don't feel good about this. I feel I am betraying some trust."

"My son is dead. I don't even have his remains to pay my last respects to. There are many people wanting answers, and there will be many more. Glenn, my son considered you a dear friend. In his honor, please tell me what he told you."

Glenn looked at Fred squarely in the eye. "He told me he did it to appease Annie. He was trying to make up for her having to sign a marriage contract."

Fred shook Glenn's hand. "I thought as much. You are a good man."

*

It was getting dark, and the last of the boats were returning to the harbor. Johnny Griggs, Fred, and a few others waited at the Anchor Inn. A younger lad ran between the dock and the hotel, reporting on each boat.

George's body had not been found.

"Supposed to be calm for the next forty-eight hours. Should make things easier for the search."

Johnny looked at Fred, not expecting a response.

"I have asked some associates in Detroit and Toronto to get up here. They will be arriving later tomorrow. Better equipment, more experienced." Fred asked Denise for a double bourbon. "I am thinking about a submarine."

Johnny tried to hide his amazement. "A submarine, really? From Detroit?"

"Yes, but Captain Simon thinks it would take at least two weeks to finalize and get it here by rail. I hope this ordeal is long over by then."

Fred downed his drink and motioned for another. "Johnny, you grew up in these waters. Tell me truthfully, how bad was it?"

"It was certainly the roughest I'd seen it this year. I would not have gone out it my boat, and it is twice the size as yours. Mr. Rausch, the size of the boat has a lot to do with it, but it's the skill of the captain more than anything."

Fred held his glass with both hands, twisting it back and forth. "And from what I'm told, the boat was driven by Annie, then her friend Frank. My son and Brian were incapacitated."

"That's what I understand as well. And if I may say, both Annie and Frank have spent their lives here. They have respect for the channel. They know how ugly it can get. Frank got the boat safely to harbor, no easy feat."

Fred put his glass down with enough force to make heads turn. "With one less passenger than he started with."

*

The thought of George being crazed in pain weighed on Annie. If the burning pain was unbearable, the cold water would be an option, albeit a bad one. But if you are not rational, any action is possible. There were two other rational possibilities. Brian was the first; George's eyes rarely left Brian the entire time he was in the boat. Perhaps he just couldn't live with what he had done. The suffering he had caused, even thinking he had killed someone. The other thought: did George have another vision?

Neither she nor anyone else would never know.

For the first time, Annie felt a smile come to her face. Frank had appeared at her door. His head was bandaged and his left eye was swollen shut. He had tape over the bridge of his nose and was supporting himself with a cane.

"Ready for a visitor?"

"I'd hug you if I could. Oh, Frank, I'm so happy to see you up and around. Where's Claudette?'

"Home. I was told this morning I can go home in a day or two, so she went ahead to relieve her mother from babysitting duties. How are you feeling?"

"Physically, I'm okay."

Frank limped to the corner chair and put his cane against the wall. They looked at each other, saying nothing. If thoughts were visible, the room would have been busting at the seams.

"I'm sorry, Annie, I don't know where to begin. I don't know what to say."

Annie picked up the newspaper from her side table. She read out loud, "'Foul play has not been ruled out.' That is what is on the world's mind right now, Frank. Forget that I've lost my husband. Forget that a friend was near death, still in serious condition, and another is all smashed up! All the world and *George's family* want to hear is how I murdered my husband to get his money!"

Annie dropped the paper on the bed and pulled a pillow over her face. In a muffled voice she scratched out, "Why, Frank, why did he stand up? If he didn't he would be here right now, sitting on the end of this bed."

Frank grabbed his cane and struggled to the corner of the bed. "Annie, even if we did know why he stood up, and we never will, there will always be speculation."

That was more than Annie expected to hear. The pillow was no longer in front of her face. Frank was looking at the floor.

"I know there will be, but that is not what I was asking you. I was asking you why *you* thought he stood up."

"I have no idea other than he was knocked senseless by the blast, or maybe the pain."

Annie leaned as far as she could toward Frank. "It almost sounded like you were alluding to something else?"

Frank looked at Annie with his one eye, making it difficult for Annie to read his face.

"Like what? What are you suggesting?"

Annie stared into his one good eye. She said nothing.

Frank slowly stood and caned his way to the door. Annie waited for him to say something.

He hobbled away, leaving her and the room full of thoughts.

Chapter 30

Annie had temporarily moved back in with her parents to convalesce.

There was no way she was going back to the lodge. She had thought about meeting with Fred, but the sounds of Mattie screaming in the background during their last communication were still very much alive.

It had been over two weeks since the fatal day, and George's body had not been recovered.

Little Current was busy. Newspapers from Sudbury, Sault Ste. Marie, Toronto, and of course Detroit had sent people to cover the story. Annie and her family had been continually hounded. Her lawyer had instructed her to remain silent and agreed a meeting with Fred was not advisable.

She said nothing.

*

Fred was growing impatient. He decided to move ahead with the submarine. Captain Simon and his two-man sub were to arrive by rail in six days. Fred hoped it wouldn't be needed, but fourteen days of searching had produced nothing. The expenses were piling up; scads of boats headed out every morning, dragging the waters for miles around Honora Bay.

"I am not stopping until we find him, Mattie. I don't care if it takes months. I am here until the water freezes if need be."

Mattie had never left Michigan. "Fred, we need closure on this nightmare. He needs to be buried here, where he belongs, with us. Our legal team also wants him recovered for estate purposes."

"Mattie, I have not said a word to Annie or her family."

"Nor will you! I am contesting everything to do with the agreement! She will get nothing if I have anything to do with it."

"She is his wife. She gets a widow's allowance. It's the law."

"Lawyers, Fred, we pay for the best. Forget that now. Let's just find our boy and bring him home."

*

It was from a spy novel.

Annie waited for the late August sun to set, then walked in the cover of darkness to Johnny Griggs's house. Johnny had been a true friend since the accident, playing double agent, not saying a word to Fred about anything he was doing for Annie.

Tonight, he had opened his doors to Claudette so Annie and her could have some time to talk without having to look over their shoulder at parents or the press.

"Brian's coming home in a week. He just found out today."

The news went in one of Annie's ears and out the other.

Johnny poured them a drink and left for the hotel. Claudette wasted no time. She lit a cigarette and pulled her chair closer to the kitchen table.

"Any word from Fred?"

"None. Christopher, the lawyer, has put the gag order on me. I don't expect I ever will hear from him. It would be hard for him. It would be hard for me too. You know I really like him;

he's a nice man. Besides, I'm sure Mattie has laid down the law, the bitch."

Annie reached down and pulled two telegrams from her purse. She held them in front of her face so only her eyes appeared over top. "They are from Dr. Langer."

Claudette had no expression, looking almost bored with Annie's theatrics. "I'm supposed to be surprised? I'm pissed off you waited until now to tell me."

"He wants me to come to Detroit so he can work on my cuts."

Claudette pulled her skirt way up and crossed her legs, showing miles of skin. "I am sure he does!"

For the first time since George disappeared in the channel, Annie laughed out loud. A real laugh, emotional. A psychiatrist would define it as a release, a big step forward. Even an indication of moving on.

"So how are you going to do that? When are you going?"

"Claudette! I'm not going!"

Annie took a drink, adjusted her hair and said, "Not yet, anyway."

She wanted to ask Claudette something much more important. She stared into Claudette's eyes.

"Yes?"

*

Anybody that owned a boat big enough to handle the North Channel had registered with Johnny Griggs at one time or another over the past two weeks. They were from all over the island. They were from as far away as Toronto and Detroit.

The $1,500 offered for George's body was close to a year's wages for most people. Plus $2.00 to $2.50 a day per person made it financially attractive.

It was still the Depression.

The locals, the real salts, had an advantage. What they lacked in the sophistication of the big-city boats they made up in local knowledge. They knew the shoals, the currents, and the prevailing winds. They also knew how quick the weather could turn. Many times, the worst day to drag was when the sky was cloudless and the sun was high. In Canada's north, high pressure often brought high winds. Then on a day when the water was flat, a thunderstorm would appear in minutes, stranding draggers five miles from nowhere.

No one knew that better than Al Ryder and Wes Bates. They had been on the job since the story broke.

Both had commercially fished around Manitoulin Island for years. They had as much or more experience than anyone who had entered the chase.

They only had one thing against them. The Depression had hit them hard, and their boat showed it. They were the last to get out there in the morning and the last to come in at night. Not because they started late; their boat couldn't go more than five miles per hour, flat-out.

But it wouldn't be how fast you got *there*; it would be knowing where there was.

*

Glenn pulled into the lodge with his lights off. He pushed his truck door closed, making no sound. The only lights were reflections off the water from the other side of Mudge Bay.

He was alone except for the crickets. And the noise from the swaying pines was the only other sound. He wasn't here on Fred's wishes. He wasn't looking for anything that might shed some light on what happened that horrible day two weeks ago.

He was here to see George.

Lamp in hand, he walked by the roped-off area. The gaping

hole in the side of the carriage house looked more horrific than ever in the dark of the night. He expected to hear screams of pain and terror, but there was only the rustling of the trees.

He moved toward the back door, a door that was never locked. He looked to the shoreline where one night he and George approached a spirit that turned out to be Fred, trying to be funny. It was the shoreline where so many sailors over the years saw a campfire in front of a cabin that was never there when they returned.

There was nothing to see there tonight, just the waves rolling under an empty dock.

He opened the door to a pitch-black kitchen. The light from his lamp showed everything in place; nothing had been touched. The family room was as it should be, and there was no noise, nothing to be seen. He shone the light to the corner of the room where George had seen a presence on several occasions; there was nothing.

He sat on the couch and snuffed out his lamp.

"George?"

He waited and waited. An hour went by. He sat motionless in the dark; the occasional flicker from the bay was the only light.

He would try again. He would be back. This was George's place, for eternity.

He bent over and lit the lamp. The lamp illuminated the picture over the mantle. George's face looked down at Glenn, as clear as last time he saw him.

Glenn started crying. "Oh George, you are here."

George's head tilted to one side, not focusing on Glenn. He stared vacantly across the room. He was smiling; he was happy.

The face disappeared.

*

Annie spoke from behind her drink. "How's Frank feeling?"

"He gets these headaches, poor guy, they knock him down for a few hours. The other thing I'm noticing is his memory. More short-term stuff."

Annie walked over to Johnny's bay window. "Claudette, did you ever talk to Frank about, you know, what we *never* talked about."

Claudette moved over to the window, looking straight ahead. "There's a whole world out there that wants to know what really happened, isn't there?"

Annie took a drink. "Don't mess with me. Did you talk to him or not?"

"Yes, I talked to him that night, driving home from the lodge."

"And?"

"He wanted no part of the discussion. He was shocked I would even consider such a thing."

Annie took an exaggerated, deep breath but said nothing and walked back to the kitchen table.

Claudette, still looking into the night, said, "I tried to bring up the subject again that night in bed. I did my best, and when I say I did my best, most men would have paid for what I did! But he wanted no part of the discussion."

Again, Annie remained silent.

"Although sometimes people do change their minds. You know, some people need more time to think it through. Or maybe something to make them see it in a different light. Maybe, like a hit in the head?"

Claudette held her glass up, trying to hide her face behind it. "He has said nothing to me. I guess Frank would be the one to ask, Annie. That is, if you really want to know."

*

Annie and her father were trying to ignore the newspaper lying open on the round oak table. However, "Mystery Surrounds Young Millionaire's Death" splashed in a bold font made that impossible.

It had taken four hours to drive to Sudbury from Manitoulin Island.

"Mrs. Rausch, my condolences for your loss."

"Thank you. This accident is receiving so much attention, my head is spinning. George's mother, Mattie, is the driving force with the press. I believe she is convinced I killed her son. She thought I was a gold digger from the first time we met."

Mr. Mahon didn't flinch, as if Annie had not spoken a word. "Mrs. Rausch, you are entitled a widow's allowance of five thousand a month."

Annie couldn't help adjusting herself in the chair, displaying a somewhat relieved, pleased, expression.

"It is my understanding that your husband's body hasn't been found?"

"That's correct."

"The monthly allowance begins when it is found. We can file a petition to accelerate that, but that will take weeks. Hopefully, he will be recovered soon."

"Mr. Mahon, is five thousand an appropriate number?"

The lawyer pushed back his chair, walked around his massive desk, and sat down beside Annie. "I am so glad you asked that question. In my opinion, given the wealth of the Rausch family and the life you have become accustomed to, that number doesn't come close to what you are entitled to. Personally, I feel it is an insult to you, my dear. I will begin drawing up papers that will be filed in Michigan shortly. I am thinking of an amount closer to thirty thousand a month."

Annie could not hold back raising her eyebrows, her mouth curling up at the corners. "I see. As luck should have it, I will be able to file with you in person, as I will be traveling to Michigan as soon as my husband's body is found. Unfortunately, I am in need of cosmetic surgery to repair the wounds I sustained in the explosion. My surgeon's practice is in Detroit."

Chapter 31

It was a safe bet there had never been a two-man sub in Little Current.

There was now.

September 6th, twenty-two days since the tragedy.

Still no body.

Captain Simon said the sub would be ready by midday on the seventh. Fred couldn't wait until it was in the water. He was tired of the Anchor Inn, no disrespect to Mr. Griggs.

He had also passed the ten-thousand-dollar mark in expenses. A ton of cash in 1938.

The water was choppy, and Wes Bates and Al Ryder had decided to take the day off. True, they were passing on a day's wages, but dragging would be tough work. They would start fresh in the morning, ready to go by sunrise.

Wes and Al had put in twenty-one consecutive twelve-hour days. Al was thrilled they had taken the day off; he was beat. Wes, on the other hand, had a birthday girl on his hands. As much as he wanted to sleep for twelve hours, his wife of eighteen years deserved a night out for her birthday.

Hey, he had been making three bucks a day for twenty-one days in a row — he was flush.

They drank and ate at the Anchor. More drinking than

eating, but what the hell, they were celebrating a birthday. The hotel was packed, as it had been since the body search began. Johnny and Wes had been friends for years, both long-time Little Current residents.

"Did you see that sub?"

Wes was smiling at Johnny, pondering the question. "I don't get it. You still need to know where to look?"

Johnny laughed. "You don't have fifty million dollars!"

"And I never will. You know, Johnny, that body could be twenty-five miles from here or stuck on the bottom, buried in mud. We may never find him."

Johnny looked around the hotel to see if anyone heard what Wes just said. "Don't let Fred Rausch hear you say that; he'd have a breakdown!"

Johnny gave Wes's wife a happy birthday kiss and continued to work the room.

*

Wes was sound asleep. He and the Mrs. had drunk more than their share.

It was 4:00 a.m.

Wes had another thirty minutes of slumber when his wife woke him up.

"I had a dream you won't believe!"

Wes rolled over, rubbing his eyes, wondering what was going on.

"I just saw George Rausch! Plain as day, he was bouncing across the waves. Half his body in the water, his arms stretched straight out. Like he was asking for help!"

Wes laughed. "I didn't realize you were that smashed? I'm glad you had a good birthday."

"Listen to me, I saw him! He will be there for you, today!"

Wes decided he couldn't get back to sleep. His wife's excitement was contagious — he was fully awake. "I hope you're right, honey, we could use the money. Did he happen to mention what time he would be available?"

"I'm serious, you dope! This ain't a joke!"

*

Al was already in his twenty-eight-foot fishing boat when Wes arrived. Al was looking at the striped sub being prepared to set sail later that day.

"Kind of looks like a zebra, doesn't it?"

Wes laughed, shaking his head in disbelief. "Well, Al, talking about crazy things, wait till you get a load of this! The wife had a dream last night. Said she saw George Rausch's ghost or whatever dancing across the water with his arms stretched out! Here's the best part, she said we are going to recover him today!"

Al laughed and continued to coil some rope. "That's a good one! She didn't happen to say *where* he was doing this jig, did she?"

Wes untied the bowline. "September 7th, Al. My lucky number is 7."

"Well, if it's going to be lucky for us, Wes, it better be lucky early. It's choppy now, and the wind is supposed to be howling by noon."

They pulled away from the dock and were at top speed in a matter of seconds, five miles per hour. They watched boat after boat pass them, all hoping today was the day they would land "dancing George Rausch."

*

Annie was washing breakfast dishes; her mother was drying.

"I told Mr. Mahon to proceed with the settlement filings in Detroit. He believes it's in my best interest, and he should know. I mentioned I would be there in person as soon as they recover the body."

Annie's mother looked sideways at her daughter. "Keep going."

"What?"

"There's more you want to talk about, hopefully."

Annie stopped washing, dried her hands, and folded her arms in front her.

"Dr. Langer, perhaps?"

Annie's mother walked to the kitchen table and handed Annie an envelope filled with telegrams.

"These came to the post office yesterday. They arrived at the Mindemoya Hospital days after you were released. Your father picked up the mail. I don't know if he read them or not. Annie, what you do is your own business. But if you want to file petitions, whatever that means, and not raise any more suspicion, you better keep Dr. Langer under wraps. Annie, I saw how he looked at you. Medicine is not on his mind!"

"Mom, he is a highly respected plastic surgeon and offered me his services. Once George's body is recovered, all gloves are off. You should have heard Mattie screaming! The names she called me. This is going to get ugly in a hurry. Dr. Langer is the least of my worries."

Her mother took off her apron and threw it on the table. "You have changed, Annie. I know Mattie thinks it's only ever been about the money. But don't make it worse by exposing another man!"

"There is no other man!"

"I know that, but why give them more to think about? They already think you murdered him!"

*

"I've got something!"

Wes handed Al the rope. The boat was rolling in the choppy water.

"Feels too heavy, but let's see."

Ten minutes later, it was nearing the surface. Wes spotted an odd shape and pulled hard on the rope.

"A log. That's not going to win any prizes."

It was 7:30 a.m., and the wind was picking up faster than forecasted.

"We have another hour, maybe two."

Wes pointed off the starboard bow. A government tugboat was on a course that intersected theirs. Al swung his boat around, allowing the tug to chug by their port side.

"There are a lot of seagulls following that tug."

"Maybe someone is throwing stuff off the boat. Maybe they cleaned some fish, who knows."

They watched the tug cruise out of sight. Two or three other boats had given up the chase for the day and were starting the ten-mile ride back to Little Current.

"One more drag Wes, that's it."

Wes didn't hear what Al said. He still had his eyes on the seagulls.

"They left the tug, Al?"

"What?"

"The gulls are landing over there."

Al circled the boat behind the seagulls. Wes leaned over the bow, placing both hands on top of his head, not believing his eyes. He turned to his buddy.

"That's him, Al, that's him!"

His wife's dream had become a reality. George Rausch had surfaced. Twenty-three days of searching were over.

His body was rolling on top of the three-foot waves. He was wearing pants and running shoes. The shirt was gone, and all exposed skin was sickly white and covered in mud. The waves were considerable and increasing in size.

"Get a line on him, now!"

Wes threw a rope over the body and started pulling him in.

"You have to give Frank credit. We can't be half a mile from the location he gave the police."

"He's been in the mud a while; the current finally moved him, I guess, and his air brought him up."

The two stood staring at George. Al put his arm around Wes and said, "We just came into a lot of money, my friend. Most valuable thing we will ever pull out of this channel."

Wes leaned over the body. "He doesn't look that bad."

"What are you talking about? He's been under 120 feet of water, stuck in mud, for three weeks!"

"No, look. All we heard about was the huge dynamite blast. Brian and Frank were all blown up — Brian nearly died! He has little cuts on his head; his arms and fingers are fine. Sure, they are white and frayed at the end, but that's the water or the seagulls. He sure doesn't look like he had serious injuries."

"What are you saying?"

"There's been lots of talk about 'foul play.' The appearance of this body? It's only going to fuel that story!"

"No matter to me. We are $1,500 richer. Let's get him back before these waves take us down!"

*

There was a crowd gathered around the sub. Captain Simon's crew were preparing to lower it into the water.

Wes and Al pulled by the sub to Al's slip. The young lad who had been running between the dock and the hotel for over three weeks stared into the boat. He started hopping around like his pants were on fire.

Since Little Current became a town, no news had traveled faster. Wes and Al were the week's biggest celebrities. The press wanted all the details of the find. All the locals wanted to know was what they were going to do with all that money.

It was late morning. The body was in the coroner's office. The Rausch plane landed in the harbor in front of hundreds of people.

Under police guard, Annie arrived with her father. They were hustled out of sight. No one saw Fred arrive, but people did see him leave. He was in the coroner's office less than an hour. He jumped in a car driven by an associate and was gone.

Later that day, the remains of George Rausch were loaded into his plane. It took off to the west, traveling over *his* Maple Point for the last time, back to Rochester Hills. In a statement from the coroner's office, Dr. Eaton said a jury had met earlier in the day. They had agreed to continue the inquest on October 12th.

*

Claudette handed Annie a tissue. "He said nothing?"

"He wouldn't even make eye contact with me! I tried several times, but he just looked down, his face in his hands most of the time. Fred had the pencil-neck sitting beside him, signing stuff and asking questions. He wanted George's body released to his custody, immediately. Fred didn't say one word."

Annie's father, sitting on the far side of the living room, nodded at Claudette in agreement.

"What did he do when they said the inquest would continue in October?"

"Nothing. I'm not even sure he heard the words. You know,

he seemed disinterested. I saw a man that didn't care what happened. His son was dead, and it didn't matter how or why. He wanted his son's body, and he wanted to go home. That's what I saw."

"So, what happens now?"

Annie stood and walked to the middle of the room. "You know what happens now, Claudette. I get on with the rest of my life, just like Fred is going to do. I am going after what is legally mine, and that's that. If that requires me fighting with Mattie and the Rausch family, so be it. I have hired the best lawyer I can to look after that."

Annie stopped talking and looked at her Mom and Dad, tears welling in her eyes, "And I hope that sweet man, the first real love of my life, rests in peace. I did love him, you know. This has been a nightmare, and it's not over yet."

Chapter 32

George Rausch was laid to rest in the family's mausoleum on September 10th in a private family service. No press, no photographers. Annie Rausch was not present for the burial of her husband. It was not her choice.

She was not invited, adding further speculation to the mystery surrounding George's death.

It was what the Rausch family wanted, or at least half the family.

It was the same day the Rausch family lawyers received notice that Annie was contesting the marriage agreement. She demanded the five-thousand-dollar *monthly* widow's allowance begin immediately and continue until the court made final decision on the will.

*

A few weeks had passed, and Annie was breathing a little easier. Both Little Current and Gore Bay had, for the most part, returned to normal. She was still approached by people, but most were friendly, offering condolences and encouragement.

Brian's recovery had been tough.

The prognosis was good, but it would take time, months,

until he was back to normal.

Annie had not seen Brian since the accident. Doctors had finally given him the green light to see visitors. Annie walked up Elm Street, as she had done hundreds of times before, to the last house on the right. The one that needed painting, that needed a new roof and so many other things.

But this time was different. She didn't feel like she was visiting close friends.

Vivid memories of the accident filled her head. Brian near death, his blood pumping all over the boat. George's face, watching Brian bleeding. Lillian screaming in horror. That look on her husband's face was haunting; it would stay with her forever.

Was that it?

Was it the thought that Brian would blame George for his suffering? It was George that blew everyone up. Why wouldn't he blame George?

But she had nothing to do with it. She wasn't even there when George decided to start tossing dynamite around. And Brian knew that; they both ran down *after* they heard the first blast. But then again, George was gone and she was left holding the bag.

The bag of money.

Lillian greeted Annie with a big hug. She kissed her on the cheek and whispered, "Honey, you are his first visitor. He is speaking very deliberately and having trouble with his volume control. Be patient with him."

Annie was not prepared for how Brian looked.

His shaven, grossly discolored head had a significant depression on one side. He was thirty pounds lighter. Brian had always been thin; it was weight he couldn't afford to lose. His face was drawn, anemic in appearance.

He sat in a wheelchair, covered in a blanket. He had aged

twenty years in a matter of weeks.

Annie felt Lillian's hand patting the small of her back, prodding her to say something. She couldn't; she was lost for words.

"Look who's here, honey?"

Brian had not taken his eyes off Annie since she walked into the room. In a voice that was stronger than Annie expected, he said, "I didn't lose my sight! Hi Annie, you seem a little shocked?"

Annie, as uncomfortable as one could be, said, "No, no, Brian, I'm just filled with a million thoughts. I'm so happy to see you!"

Brian continued to stare, no smile, no movement at all. That was the freakiest thing for Annie. Only his lips were moving, but he spoke clearly, louder than normal.

"The doctors have told me to keep my head as still as possible. It's a pain in the ass."

Lillian adjusted the blanket. "He has improved so much in the last seven days. They say complaining is a sign of getting better. Well, if it is, he sure is recovering!"

Annie was trying to act normal. She was failing, miserably. He looked awful; she couldn't get past it.

"I read the inquest goes in a few days. You have a lawyer?"

"Yes, Brian. Mr. Mahon from Sudbury."

For the first time Brian moved his arm. Annie went white, expecting blood to start pumping out of it. He pointed at the table. Lillian handed Annie a piece of paper.

"They want me there. They want me to tell them what happened!"

Annie looked at Lillian, then at Brian. "You are not going, right? I mean, you can't go in your condition."

In a much louder, agitated voice, he said, "Even if I could, I don't remember shit! I remember seeing George holding a stick of dynamite. The rest is — fuck — only the stuff I read in the paper."

Lillian held his hand. "I think that's enough talk for today, honey. The doctor said no excitement, to keep your blood pressure down. Annie, I think you should go now, sweetie. Maybe come back tomorrow."

Brian moved his wife's hand out of the way. "Annie, I need a favor. I can't afford any big-shot lawyer. Can you ask Mr. Sudbury to help me?"

"Of course, Brian. I will call him today. You don't worry about that."

Lillian grabbed Annie by the arm. "Okay, Brian, Annie's leaving now."

Annie pulled away from Lillian and kissed Brian on his bruised head. "I will look after that, rest and get better."

Brian grabbed Annie's hand and feebly attempted to pull her closer. "I don't remember anything! Nothing! Tell your lawyer that."

He sat back and put one hand on top of his head, in obvious pain. "You look good, Annie. You are *very* lucky; you don't look any different than you did before the accident."

*

The inquest was scheduled to begin at 10:00 a.m. on October 12th.

In three days.

Annie had been friends with Claudette since grade school. Frank and Claudette had been together since they were fourteen. For the first time, Annie was going to see Frank behind Claudette's back.

Would Frank tell Claudette about the meeting? Maybe — probably. But it didn't matter to Annie. She had to talk to him.

Her lawyer had told her to. And he had told her what to say.

They had agreed to meet at Low Island Park in Little Current. It was out of the way, isolated, a few picnic tables on the shore of the North Channel. You looked across a small channel to the mill on Picnic Island. They would be alone, guaranteed.

"You look good, Frank. You look like your old self."

Frank pulled his hair back, exposing an ugly scar on his scalp line. "I have three of these, but I've let my hair grow to cover them up!" He giggled nervously, smiling at Annie.

"First time."

"What?"

"First time I think we have ever been alone."

Annie's mother felt she had changed. If she were present for this conversation, her belief would be validated.

"Frank, they are going to ask you what happened. Fred Rausch and his legal team are going to be there."

Frank was running the risk of getting splinters in his ass, he was shifting around so much. "So?"

"Well, Frank, I want to know what *really* happened."

Frank's eyes widened, his hands stretched out in front of him. "You were there! You were in better shape than me! What the hell are you talking about?"

"Frank! I know what Claudette talked to you about!"

Frank got up from the table and lit a smoke. "And Claudette told you, Annie, it went in one ear and out the other! Fuck you, Annie, I could never do that! And even if I wanted to, I couldn't have!"

"Of course, you could have! You did! You flipped George out of the boat!"

"I don't remember it like that. I was trying to keep the boat on top of the fucking water! Do you remember the size of the waves?"

Fred's face was beet-red, his voice screeching out the words.

Annie walked around the table, putting her arms on his shoulders. "You didn't turn the boat deliberately?"

Frank took a long drag on his smoke. "I was trying to keep the boat from capsizing. What happened to George was a horrible accident."

Annie looked deeply into his eyes. "You are lying to me."

Frank turned and walked down to the water. He stood staring at the waves lapping over the flat rocks. The very water where ten miles to the west this all happened — or didn't.

Annie followed him down and stood beside him, both looking across the channel at the Mink Islands.

"What do you want from me, Annie?"

Annie pulled a bank statement from her pocket and handed it to Frank. It was notification that five thousand dollars had been transferred from a Detroit accounting firm to Mrs. Annie Rausch.

Her first *monthly* widow's allowance payment.

Frank read it, then read it again. He handed it back to her. Still not looking at her, he said, "I'm happy for you."

Annie put the paper back in her pocket. "I am going to receive that amount *every* month. Do you hear me? Every month! Frank, I don't want to know what happened. I really don't. Not ever. My lawyer told me to push you for the truth. I'm sorry honey, I am. At the inquest, the Rausch lawyers will do everything possible to find some indication of foul play. If they can find even a hint, there will be a trial. I don't get any money, and one or all of us will be going to court."

Frank lit another cigarette from the one he was still smoking. "I told you, Annie, I was trying to get us to Little Current alive."

Annie moved in front of him. "You received a few hits to the head, you were bleeding profusely, in severe pain, and it probably affected your memory."

Frank looked at Annie, this time his eyes focused, leaving

nothing to the imagination. "Is that what you want from me, Annie?"

"It's what Mr. Mahon wants."

*

It was October 12th.

Annie and her lawyer were seated, waiting for the arrival of the Rausch contingent.

Annie's lawyer was handed a notice from Mr. Humphries, the person in charge of the inquiry. It confirmed the list of people who would be asked to testify.

Annie looked at the list and quickly whispered, "No Fred?"

"He wasn't there. He doesn't need to be here."

Included in the list were attending physicians, coroners, police officers, and Frank and Lillian. Brian had signed a statement that would be submitted with his wife's testimony.

Annie was surprised to see Glenn enter the room.

"What is he doing here?"

"A Rausch request."

Shortly after, Wes and Al, the two men who had recovered George's body, entered.

Mr. Humphries opened the inquest. "No one is on trial here today. We are here to review the facts. The purpose is not to determine *why* George Rausch died, but *how*, when, and where. Hopefully the jury will be able to make a decision based on the findings of this inquest."

Annie looked across the room at the Rausch legal team. All she could see was Mattie glaring back at her. But that was impossible; she wasn't there.

Not in person, anyway.

Chapter 33

Mr. Humphries read something in front of him, then pulled his glasses off and peered across the table at Lillian. "It says in both the police and medical reports that you were totally untouched by the explosion."

Lillian looked like she was going to pass out at any minute, shaking, like the inquest was taking place outside in February. "That's right. I came down after the second explosion."

"So, you were by far the most alert person in the boat?"

"I was caring for my husband; I thought he was dead. I believe the doctor said I was in a mild state of shock."

The coroner read the medical report again. "It says, 'could have been suffering from' ... but anyway, tell us your recollection."

"Annie was driving the boat for over an hour. George was in the back seat with Brian and I. Brian was in the middle. The waves were four feet high. I thought we were going to capsize many times. Annie said her arm was too sore to continue, so Frank, who was in the front with her, took over. Another thirty minutes went by. I looked up, and George was standing up with his foot on the side of the boat."

"Did anyone attempt to sit him down?"

"The water was too rough. The next thing, the boat lurched

and he went over the side."

A Rausch lawyer handed Mr. Humphries a note.

"What caused the boat to lurch?"

Lillian wasted no time. "The waves, of course. The boat had been doing that for hours. This was a huge roller, a really strong one."

Lillian was done her testimony. The medical testimony given earlier had laid to rest any concerns about Brian's involvement.

The Rausch team were huddled outside during the fifteen-minute recess.

Mahon said, "They are going to supply Humphries with all sorts of questions for Frank."

Claudette was sharing a smoke with her husband, looking at Annie. Mahon continued, "The medical report given on Frank helped a lot."

Annie looked at her lawyer. "Frank will be fine."

The inquest reconvened with the recalling of the acting coroner, who released George's body the same day as he was found.

"The injuries on the body would not have caused death. There was no head trauma other than small cuts that would have required a minimal amount of stitches. His shoulder had a partial separation. He had chemical burns on his back and shoulders and arms, none of which could cause death. In my opinion, if he had made it to Little Current, he would have survived, no question."

Mr. Mahon looked over at Annie. "Here we go, the note I gave Humphries."

"In your opinion, Doctor, would the chemical burns you mentioned be painful enough to make someone jump into the water?"

"Impossible to say. Everyone's threshold is different. The pain could be severe for one and tolerable for another."

Mahon slumped a little in the chair and whispered to Annie, "Not the best answer, but it gives the jury something to think about."

Frank was next up. He looked calm, ready to go.

"The medical report states you had a severe concussion and required forty-five stitches to close three wounds in your head."

Frank pulled his hair back. "Yes, sir. Have a look."

The first chuckles of the hearing cascaded across the hall.

"What do you recall of the event?

"Lillian gave an accurate account. I don't remember how long I was driving for. I remember the water. As rough as I have ever seen it, and I have been here my whole life. I was trying to keep the bow forward; we could have tipped a hundred times. I will give Annie credit, she did a great job driving the boat. I heard Lillian scream, I looked over my shoulder and saw George standing like he was about to jump."

Humphries interrupted, obviously with a well-timed question from team Rausch. "And by turning to look, you turned the boat suddenly and George fell out!"

Mahon held his breath, watching the expressions of the jury. Annie, on the other hand, was focused on Claudette, seated in the back of the hall. Annie was looking for something, anything, to show on her face.

"As I said before, I was trying to keep the bow forward. A huge swell knocked us sideways, and I corrected, keeping the bow forward. I wasn't thinking too clearly, I was going on gut feel."

Mahon exhaled, wanting to give Frank a hug.

The last person of the hearing was Annie Rausch.

"Why did you give the wheel to Frank?"

"My arm was throbbing so badly, I couldn't continue."

"When you saw your husband standing in the back, why didn't you try to grab him, make him sit down?"

"As you have heard from the others, the waves were so big, it was impossible to stand. I couldn't stand, and my arm was weak from holding the wheel. I just wasn't physically capable."

Annie looked over at her lawyer. He had a pitiful expression, shaking his head. Annie started crying, making no attempt to hide her head, the tears visible to all.

"Is there anything else?"

Humphries shook his head and told Annie to go back to her seat.

There was nothing for the next fifteen minutes.

"The jury will consider today's testimonies. If a clear decision can be made, it will be communicated in due course."

Claudette and Frank waited for Annie to say her goodbyes to Mr. Mahon.

"He said, 'You done good, boy!'"

Annie was looking directly at Frank while hugging Claudette.

Frank was lighting a cigarette from the one he had going. Claudette watched Annie's lawyer drive his black Cadillac toward the swing bridge.

"Nice car that man drives. Listen, I was nervous for you guys! Those Rausch lawyers didn't look too happy."

Annie said, "Let's go to the Anchor, I'm buying dinner."

Annie walked over to Johnny and asked for the table in the corner. She slipped him a few bills. "Can you keep the newspaper guys at bay, please, honey? We want to have a nice dinner."

The table was beside the vacant spot on the wall, where George's picture once hung. Annie looked at the discolored section of the wall, thinking about the fireplace at the lodge.

Claudette noticed the tip. "Look at you, rich girl. Good for you."

Annie took Frank's hand. "Thanks sweetie, you are a good friend."

She called Denise over. "Four double bourbons, Denise, and

if Johnny's not looking, have one yourself!"

Claudette smiled at her friend. "You're in a good mood. Feeling pretty confident?"

"Actually, I don't know what I'm feeling. But there's nothing I can do but wait, so let's relax."

Johnny came over to the table and whispered something in Annie's ear. Annie looked at Claudette, shrugging, and followed Johnny to the bar.

"I have never seen the guy before in my life. I'm sure he was with the Detroit group."

Johnny handed Annie an envelope and walked away.

I'm trusting you will keep this confidential. I am taking a huge risk. I am counting on your character. I wanted to tell you personally, but circumstances would never allow it. I always thought you loved George, and I still do. I know you are a good person. Whatever happens financially is out of my hands. I want you to know this. I don't care what happened. All I want is my dear George to rest peacefully. I want this behind me. It was a terrible accident, and I want it remembered as that and only that. I am sorry for the pain and suffering you and your friends went through. He was a wonderful human being, and I will never get over the loss. He was my best friend. He loved you unconditionally, never doubt that. Destroy this note, please, for George.

Goodbye, Annie

She was a mess, alone, standing in the dim light at the end of the bar. She read the note over and over. Annie had liked Fred from the first time she met him. He made Rochester Hills feel like home. He offset the sandpaper he was married to.

If only there was some way she could contact him.

She went into the lady's room, tears flowing freely, watching the ripped pieces of paper flush out of sight.

"Where the hell have you been? God, we thought someone

kidnapped you."

Annie drank her bourbon like a sailor of fifty years. She remembered almost puking on it years ago at the lodge when she tried it for the first time. Tastes change, in so many ways.

"Some reporter told Johnny he was an old friend of my father's. I talked to him for a few minutes and realized he was full of it."

The three had a nice dinner, including several drinks. Frank and Claudette had no idea about the letter; Annie did a masterful job. Two times reporters approached the table. Both times Johnny was there like the sheriff of the small town, protecting his friends.

"I hope you know I won't forget you two."

Claudette looked over her glass. "You going somewhere?"

"Don't make this difficult. You know what I mean."

Annie paid the bill, and the three, holding on to each other, walked up Worthington Street. They made it as far as the church on the west side of the road and sat on the steps. Frank and Claudette watched Annie, trying to stand without falling down. She held the railing and looked down at her two friends. Suddenly her face was not jovial. She looked businesslike, her eyes sober.

"I am going to say this once, and you will never hear it again. Regardless of what comes out of today's inquest, I never want to know what did or didn't happen. You two will never talk about what did or didn't happen. The only thing I will ever know for sure is I lost my husband. Today's hearing only confirmed to me how much I want to move on. You two will be looked after because you are my friends and for no other reason. I love you both."

Annie walked down the steps and crookedly into the night.

*

"Annie! Annie! Wake up, it's Mr. Mahon on the phone."

She ran to the phone, still asleep. A few seconds and her expression said it all.

Her father and mother watched her slide to the floor against wall. They watched their little girl smile, followed by tears of joy.

Mr. Mahon had passed on the verdict from the coroner's office.

"Accidental death by drowning."

The coroner's office decision was big news in all the papers across North America. Telegrams poured into the Arnold home. Telegrams from people Annie knew and people she didn't know.

Annie sat on the end of her bed, reading the most recent from Dr. Langer.

I'm very happy to read yesterday's decision. It must be a great relief to you and your family. I hope now you will get to Detroit so we can repair your injuries. Please call me anytime, you have both numbers. I hope to hear from you soon, Annie.

William

A few days later there was another call from her lawyer.

"It's heating up now, Annie. Their position is you will receive $250,000, and all monthly widow's allowance will be deducted from the total when settled."

"What now?"

"We will say you are due a minimum of twenty-five percent of the ten-million-dollar trust fund George would have received at age twenty-five, plus the lodge. In addition, your monthly allowance of five thousand will be increased to thirty-three until the settlement."

"Wow, when are we filing?"

"Two weeks, November 15th, probate court, just outside of Detroit."

"So, I will be able to get to downtown Detroit?"

"Easily, quick limo ride."

Annie was at the post office shortly after she hung up the phone.

The telegram, on its way, read, *I will be there November 15 for a few days. I hope you can schedule my surgery for then.*
Annie

*

The winds of early November were rarely kind on Manitoulin Island.

Lillian, head down, carried her two bags of groceries along Water Street. Not looking where she was going, she walked directly into an older man coming in the opposite direction.

Groceries spilled onto the sidewalk.

"I'm so sorry, my fault."

The man, bent down, helping Lillian.

"No problem at all. Here, let me help you."

With everything back together, Lillian walked to the corner with the man now walking beside her.

"Are you sure you can manage?

Lillian was starting to feel a little uneasy. "Yes, yes, I'm fine, thank you."

The man grabbed her arm and reached inside his breast pocket. He placed a small, tightly wrapped package in her grocery bag.

"Now, Lillian, you get right home to Brian. Don't stop for anyone. You tell Brian he never speaks again about the accident to anyone! Ever!"

The man hopped in a car and drove away.

Chapter 34

"Slow down! Slow down!"
Annie could not make sense of Lillian's ranting over the phone. She couldn't tell if she was crying, laughing, or what.

"I will be over as soon as I can. I need to do something first. Settle down, honey, everything will be fine!"

*

The Rausch family, Fred to be precise, had retained Glenn's services to keep an eye on things at the lodge until the courts had made their final decision.

He kept the grounds impeccable and ensured the site was secure. There had been some evidence of people nosing around the property, but nothing had been disturbed.

Glenn also kept an eye out for George.

He had only seen George's presence once in more than ten visits to Maple Point.

Over the past few weeks, he had filled several boxes with George's personal belongings and sent them to Fred in Rochester Hills.

He had two boxes that belonged to Annie. He had made arrangements to drop them off at the Arnold home. Glenn had no issue with Annie or any anxiety about seeing her face to face. Annie, on the other hand, had always felt Glenn held her in contempt. The gold digger that never really loved her husband. The woman who would do *anything* to get his money.

Whether that was real or not didn't really matter now; they would soon be standing a foot apart.

"Hi Annie. It's been a while. I hope you got my telegram after the accident?"

"I did, I did, please come in."

Glenn placed the boxes on the kitchen table. "You look good, Annie. How are you holding up? I saw you at the hearing. Were you pleased with the proceedings?"

Annie thought that was an odd question.

She also knew anything she said would get back to Fred.

"I'm feeling much better, thank you. As far as the inquest, it was tough on me, you know, reliving that nightmare."

Annie was trying to determine if Glenn was on a mission for Fred or just being a good guy.

George loved Glenn.

She remembered him saying he was "one of the nicest people I have ever known, a true friend." Annie decided to cautiously open up.

"The whole thing has been so hard. The foul play stuff, such stress. It's been awful." Annie tried for the best eye contact possible. "I miss him. I miss him, every day."

Glenn looked around the kitchen. "Can I sit down?"

Annie pulled out a chair.

"I want you to know something, Annie. I told George a long time ago, it was never you that concerned me. It was everyone else."

Annie sat, totally confused. "What?"

"I told him his wealth was so vast, it could make people do terrible things. Do anything to get at it."

"What are you saying, Glenn? Are you saying my friends would do terrible things?"

"I'm not accusing anyone, Annie. I'm telling you what I told George. He should never be concerned about you."

Annie was more confused than ever. It sure sounded to her like he was accusing her friends and at the same time giving her a backhanded compliment.

"I guess I should be going."

Annie was uncomfortable. Was he sending a message that he knew what really happened? He couldn't know — nobody knew, *she didn't know* if anything happened. More disturbing was George had never told her what Glenn had told him.

Then, to blow her mind totally out of shape, Glenn opened the front door and said, "I know you don't believe in the island's power or mystery, but I saw George at the lodge the other night, as clear as I am standing here. He was looking out of the painting over the fireplace. He was smiling. He is happy, Annie. He's where he will be happy, for eternity."

Annie felt her mouth hanging open.

"Take care of yourself, Annie. I hope we see each other again sometime."

*

Annie wasn't sure what end was up walking over to Brian and Lillian's. She didn't know if her mind could handle any more bending.

The door swung open, and Lillian hugged Annie so hard, she had to tell her to let go.

"Honey, geez, you were choking me!! What the hell is going on?"

Lillian flung herself at her again. "Oh Annie, I love you!" She stepped back. "But why all the drama, honey? You could have just knocked on our door!"

Annie feared her mind was going to pop like a birthday balloon. She yelled, "Okay, stop! Lillian, what the fuck are you talking about? Start making some sense."

Lillian dragged Annie into the living room. Brian was staring at Annie. She couldn't believe her eyes — Brian was grinning! Almost a full-grown smile. He held out both arms from his wheel chair. "You saved our lives. Thank you, bless you, Annie."

Lillian handed Annie a leather pouch. She was laughing, crying happily. "Oh, Annie!"

Annie opened the pouch and for the second time in less than an hour felt her chin drop.

"How much money is in here?"

Brian, still grinning, said, "Like you don't know."

Lillian laughed and laughed.

"I don't know! I have no fucking idea! I didn't give you this!"

Annie's face was one of panic; it cut off the room's euphoria instantly.

"Annie, quit joking, you are not being funny."

"Lillian, where did you get this?"

Lillian went pale and moved beside her husband. His grin had vanished as well.

"A man, an older man, shoved it in my grocery bag and told me to get home to Brian. He knew both our names, that's why I assumed it was you. He said, 'You never speak to anyone about the accident again, ever.'"

The light went on in Annie's head, calming her considerably. The calm unfortunately had not reached Lillian and Brian.

"I know who it is from. But the three of us have to find some religion here, in a hurry. Fred Rausch never wants to hear about his son's 'accident' again. He wants all the speculation to go away. He wants his son to rest in peace. George is gone and never coming back. He wants the world to let it go. Knowing

Fred, he is also sorry about what happened to Brian."

Lillian and Brian were in shock.

Again.

Annie sat at the table, flipping through the cash in the pouch. The room was like a tomb.

"Ten thousand dollars?"

Lillian nodded. "Enough to buy two houses."

Annie looked at the two of them and put her coat on. "No one will ever hear a thing from me. I'd stay quiet if I were you."

Annie kissed both of them and left.

Lillian grabbed the pouch and kneeled down in front of her husband. "What do you think, honey?'

Brian looked at the pouch then back at his wife. The grin returned to his face. "I think we are rich! Quietly rich!"

Lillian shook her head in disbelief, mesmerized by the money. Brian touched her on the shoulder. "But you know, honey, if Annie did have anything to do with the accident, that was a hell of a story."

*

It was November 16th. Annie woke up in a bed the size of a football field. She was in a suite at the Detroit Hilton. She'd had dinner the night before with her lawyer.

Mr. Mahon was a nice man but dry as toast. It had been a boring night. They had filed, as planned, earlier that day.

Annie's surgery was scheduled for ten in the morning the following day. She was to be at Dr. Langer's office at three this afternoon for a pre-op consultation.

She was shaking in the back of the limo. Annie had no idea what to expect. She was feeling nerves she never knew she had. However, the ride through downtown Detroit in a stretch was a nice touch. Not even with George could she remember being in a car this big.

This was part of Mr. Langer's foreplay, something she was more than ready for. Something her mother had talked to her about, at length, before she left. The talk was so bad, she had to remind Mom she was twenty-one years old, widowed and capable of looking after any eventuality.

"Annie, you look great! How are you?" William held out his hand.

"It's nice to see you after all this time. I'm doing pretty well, considering."

"I'm so sorry, Annie. Telegrams are okay, but they don't express my real feelings for your loss. No one should have to go through what you have endured."

Annie was reminded the doctor was older, eight or nine years for sure. But he was good-looking, very good-looking.

"Is this surgery going to hurt?"

He laughed. "You will be asleep, so no, it won't."

A nurse came into his office.

"Annie, my nurse will take you into the examining room. I will be in shortly."

Annie noticed the night-gown on the examination table. This was going to be awkward.

The nurse raised her gown, exposing all of her leg. Annie was mortified while William concluded a lengthy examination of the injured areas.

"Two, maybe three surgeries, Annie. Can't possibly be done in less."

Dr. Langer walked Annie to the elevator.

"Thank you, doctor, I will see you tomorrow."

"Annie, as your doctor, I cannot ethically ask you out on a date. But I will be eating across the street from the Hilton at a small restaurant called The Oaks. If you are there, say, at 7:00 p.m., I will be there. It won't be late; I am in the O.R. all day tomorrow."

They both laughed.

"I would love to have dinner with you. I will see you at seven."

As Annie's mother had noticed, Annie had changed. She was not a shy girl; she was capable of speaking her mind, articulating exactly what she wanted.

*

"Does the Rausch family know you are looking after my surgery?"

William took his time with the answer. "They do not. Does that matter?"

"Do you still see them regularly?"

"You didn't answer my question, Annie. But I see Mattie at the school board meetings."

"Do you see Fred?"

"Only at social functions, and they are few and far between."

"I don't care whether they know or not."

They finished dinner, and Dr. Langer walked Annie across the street to the Hilton. Annie held out her hand and thanked him for the evening.

"Goodnight, Annie, see you tomorrow afternoon."

The doctor walked away; Annie was still watching him.

"William, could I ask you for a nonmedical favor?"

"Anything!"

"Mattie can never know. Could you tell Fred I'd like to talk to him?"

Chapter 35

It had been a week and two successful surgeries since Dr. Langer contacted Fred.

He had not replied.

Annie knew most of the staff at the Hilton by first name and had become something of a celebrity. She was due to go home tomorrow.

Annie had mixed feelings about Fred's lack of communication. There were so many things in play, weighing on his decision to see her or not.

Arguments were being heard from both sides regarding the validity of the marriage contract. Mr. Mahon felt they would have decisions on that and the will immediately after the holidays.

The note she received from Fred weeks ago was definitive, ending in *Goodbye, Annie.*

The strange man giving Lillian money and a warning was so out of character for him. It even had Annie thinking, maybe it wasn't Fred at all. But who else could it be?

And then there was Glenn. How much contact did those two really have? Did he tell Fred he went to her house? Did he tell Fred about seeing George? Maybe that was the final straw. He would distance himself from the entire tragedy, and especially

Manitoulin Island, forever.

Dr. Langer had Annie's gown undone. She was on her side, looking at him while he inspected his last surgery.

"Like what you see?"

Dr. Langer stepped back and took off his gloves. He looked at her and smiled. "I do, very much. The small amount of discomfort you are feeling will be gone in a week to ten days. I am quite sure in time you will not be able to tell where the original injuries occurred. Unless there is a complication or some abnormality in your healing, I don't think I need to see you again."

Dr. Langer was standing in front of his desk. Annie, in a new full-length fur, was adjusting her hat and gloves.

"I guess this is my last chance to have dinner with you. Say seven? We can dine at The Oaks again."

"That would be wonderful, My train leaves early in the morning."

*

It was a miserable day on Manitoulin Island. The freezing rain was going sideways in winds reminiscent of August 15th. Claudette's expression was consistent with the weather. She stomped into the Anchor, cursing and swearing, collapsing in a chair.

Lillian was dressed in a new coat, with new boots and new gloves.

Claudette was so cold that she didn't notice at first. Then the sirens went off. Her eyebrows raised, mouth open, she pointed at the coat now lying on the chair.

"Hello?"

"You like it?"

"Cute. Okay, but out with it!"

Lillian had rehearsed with Brian. She was expecting Claudette's cross-examination.

"A present from Annie. She gave Brian and I some cash to help us out."

It was a good thing it was winter and the Anchor was near empty. Claudette looked ready to smack someone. She yelled, "She did, did she?"

"Now, Claudette, we both know Annie has always been more than generous with us. I'm sure she will do the same for you when she gets back."

Claudette sat stewing, glaring at the new coat.

*

Annie stood in front of the floor-length mirror, liking what she saw. One of her new dresses exceeded expectations.

It was 6:00 p.m. when the concierge called her room.

"Your car is here, Mrs. Rausch."

She was taken back. The restaurant was fifty feet, across the street. She assumed it was a last surprise from the doctor.

The doorman opened the limo door. Fred smiled within.

"Hello, Annie. Let's go for a drive."

They headed toward the water. She glanced at Fred, uncertain what to say.

"I didn't know you were seeing Dr. Langer. I was surprised when he called."

Annie was hoping he meant professionally seeing him.

"He is the only plastic surgeon I know. I have you to thank for that."

Fred was looking ahead, not at Annie. "I am not comfortable here, Annie, as you can well imagine. But as I said in my note, I am trusting you. What did you want to talk about? Our time is limited."

Annie turned and faced Fred, hoping he would reciprocate. "I wanted to thank you for what you did for my friends, Brian and Lillian. That was very kind of you."

Fred continued to look forward. "It wasn't totally charitable. As I said, I want this over. I don't want to live this hell again. It was preemptive, in case people try to seek damages for the accident."

Annie tried again to get Fred to look at her. "I wanted to tell you in person that I loved your son. I want you to know that."

Fred turned to Annie for the first time, but said nothing, his eyes piercing.

"Fred, I know you don't believe in ghosts and goblins. I don't either, but Glenn told me he saw George."

Annie started to cry. "He said he was happy."

George lowered the privacy window and ordered the driver back to the hotel. He continued to look at Annie, his face reddening. The car pulled up in front of the Hilton.

"Did Frank kill my son?"

"What? How could you ask that?"

Fred moved closer, raising his voice. "You replaced Glenn with Frank because he needed the money, right?"

"Yes, but..."

"Tell me, Annie, for George's sake, did Frank cause his drowning? Was that the deal you made?"

Annie was scared. Fred was consumed by rage. She reached for the door.

"Fred, why are you doing this? The boat lurched, George went over the side!"

Annie opened the limo door and ran inside the hotel.

*

Annie was huddled at a corner table in the Hilton bar. A double bourbon was gone, another was in front of her. She sent a doorman across the street, informing Dr. Langer she wouldn't be joining him for dinner.

She was trying to rationalize Fred's behavior. The note said he knew she loved him.

So why the accusation? Why had he changed so much since the note he sent her? Perhaps too much time to think?

It had to be Glenn.

He had to be filling Fred's head. It made sense now. Fred didn't flinch when she said Glenn saw George and he was happy. Glenn had already told him.

*

"I was worried. Are you okay? What happened?"

Dr. Langer had surprised her.

Annie had to think fast. William was not to know anything — about anything.

"I'm sorry, William, I have had an emotional evening. Fred Rausch showed up unexpectedly. I just wanted to say goodbye to him in person. It turned out to be much more than I thought it would be. I was not up for dinner, I'm so sorry."

"Don't give it a second thought. Perhaps a nightcap? Or are you too tired?"

They talked for a bit and enjoyed a last drink together. Dr. Langer walked her to the elevator.

"I would like to see you again. Next time as William and Annie."

"I'd like that. I need some time. I want to get this legal ordeal behind me. I'm sure you understand."

William smiled, and Annie moved closer. He held her tightly, their first kiss igniting the spark felt years ago in the Rausch home. They both knew it was the beginning of something worth chasing.

*

Frank was doing some light mechanical work at the local garage. It was good for him to get back at something, and Lord knows they needed the money.

It had been ugly for three straight days. Rain and snow, with high winds. Frank liked the work, hated the fifteen-minute walk home.

He was locking up when bright lights from a pickup illuminated the front of the shop. Frank couldn't make out who was driving.

The window rolled down, and Glenn's head popped out.

"I'm too late, damn."

Frank walked over to the window. "Hi, Glenn, what's the problem?'

"Brake light, no big deal, I will come back in the morning."

"I don't mind, come on in."

Glenn backed the pick up into the bay, and in two minutes the light was replaced and Frank was cleaning his hands in the sink. He turned to see Glenn locking the door from the inside.

"What are you doing?"

"You and I need to have a little talk."

Glenn moved quickly, standing so close, their noses were touching.

"The Rausch family doesn't believe it was death by drowning. They think you did it, Frank. They think Annie put you up to it."

"Get out of my face. Let them think what they want. You should know better, Glenn!"

"It doesn't matter what I think, but it's going to matter a whole lot to you what I tell Mr. Rausch."

Glenn pushed a tire iron into Frank's throat, forcing him against the wall.

"Did you do it, Frank? Did Annie pay you?"

Frank tried to push back, but Glenn was too strong.

"No! Annie loved him."

Glenn looked into Frank's eyes, but Frank didn't flinch.

Glenn let go, throwing the tire iron on the floor. He slowly walked over and washed his hands. Frank collected himself, rubbing his throat.

"You know, Frank, Fred Rausch can be very persuasive. His son's death changed him. He wants to know what happened."

"I told you what happened. I told the world what happened!"

Glenn walked to the door and unlocked it, opening the bay door.

"Then I'm glad, Frank. I can tell Mr. Rausch we had a nice chat. Remember, he just wants his son to rest in peace. Like I do. George was my friend, a wonderful man. We will never talk about it again. This night, the accident, nothing. It's over."

*

"You get your fucking ass over here now! I don't care if you just stepped in the door or not."

Annie's bags were outside her parents' house. She was still wearing her fur, hanging up the phone.

Frank was waiting, holding the door open. He grabbed Annie's arm and hustled her down the stairs. Claudette was sucking on a cigarette. Its ember was the brightest thing in the room.

"I was almost killed last night!'"

Frank paced the room and Claudette chimed in, "Forget to pay someone off? Fuck, Annie, you are like blood to me. And you leave us out in the cold? Frank almost dies? Again! What the hell is going on."

"What happened? If you didn't notice, I have been in Detroit for two weeks! Now, both of you calm down and talk to me."

"Fucking Glenn attacked me last night, wanting to know if you paid me to flip the boat."

Annie covered her face with her hands. Fred's limo ride was now front of mind. Claudette screeched, "You gave Brian money and not us!"

"Okay, okay, settle down and listen to me."

Annie started with her ride in Fred's limo. She explained how out of control he looked. How he yelled at her with a crazed look, demanding to know if she had Frank flip the boat.

"I didn't know until last night how much Glenn was working for Fred. Now we know. Fred paid Lillian and Brian off. He wanted them silent. He wanted them never to think about going after him for damages. He wants his son to rest in peace. He never wants to relive any part of this, ever again."

"Lillian said you gave her the money."

"I guess that's what she decided to say. Fred gave her the money and told her never a word about it; it's over."

"That's what Glenn said last night."

Annie exhaled and shook her head. "I said you guys will be looked after, as friends, people I want to share my good fortune with."

Claudette's hysteria had subsided. She sat on Frank's knee. Annie hugged the two of them.

"George is not coming back. Glenn will tell Fred he doesn't think there was any foul play. It is over. This time for sure. Trust me, it's done."

Claudette's head was still buried in Annie's shoulder.

"Honey, how much did Lillian get?"

Annie smiled. "I'm not exactly sure, but you guys will do better — much, much, better."

*

Frank took a long time to settle down. He crushed out his last of twenty cigarettes and crawled into bed.

He and Claudette lay awake in the dim, smoky light. Several minutes and many thoughts later, she said, "Frank, how much do you think Annie will give us?"

Frank didn't move, his eyes closed. "Enough, sweetie, way more than enough."

He leaned over, kissed his wife goodnight, and turned his back to her.

"How do you know that for sure?"

Frank didn't answer; no one really wanted to know.

Epilogue

On January 10, 1939, Annie Rausch was awarded the lodge and just under two million dollars — one fifth of George's ten-million-dollar trust.

The average wage at the time was still under two thousand dollars a year.

In September of that year, Annie attended college in St. Thomas, Ontario. She wanted to gain some financial skills to look after her money. She dated Dr. Langer exclusively soon after the settlement. One year later, Annie and William Langer were married.

Annie sold the lodge a few years later.

One summer, Mr. and Mrs. William Langer decided to take a cruise in Georgian Bay to visit Annie's parents.

On the trip, they traveled along the north shore of Manitoulin Island. It was just after sunset. They sailed past Maple Point. It was the first time Annie had been back there since the accident. Annie and her husband stood on the deck, under the stars, looking toward Mudge Bay.

Annie started crying. Her husband asked her what was wrong. She said nothing.

She saw a cabin in front of the lodge. A fire was burning, throwing wild colors into the air.

Annie would never return to Maple Point again.

Just as well, because if she did, *the cabin wouldn't be there.*

Please visit my website:

www.ronaldmccormack.com

There you will find my biography, as well as my blog containing factual articles pertaining to this tragedy.

34688390R00183

Made in the USA
Columbia, SC
30 November 2018